The New York Times

IN THE HEADLINES
Police in America
INSPECTING THE POWER OF THE BADGE

THE NEW YORK TIMES EDITORIAL STAFF

Published in 2021 by New York Times Educational Publishing in association with The Rosen Publishing Group, Inc.
29 East 21st Street, New York, NY 10010

Contains material from The New York Times and is reprinted by permission. Copyright © 2021 The New York Times. All rights reserved.

Rosen Publishing materials copyright © 2021 The Rosen Publishing Group, Inc. All rights reserved. Distributed exclusively by Rosen Publishing.

First Edition

The New York Times
Caroline Que: Editorial Director, Book Development
Cecilia Bohan: Photo Rights/Permissions Editor
Heidi Giovine: Administrative Manager

Rosen Publishing
Megan Kellerman: Managing Editor
Greg Tucker: Creative Director
Brian Garvey: Art Director

Cataloging-in-Publication Data
Names: New York Times Company.
Title: Police in America: inspecting the power of the badge / edited by the New York Times editorial staff.
Description: New York : New York Times Educational Publishing, 2021. | Series: In the headlines | Includes glossary and index.
Identifiers: ISBN 9781642823271 (library bound) | ISBN 9781642823264 (pbk.) | ISBN 9781642823288 (ebook)
Subjects: LCSH: Police—United States—Juvenile literature. | Law enforcement—United States—Juvenile literature. | Police brutality—United States—Juvenile literature.
Classification: LCC HV8139.P655 2021 | DDC 363.2'30973—dc23

Manufactured in the United States of America

On the cover: Metropolitan police in formation during a Columbus Day procession, Washington, D.C.; Vincent Fournier/Gamma-Rapho/Getty Images.

Contents

7 Introduction

CHAPTER 1

Police and the Community: Connecting, Serving and Protecting

10 The Point of Order BY NICK PINTO

15 New York Police to Use Social Media to Connect With Residents
BY BENJAMIN MUELLER AND JEFFREY E. SINGER

19 In New York, Testing Grounds for Community Policing
BY J. DAVID GOODMAN

27 New York Police Will Retrain Security Staff at Homeless Shelters
BY NIKITA STEWART AND JOSEPH GOLDSTEIN

30 Defining the Role of the Police in the Community BY ALINA TUGEND

33 Female Police Officers Save Lives BY AMY STEWART

36 Supreme Court Considers a Thorny Question of Free Speech and Police Power BY ADAM LIPTAK

39 Barr Says Communities That Protest the Police Risk Losing Protection BY KATIE BENNER

CHAPTER 2

Assessing Racial Profiling and Bias

42 What Racial Profiling? Police Testify Complaint Is Rarely Made
BY JOSEPH GOLDSTEIN

47 Are Police Bigoted? BY MICHAEL WINES

52 Class-Action Lawsuit, Blaming Police Quotas, Takes on Criminal Summonses BY BENJAMIN WEISER

56 A Struggle for Common Ground, Amid Fears of a National Fracture BY JACK HEALY AND NIKOLE HANNAH-JONES

60 Police and Protesters Clash in Minnesota Capital BY MITCH SMITH

62 President Obama Urges Mutual Respect From Protesters and Police BY MARK LANDLER AND NICHOLAS FANDOS

65 When Police Officers Vent on Facebook BY SHAILA DEWAN

69 'I Was Wrong,' Bloomberg Says. But This Policy Still Haunts Him.
BY EMMA G. FITZSIMMONS AND JOSEPH GOLDSTEIN

CHAPTER 3

Efforts at Reform: Examinations of Training, Principles and Practices

76 Police Training and Gun Use to Get Independent Review
BY CARA BUCKLEY

79 In Police Training, a Dark Film on U.S. Muslims BY MICHAEL POWELL

83 Obama Puts Focus on Police Success in Struggling City in New Jersey BY JULIE HIRSCHFELD DAVIS AND MICHAEL D. SHEAR

88 Long Taught to Use Force, Police Warily Learn to De-escalate
BY TIMOTHY WILLIAMS

93 Training Police in Social and Communication Skills
THE NEW YORK TIMES

95 Police Leaders Unveil Principles Intended to Shift Policing Practices Nationwide BY AL BAKER

99 New York Police Illegally Profiling Homeless People, Complaint Says BY NIKITA STEWART

101 A Strategy to Build Police-Citizen Trust BY TINA ROSENBERG

107 Barriers to Reforming Police Practices BY TINA ROSENBERG

114 Changes in Policing Take Hold in One of the Nation's Most Dangerous Cities BY JOSEPH GOLDSTEIN

119 I'm a Police Chief. We Need to Change How Officers View Their Guns. BY BRANDON DEL POZO

CHAPTER 4

The Tech Side: Body Cams, Data and Surveillance

122 Police Use Surveillance Tool to Scan Social Media, A.C.L.U. Says
BY JONAH ENGEL BROMWICH, DANIEL VICTOR AND MIKE ISAAC

125 New York Police Say They Will Deploy 14 Drones
BY ASHLEY SOUTHALL AND ALI WINSTON

129 Cleveland Police Officer Contacted 2,300 Women Using Work Computer, Authorities Say BY JACEY FORTIN

131 Police Body-Cam Video Appears to Show Willie McCoy Sleeping Before He Was Fatally Shot BY JACEY FORTIN

134 Tracking Phones, Google Is a Dragnet for the Police
BY JENNIFER VALENTINO-DEVRIES

143 Police Data and the Citizen App: Partners in Crime Coverage
FEATURING ALI WATKINS

147 How the Police Use Facial Recognition, and Where It Falls Short
BY JENNIFER VALENTINO-DEVRIES

155 New Jersey Bars Police From Using Clearview Facial Recognition App BY KASHMIR HILL

158 Have a Search Warrant for Data? Google Wants You to Pay BY GABRIEL J.X. DANCE AND JENNIFER VALENTINO-DEVRIES

CHAPTER 5

Abuse, Deadly Force and Accountability

162 Activists Wield Search Data to Challenge and Change Police Policy BY RICHARD A. OPPEL JR.

167 Activists Say Police Abuse of Transgender People Persists Despite Reforms BY NOAH REMNICK

172 4 Years After Eric Garner's Death, Secrecy Law on Police Discipline Remains Unchanged BY ASHLEY SOUTHALL

177 The Lawyers Protecting the N.Y.P.D. Play Hardball. Judges Are Calling Them Out. BY ALAN FEUER

182 Fort Worth Officer Charged With Murder for Shooting Woman in Her Home BY MARINA TRAHAN MARTINEZ, NICHOLAS BOGEL-BURROUGHS AND SARAH MERVOSH

187 Philadelphia Police Inspector Charged in Sexual Assaults of Officers BY AIMEE ORTIZ

190 Police Officer Charged With Murder in Killing of Handcuffed Suspect in Maryland BY NEIL VIGDOR, MARIEL PADILLA AND SANDRA E. GARCIA

193 A Black Police Officer's Fight Against the N.Y.P.D. BY SAKI KNAFO

213 Glossary
214 Media Literacy Terms
215 Media Literacy Questions
217 Citations
222 Index

Introduction

THE MISSION STATEMENT of the New York City Police Department, the largest police force in the United States, reads: "The mission of the New York City Police Department is to enhance the quality of life in New York City by working in partnership with the community to enforce the law, preserve peace, protect the people, reduce fear, and maintain order." Perhaps the most crucial phrase in this mission statement is "working in partnership with the community": If the police are disconnected from the communities they are meant to serve and protect, how effectively can they accomplish their goals?

This is the underlying question that drives much of the analysis of police conduct in the United States, and it is something police forces across the country continue to grapple with. Efforts to incorporate "community policing" — assigning officers to work regularly in a specific area so they form a rapport with the local community — have had mixed results in different regions. This approach is especially necessary in high-crime communities, as trust and communication between police and civilians may make a significant difference in reducing crime in those areas.

It's worth noting that increasing the amount of time specific officers spend in a community is not the same as increasing police presence in that community altogether. Increased police presence in a community that distrusts the police might elevate tensions, particularly in minority communities. In such cases, as journalist Tina Rosenberg writes, "it is important in itself to reduce the sense that police are an army of occupation." Given the historically fraught relationship between police and minority citizens, accomplishing this is no easy feat. So what can police forces do to build trust with the public?

JOSHUA LOTT FOR THE NEW YORK TIMES

Police officers watch demonstrators block Interstate-94 as they protest the fatal police shooting of Philando Castile in St. Paul, Minn., on July 9, 2016.

To answer this question, police are tasked with examining the structural bias, racism and use of force that pervades American law enforcement. One of the major obstacles in reckoning with these issues is that evidence of these problems is often not well-tracked or such incidents are dismissed as one-offs that are not representative of the police as a whole.

Even so, efforts at police reform persist. Law enforcement leaders have proposed changing training methods to prioritize de-escalation tactics before resorting to force. The expansion of tech tools at officers' disposal, from tracking information to facial recognition software to surveillance drones, has the potential to better prepare police to handle specific situations more safely. However, lack of government resources or support can impede the changes law enforcement officers push for, and the flaws of certain tech tools raise concerns about privacy and racial bias.

As all of these issues persist on the larger scale, individual tragedies of deadly force continue to occur. The unnecessary killings of black citizens and police officers alike are reported with alarming frequency, leaving civil rights organizations, victims' families and individual officers searching for justice. How can instances of police abuse and deadly force be addressed so the loved ones of victims can heal? What is the process of trying to enact real change within a police force so that these incidents can be prevented from happening again? The following articles chronicle efforts across the country to answer these questions, and to determine what police need to protect and serve as well as what communities need from law enforcement.

CHAPTER 1

Police and the Community: Connecting, Serving and Protecting

Specifying the role of the police in a given area is no easy feat. Every community has distinct needs and requires a custom approach to service-related activities, maintaining order and curbing crime. This chapter details some of the strategies police have used in different areas, as well as assesses the basic history of the police, from the nine principles of policing to bringing women onto the force. Tensions regarding race relations, police presence and the freedom to criticize police practices are also explored.

The Point of Order

ESSAY | BY NICK PINTO | JAN. 13, 2015

THE QUESTION OF whom the police serve, and whose order they impose, is once again up for debate. But it is as old as policing itself. A political cartoon by Charles Jameson Grant, sold for a penny or two on the streets of London around 1834, depicts the British secretary of state addressing members of London's recently formed Metropolitan Police Force. "My lads," he says, "you are always justified in breaking the heads of the public when you consider it absolutely necessary for the maintenance of the public peace." The assembled constables, a rough-looking crew, appear perfectly capable of such a task. "By Jasus I wish your honor would give us a few throats to cut," one says, "for we have had enough of breaking heads."

Just about five years old at the time, the Metropolitan Police had already earned a handful of unflattering nicknames, as noted in the cartoon's title: "Reviewing the Blue Devils, Alias the Raw Lobsters, Alias the Bludgeon Men." Britain's soldiers were colloquially known as lobsters, because they wore red coats, so in an effort to quiet fears that the police would be a kind of occupying army, the Metropolitan Police wore blue instead. Many early opponents of the police suspected that the difference was only cosmetic; they worried that it would take only a little hot water for the men in blue to show their true color.

London in the early 19th century was a sprawling and disorderly metropolis, divided into scores of parishes, each responsible for hiring its own night watchmen and constables. In cases of great civil disturbance, order was restored by the army. In 1829, after years of opposition, the home secretary, Sir Robert Peel, finally persuaded Parliament to institute a professional police force in the rapidly growing areas around the capital. Skeptics saw the police as a tyrannical import from the Continent; Paris, Vienna, Berlin and St. Petersburg had already created local police forces, and they were regarded as agents of state oppression. To address these criticisms, Peel took pains to distinguish his nascent police and demonstrate that the Met would be answerable to the people, not the king or private interests. Not only would they wear blue, but, like many ordinary citizens, they would also sport top hats. And they would not, except in rare circumstances, carry firearms.

Peel's vision was highly influential in the formation of the New York City Police Department in 1845, and he is now regarded as a father of modern policing. Peel's name is perhaps best known in association with the nine principles of policing, which remain fixtures in police academies throughout the English-speaking world.

The first of these principles outlines the role of police in society: "To prevent crime and disorder, as an alternative to their repression by military force." But in pursuing the first principle, officers must also remember the second: "The power of the police to fulfill their functions and duties is dependent on public approval of their existence, actions and behavior, and on their ability to secure and maintain public respect." The democratic nature of the institution is further emphasized in the seventh principle, which states that "police are the public and that the public are the police, the police being only members of the public who are paid to give full-time attention to duties which are incumbent on every citizen in the interests of community welfare and existence."

The British Parliament at the time of the foundation of London's Metropolitan Police Force was dominated by landed aristocrats and business interests. Facing pressure from the disenfranchised middle and lower classes, Parliament passed the Reform Act of 1832, extending the vote to middle-class landowners while continuing to exclude the poor. In subsequent years, an increasingly organized working class kept the pressure on, often through large demonstrations. In 1833, nearly half the police force, or about 1,700 men, were deployed to a demonstration of as many as 4,000 people called by the National Union of the Working Classes. The event devolved into violence on both sides, and one constable was killed. Assigned to keep order in such a charged environment, the police were inevitably viewed as political.

Peel and his two police commissioners, Lt. Col. Charles Rowan and Barrister Richard Mayne, understood that the success of this new order-keeping force depended on the impression that this was not the case. "The force should not only be, in fact, but be believed to be impartial in action, and should act on principle," Rowan and Mayne wrote in their first report to Peel. But when the police were deployed by a government answerable only to the top 20 percent of the population, their implicit politics were unavoidable, even when police conduct was exemplary.

The police soon took on duties like telling vagrants to move along and regulating public drinking, gambling and other forms of vice frowned upon by the ascendant classes. The vision of order so appealing to business and property owners could easily look like repression to those on the other end of the constable's truncheon. Rowan and Mayne stressed the need for their force to be solicitous of "respectable" citizens. Those who did not meet this standard often felt the police were working against them rather than for them.

THE ATTRIBUTION OF the nine principles to Peel himself is historically dubious — it's more likely that they were written by Rowan and Mayne and credited to him — but that does nothing to diminish their continuing influence. Chief among Peel's modern-day disciples is William J. Bratton, the police commissioner of New York City. Bratton refers to Peel constantly, even claiming to always carry a copy of the nine principles with him.

At a $1,250-a-table business breakfast forum in the Roosevelt Hotel in Midtown Manhattan in September, Bratton once again invoked the foundational text, dwelling little on the document's focus on humility and egalitarianism and instead expounding largely on the first principle.

"In the '60s, '70s and '80s, we as a country, and a profession, drifted away from the emphasis on prevention and focused most of our time on trying to respond to the growing crime and disorder problems," Bratton said. "And we failed. We also almost totally abandoned the idea that our role is also to prevent disorder, the so-called quality of life." The resulting chaos, he argued, gave way to the sky-high crime rates of the early 1990s. "A safe city means business thrives," Bratton told the assembled business leaders, as they erupted into applause.

During his first term as police commissioner, under Mayor Rudolph Giuliani, Bratton pioneered the "broken windows" style of policing, focusing on relentless enforcement of minor violations, a strategy widely credited for the city's dramatic drop in crime. Not all New Yorkers have had such unqualified enthusiasm for the N.Y.P.D.'s imposition of order. Mayor Bill de Blasio rode into office last year after campaigning against the department's stop-and-frisk policy, which overwhelmingly affected black and Latino New Yorkers. Nearly 90 percent of those stopped were innocent of any wrongdoing. Recently, long-simmering frustrations with broken-windows policing boiled over into protests when news broke that there would be no charges in the death of Eric Garner, who perished in an encounter with law enforcement that began because he was suspected of selling loose cigarettes.

Most people now think of the police primarily in their role of crime fighting. But it is at least as much their other original mandate, the prevention of disorder, that perpetuates the suspicion many hold for them. Order is a subjective thing, and the people who define it are not often the people who experience its imposition. In the 186-year history of modern policing, class and race have always shaded how citizens feel about the agents of law enforcement. From 19th-century London, through Jim Crow and the civil rights era, to the age of broken windows and stop-and-frisk, the definition of the public to whom the police are accountable has constantly shifted. Peel's apocryphal principles, like so many of our foundational documents, remain more aspirational than descriptive.

NICK PINTO is a journalist living in Brooklyn.

New York Police to Use Social Media to Connect With Residents

BY BENJAMIN MUELLER AND JEFFREY E. SINGER | MARCH 25, 2015

THE NEW YORK Police Department has faced its share of pushback on social media, most memorably when it solicited photos of police interactions on Twitter under the hashtag #myNYPD. Images of aggression by officers upended that campaign.

Now, the department is seeking to turn New Yorkers' penchant for online complaints to its gain by crowdsourcing their concerns. It has even consulted another sector troubled by social media gripes — the airline industry — to become more responsive to problems voiced online.

"They're very good at managing customer complaints," said Zachary Tumin, deputy commissioner for strategic initiatives and leader of the department's social media efforts, who visited Delta Air Lines' Atlanta headquarters this month. "That's an area we need to explore."

The department's fleet of commanding officers has found its footing on Twitter in recent months, using the site to herald arrests, announce transportation delays and spread information about suspects. Now, the officers are planning to use that online visibility to draw ground-level information on crimes and conditions, a potential boost to a department seeking to align its "broken windows" crime-fighting objectives with local communities' needs.

In a pilot program starting next month in the 109th Precinct in Queens, police officials will use a platform called IdeaScale to solicit tips and concerns from residents. The platform, which some government agencies have used internally as a brainstorming tool, promotes the posts that other users agree deserve attention.

In that way, officials argue, the police will be able to look beyond departmentwide priorities and focus on concerns that resonate in smaller communities.

"If this works," Mr. Tumin said, "it could be a very important tool for precinct commanders around New York to solicit crowdsourced issues that communities want us to address — graffiti, or bikes that are abandoned or still locked after a cruddy winter."

Police officials caution that the new tool will be implemented slowly, as the department works to balance easy access for residents with controls on irrelevant or sensitive information. At first, only a few thousand residents in the 109th Precinct — which includes the neighborhoods of College Point, Flushing and Whitestone — who have given their email addresses to community leaders will be invited to join.

As an example of the kind of feedback the police are looking for, Deputy Inspector Thomas Conforti, the precinct's commanding officer, will ask residents to submit suggestions and concerns about the police academy that recently opened in College Point. He said he has heard people quietly worry about the lack of public transportation and the potential for clogged traffic. IdeaScale, he hopes, will make that conversation more accessible while lifting residents' most popular ideas to his attention.

"We could establish a platform that allows residents to specifically let us know what their concerns are, and what their problems are, and gives them the opportunity to communicate with us without leaving their rooms," Inspector Conforti said. "That's what we anticipate this platform will be able to do."

He added, "We're going to tailor our nonemergency police response to it."

Inspector Conforti was among the inaugural class of the department's commanding officers to join Twitter, a decision that he credits with making residents less intimidated about bringing him their concerns. Recently, he said, he sent a team of officers to a schoolyard where all-terrain vehicles had been revving their engines, an issue he would not have known about had a resident not written to him on Twitter.

But, he added, while Twitter makes it easy to spread information, "it's not necessarily a great platform to have an interactive conversation

ÁNGEL FRANCO/THE NEW YORK TIMES

Deputy Inspector Thomas Conforti said Twitter also makes residents feel less intimidated about sharing concerns.

with people," a deficiency he hopes IdeaScale will address. Residents' comments will be visible to anyone from the same precinct who has joined, making it a more sheltered platform than Twitter, but still unsuited for personal concerns.

It helps the precinct's cause that a vocal segment of residents in this largely blue-collar area of Queens already feels comfortable collaborating with the police. Chrissy Voskerichian, the community council president in the precinct, said many people are eager for aggressive enforcement of quality-of-life crimes.

The precinct is also exploring opening an official account on WeChat, a social media application popular among Asian immigrants.

While that project faces steeper technical hurdles, Mr. Tumin said it reinforced the department's effort to reach people who tend to be more hesitant to contact the police. He said a department survey last year showed that as many as half of women in some Asian immigrant communities who had been the victim of crimes had never reported them.

"That means we're going to learn about new problems, and be prepared to put resources into fixing them," Mr. Tumin said.

Geng Hang, 44, who runs Red Apple Employment Agency in Flushing, said she has had mixed feelings about the police. She recalled when officers rebuffed her and a group of friends who were trying to report a woman missing; they discovered days later that the woman had been found dead along a riverbank.

"This would allow us to have a very convenient way for us to communicate with the police," Ms. Geng, speaking in Mandarin, said of the new initiatives. "We could then consult them on all sorts of legal issues. And not only that, so many people don't have time because they are so busy working and they spend a lot of time going back and forth to the precinct for very small matters."

Even as they said they welcomed new channels for collaboration, residents questioned whether the department was prepared to solve the inevitable technical hiccups on platforms like IdeaScale, and whether it was ultimately a tool for reinforcing police priorities or giving an outlet to those who feel alienated.

But Inspector Conforti said he would seek out criticism, posting questions on IdeaScale about specific enforcement tactics on issues such as overnight commercial parking.

"Everyone likes to think the N.Y.P.D. has all the answers," he said. "Sometimes, we might be missing something."

In New York, Testing Grounds for Community Policing

BY J. DAVID GOODMAN | AUG. 23, 2015

RESIDENTS ON THE STREET rarely return the greetings of the precinct commander. Officers complain that their overtures are usually rebuffed, but they travel even short distances by car and drive down pedestrian paths in housing developments, cruising past staring faces. Many leave the Queens precinct for meals, some crossing into Nassau County for coffee at Starbucks.

On the other side are young men who say they remain the targets of police harassment and detect no new effort by officers to connect with them.

These are snapshots of the halting progress and enduring hurdles facing the New York Police Department, the country's largest force, as it embarks on an ambitious effort to reshape everyday interactions between its patrol officers and residents of the city after a period of searing tension.

The 101st Precinct in Far Rockaway, an overgrown former beach resort dotted with Robert Moses-era public housing at the city's eastern edge, is an early testing ground of a model of so-called community policing that fell out of favor in the 1990s as crime levels hit all-time highs. The idea is as simple as it is old-fashioned: Rather than chase 911 calls, certain officers patrol only a small area. They are meant to solve problems, not simply enforce the law.

There have been some minor achievements. But breaking through walls of silence and suspicion that often keep officers and residents at a distance is no simple task. The fact that most residents are black or Hispanic and most officers white adds an undeniable hint of distrust.

"People are still hesitant to be seen talking to us in uniform," said Officer Matthew Ruoff, who came from a unit tasked with rooting out low-level crime and is now a kind of emissary for a different mode of policing. "But it's been a few months and they are starting to open up. My goal is for people to view us as more than just, Oh, those two cops."

Neither Officer Ruoff nor his partner, Gregory Lomangino, had made an arrest in weeks. Instead, on a recent Thursday, they crisscrossed their corner of the precinct, stopping to chat with a deli worker, a kebab seller and a security guard. At each stop, they radioed to report a "community visit."

The theory, in part, is that if officers are given ample time and steady beats, they can learn about local concerns, address percolating problems of crime and disorder before they boil over and, in doing so, improve frayed relations with skeptical communities. It has been endorsed on the national level by President Obama's task force on 21st-century policing.

"There's a lot riding on it," the police commissioner, William J. Bratton, said recently of the concept, which will soon be expanded from four test precincts to more than a dozen others across the city, made possible by the addition of 1,300 officers.

Other departments around the country, from Boston to Los Angeles, have tried versions of community policing over the years with varying levels of success. Now, as pressure builds for the police to ensure public safety in ways other than simple enforcement, law enforcement leaders are watching to see if New York's return to an old idea will bring new and lasting change.

"It will send a message across the country," said Chuck Wexler, the executive director of the Police Executive Research Forum, a Washington-based research group. "It's a major shift nationally — to have the biggest department in the country talking about problem solving."

Examples of the early challenges the program faces are clear to anyone who spends time with the officers.

On a recent afternoon, for example, six officers left the station house to attend a community meeting two and a half blocks away. They could have walked through the bustle of Mott Avenue. Instead they drove in a marked police van, parked and went inside.

When it was over, the officers, known as neighborhood coordination officers or N.C.O.s, piled back into the van, made a U-turn and drove back.

The meeting itself left some involved feeling disheartened. "They didn't seem interested in finding out how we could work together," said Jazmine Outlaw, 20, a resident and the president of the 101st Precinct Community Council, who was at the meeting.

SIGNS OF PROGRESS

But there have been some successes, too. Officers Andrew Hayes, 30, and Glenn Ziminski, 32, neighborhood officers who were formerly assigned to chasing drug dealers in local housing developments, gathered information on shootings in a new way: a local mother who came to an event for children to meet officers.

"It was a shock to even him and me," Officer Hayes said, comparing it to his experiences in narcotics enforcement. "The only way we knew about getting a confidential informant is to flip a guy because he bought drugs," he said. The recent breakthrough was different. "That was all based off being an N.C.O., going to a meeting, conversing with people."

For Officers Ruoff, 31, and Lomangino, 34, a demonstration of what their new jobs could entail came in June when they learned of a woman in the Arverne View apartments who had a FedEx package — lotion and a cellphone case — stolen from the hallway in front of her apartment.

The theft was assigned to the precinct's detective squad, Officer Ruoff said, but as a minor crime it was a low priority. So the officers followed up with the building's security, found video of the thief, and learned that she was known to stand in front of a nearby deli most mornings with a beer. They found her two days later and made an arrest.

Critics of the department remain skeptical that the promise of better police-community relations will be realized through patrol officers. "It's old wine in a new bottle," said Robert Gangi, the director of the Police Reform Organizing Project. "Most people do not become police officers to do social work."

In a tacit acknowledgment of that reality, the Police Department is considering how to change its recruitment strategies. The department wants more applicants who can incorporate a measure of social work into a job that has long been defined almost exclusively by a willingness to face difficult situations and confront dangerous people. Mr. Bratton's connection to community policing has its roots in Boston in 1977, when as an ambitious young officer with the Boston Police Department, he was tapped to help implement a consultant's vision of neighborhood policing, one with similarities to the one rolling out in New York: sectors with dedicated patrol cars and officers learning local issues.

"We lost that," said the consultant, Robert Wasserman, who has remained close to Mr. Bratton over the years and now has an office steps from the commissioner's on the 14th floor of Police Headquarters. "We have to sit down and engage with people on an equal basis."

DIFFICULT PROVING GROUND

Inside the 101st Precinct in Far Rockaway, the change was sudden. On Monday, May 18, officers who had been assigned to specialized units were put back on patrol and sent to four newly designed zones — Adam, Boy, Charlie and David — that more or less correspond to existing neighborhoods.

"We kind of flipped on a dime," Deputy Inspector Justin Lenz, the precinct commander, said in his first-floor office in the aging precinct station house, where, in heavy rain, water pours in from a leaky roof. A 1979 map of the area still hangs on one wall, used to highlight gang territories in what some officers call "Brownsville by the sea," a reference to the notoriously violent Brooklyn neighborhood.

The precinct, in southeastern Queens, is one of the four — including the adjacent 100th Precinct and the 33rd and 34th Precincts in Upper Manhattan — selected as the first to test the approach.

For residents battered by Hurricane Sandy and a history of high crime, change has been felt more slowly on the street.

Many complain of a crushing boredom — not a single movie theater or sit-down restaurant — punctuated by occasional violence on the one hand and police intrusion on the other.

"This is still what we're experiencing," said Milan R. Taylor, 26, who heads the Rockaway Youth Task Force, a neighborhood group with a community garden near the Ocean Bay Apartments, historically one of the area's more violent housing developments. He said he had been stopped a half-dozen times at vehicle checkpoints this year by officers from outside the precinct who did not seem aware of the new initiative.

"It's not trickling down," Mr. Taylor said.

Other young residents said plainclothes officers have mocked them on the street, pumping rap music and throwing gang signs when driving past groups gathered outside. "We could be just like this and they stop," said Keyshawn Chean, 18, standing with friends near Beach 26th Street. "There's no new program."

The policing of Far Rockaway is complicated by entrenched challenges — high poverty and a location more than an hour by train from Manhattan — that have been a part of the neighborhood's fabric since Robert Moses and the city cleared the beachfront bungalows and set down big brick blocks of public housing.

Drainage is nonexistent on some residential streets, with huge puddles in the summer and small ice rinks in the winter; the area is dotted with nursing homes and shelters; the only hospital, St. John's, is the biggest employer.

At night, a neighborhood watch team patrols the middle-class houses in an Orthodox Jewish enclave to the east. In some of the housing projects, a group of so-called violence interrupters from a local nonprofit, Sheltering Arms, is getting off the ground with funds from the mayor's office.

The downtown, along Mott Avenue, is marked by a commercial plaza with few occupied shops; businesses elsewhere in the neighborhood close early. "This should be a jewel," Councilman Donovan Richards Jr., who represents the neighborhood, said as he stood at the open mouth of the large U-shaped shopping center. "We've turned the tide, but we're not out of the dark yet."

Roughly a mile away, at the far end of an alley without a name by an overgrown lot near the beach, Joanne Rebollo, 29, watched three of her four children and two nephews play in a kiddie pool in front of her rented white bungalow, one of the few remaining, on a sweltering afternoon.

"There's nothing to do with the kids," Ms. Rebollo said of the area, where she moved in February to escape rising rents in Bushwick, Brooklyn.

The neighborhood where she lives is ringed in purple on the precinct's aging map as the territory of the G.O.A., the Gang of Apes, one of at least nine active gangs in the precinct. Some divide up single housing developments: The front side of Redfern Houses, for example, clashes with the back.

On a recent patrol, Officer Ziminski stopped in the small red-floored foyer of 14-60 Beach Channel Drive in the Redfern Houses where, as a rookie officer eight years ago, he found Rayquan Elliot, a local rapper who performed as Stack Bundles, dead on the ground, a bullet through his skull.

The murder reverberated through the community at the time, sowing despair among those who had seen the young star as a beacon, and his death as another sign of the impossibility of making it out. It remains unsolved. Despite the area's reputation for violence, crime has diminished here recently, and shootings are sharply down this year. Among residents, the most well-known murder this year — the killing of the rapper Chinx, a child of Redfern and a friend of Mr.

Elliot's who was fatally shot as he sat in his Porsche at a stoplight — occurred miles away in Briarwood, Queens.

A LESS VIOLENT CITY

In part, the community policing model can be tried again in New York because officers have less crime to deal with. "I think it's a luxury of manageable crime," Mr. Wexler said. "If Bratton were to have attempted this in the 1990s with 2,200 homicides, it would not have been successful."

Roughly a third of the major crime in the 101st Precinct, where about 200 uniformed officers now work, occurs among people who know each other, Inspector Lenz said, including robberies and felony assaults.

"It's not your moms walking on the boardwalk and gets beat down and we're trying to find some crazed guy," he said. "It's people that know each other and then they attack, and there's weapons involved. It is what it is."

Some officers have complained that the dismantling of most of the specialized precinct units took away what had been a steppingstone to the detective squad or other advanced positions. But the neighborhood officers are given time to make home visits, seen as a way to develop skills needed for detective work.

Indeed, the new approach is rooted in conversations with people in the community. But that has forced officers into interactions that some have found awkward or uncomfortable.

"Their version is somebody wasn't too friendly to them," Inspector Lenz said. "I go, So what? Obviously I don't want you to arrest them. Just let it go."

Leaders in the Police Department have yet to settle on a method for gauging the effectiveness of officers who, in the past, were evaluated on their quantifiable activity: arrests, summonses, stops. Many of the new officers come from so-called conditions units, which focused on enforcement and are being disbanded under the program.

"They are looking at 'soft activity' now," Officer Hayes said, riding in the passenger seat of an unmarked squad car, with Officer Ziminski behind the wheel. The radio chirped with calls: a reported break-in, a missing 17-year-old, gunshots that turned out to be, on inspection, just fireworks. At one point, they drove past a young man on a street corner, his face partially covered by a mask from what the officers said was a self-inflicted gunshot wound, flashing a middle finger at the car.

"Between the two of us, Glenn and I had at least a hundred collars last year," said Officer Hayes, who has since joined the precinct's anti-crime unit, a pathway to the detective squad. For a month, neither of the officers recorded any arrests.

On a recent afternoon in Far Rockaway, the six officers sat on couches in the second-floor office of the Rockaway Youth Task Force for a conversation that roamed from the Black Lives Matter movement to strategies for backyard composting to the bureaucracy of the department.

Mr. Taylor and Ms. Outlaw, the precinct community council president, described their concerns about low-level arrests that appeared to be a form of petty harassment to young minorities: tickets for bicycling, for spitting on the sidewalk, for jaywalking.

"We already got the message — we're not doing that petty stuff anymore," Officer Lomangino said. "We have stopped."

Mr. Taylor expressed frustration that the new approach seemed limited to a small number of local officers. "What do we do?" he asked. "The great work that you guys are doing is being undone by all these other things."

"I'm with you," Officer Lomangino said. "But enforcement will always be there. We're the police."

New York Police Will Retrain Security Staff at Homeless Shelters

BY NIKITA STEWART AND JOSEPH GOLDSTEIN | MARCH 15, 2016

IN AN EFFORT to reduce violence in New York's homeless shelters, City Hall has directed the Police Department to retrain some of the guards assigned to maintain order in the shelter system.

Responsibility for security at the more than 250 homeless shelters across the city is shared, with a force of about 600 peace officers working alongside about 1,000 private guards contracted by the nonprofits that operate the shelters.

Under the initiative announced on Tuesday, only the peace officers will receive the retraining by the Police Department.

The shelter system is notorious for the dangers at some of its sites, and for many homeless people that danger is what keeps them on the street or in subway cars, rather than in shelters.

At a news conference at City Hall on Tuesday, James P. O'Neill, chief of department, said the peace officers would undergo three-day training sessions while supervisors would spend five days in training to brush up on de-escalation and other tactics.

Peace officers have arrest powers and may carry nonlethal weapons, but unlike police officers, they do not carry guns.

Chief O'Neill said the training curriculum and other details had not been finalized, and that it would take six months to a year to train all of the officers. In addition to the retraining, he said, the department will work with the Department of Homeless Services to develop a plan to strengthen security.

Mayor Bill de Blasio, a Democrat, announced the safety plans on Tuesday, after a 90-day review of homeless services that he ordered as the mayor continues to grapple with stubbornly high numbers of homeless people.

CHANG W. LEE/THE NEW YORK TIMES

A man is searched at the entrance to the Boulevard homeless shelter on Lexington Avenue in Manhattan.

The city said it could not immediately provide the cost of retraining the 600 peace officers.

Shelter violence has made news repeatedly over the last year.

In January, a resident of an East Harlem shelter, a former librarian with a history of mental illness, was found dead with his throat slashed. One of his roommates at the shelter is suspected in the killing and remains at large, the police said.

Last month a homeless woman and two of her children were stabbed to death at a Staten Island hotel that the city was using to house homeless people. Michael Sykes, the boyfriend of the woman, Rebecca Cutler, 26, has been charged with three counts of murder and one count of attempted murder in the deaths of Ms. Cutler and her daughters, Maliyah Sykes, born in September, and Ziana Cutler, 19 months. A third daughter, Miracle Cutler, 2, was stabbed but survived.

Steven Banks, the commissioner of the Human Resources Administration, appeared on Tuesday at a City Council hearing, where some Council members told him they were concerned with the increase in the number of homeless people and the violence in the shelters.

The review found that domestic violence accounted for 60 percent of violent episodes in the family shelters with children and 80 percent in adult family shelters. The city will bring back a program that provided domestic violence services in shelters that was ended in 2010.

Among homeless advocates, reaction was mixed. Some supported that the city was taking steps to make the shelter system safer, while others were concerned that the city would overstep and harass shelter residents.

Some homeless people have already been wary of Home-Stat, an initiative that increased the number of outreach workers and police officers assigned to address street homelessness.

"All this will do is deter people from entering shelter," said Al Williams, 46, who has been homeless since 2012 and is a member of the advocacy group Picture the Homeless. "When there are no consequences in the overwhelming majority of cases where police kill a civilian of color, police are clearly under no obligation to treat us with courtesy, professionalism or respect."

Mr. Williams, who is currently staying at Catherine Street Shelter in Manhattan, said the retraining plan was another reckless policy that targeted homeless people and took police resources away from fighting crime, "only to put them into punishing the poor."

Mary Brosnahan, president and chief executive of the Coalition for the Homeless, emphasized the safety and services planned for domestic violence victims.

"We see time and again families seeking shelter who are reluctant to share details of a dangerous history at intake interviews, often for fear of retribution from an abusive partner or parent," she said in a statement. "Restoring in-reach programs throughout the shelter system will help identify many more New Yorkers, who otherwise would suffer in silence."

Defining the Role of the Police in the Community

BY ALINA TUGEND | JULY 20, 2016

BALANCING MORE COMPASSIONATE policing with more effective law enforcement is one of the great challenges facing a nation traumatized and divided by multiple deadly episodes between the police and black men and the killings of police officers in cities large and small.

That was one of the major themes of a panel at Cities for Tomorrow, a conference held Monday and Tuesday hosted by The New York Times.

In many poorer African-American neighborhoods, "there are two complaints — one that the cops are brutal and rude and the other that they don't do enough to stop crime," said Mark A.R. Kleiman, a professor of public policy at Marron Institute, part of New York University. "We have to learn to address both those issues."

But Professor Kleiman, a crime reduction and drug policy expert, told audience members that creating safer communities does not call for less humane policing.

"Those who are the best in crime control are also the best in controlling excesses," he said. "There is no trade off."

But there is no question that although homicide rates nationwide have gone down significantly over the last two decades, many Americans have become more and more polarized over the role of the police.

That is especially true in what has been particularly bloody month — killings of five police officers in Dallas, three in Baton Rouge, La., and the two killings of black men by officers in Baton Rouge and a suburb of St. Paul.

New responses have to be found to address the turmoil, said Representative Hakeem Jeffries, Democrat of New York, who also spoke on the panel.

"There's been a lot of tragedy, trauma and pain," he said. "We could all retreat into our ideological corners, or we could work together to address a very complex problem."

So instead of a traditional congressional hearing on the matter, that will most likely end up as confrontational, he said, the House of Representatives has formed a working group made up of "six serious members from both parties who will spend the recess talking to all sides."

"We will have to speak to people who might make us uncomfortable," he said, including members of the activist group Black Lives Matter, high-level police officials and rank-and-file officers.

The hope, Mr. Jeffries said, is that the information gathered by the working group will help develop a piece of legislation "that does something about the strained relations between the community and the police." Bob Goodlatte, Republican of Virginia, and John Conyers, Democrat of Michigan, will lead the group.

Both Mr. Jeffries and Professor Kleiman agreed that too often the young police officers who are walking the beat are being asked to address issues that arise from a multitude of causes, such as poverty, poor education, lack of jobs and housing, and isolation.

But they also agreed that such officers are not being given the tools to work within those communities.

"If you spend a lot of time training officers about where they might get shot, it might make them trigger-happy," Professor Kleiman said. "If I were going to train someone to go on the streets of New York, I would want to do a lot of mindfulness training first. It would teach them not to respond to affronts as male primate dominance challenges."

Richard Price, the author of numerous novels portraying urban America, including "The Whites," "Clockers" and "Lush Life" and a writer for the acclaimed HBO series "The Wire," said of community policing, "it's a lot harder to overreact when you know someone's name." Mr. Price, who also spoke at the conference, cited his major concerns about the effect of the latest killings of both black citizens and police.

"My fear is that police will close ranks — it's us against the world," Mr. Price said in an interview. "My other fear is that they're going to get paralyzed and not do any policing. My third fear is that it won't change anything."

"I'm not anti-police or pro-police," he said. "I'm anti-police overreacting, but police got to police."

And they also need to have zero tolerance not just for overreaction, but also for the cover-up of incidents that get out of control.

"One kind of police conduct all police don't tolerate is corruption," Professor Kleiman said. "We need to make police as intolerant of abuse and false reporting as corruption."

We also need to think beyond crime as simply the concern of the criminal justice system, he said, noting that "if there is a single thing Congress could do to control crime, it would be to triple the federal alcohol tax."

There was general agreement that, while too many Americans — especially white Americans — believe that police brutality has increased against black men and women, the reality is that what has changed is the ability to easily record and display it.

"In the African-American community, we've known about the problems of police brutality for decades," Mr. Jeffries said. "It's finally been brought to light for the majority of Americans."

During a panel about his writing, Mr. Price, who lives in Harlem, discussed the complex impact of the area's gentrification.

"They're cleaning out some very good and decent people. Whatever is exciting and new is a little bit of a death knell."

When asked by an audience member what role white people have in Harlem, he answered, "Be a good neighbor. Say hello." After taking a few shots at the upscale market Whole Foods, which is scheduled to open a store in Harlem this year ("you need to save up to buy a banana"), he also urged the questioner to patronize the businesses that "have been there a hell of a lot longer than you have. Don't put all of your money into businesses targeted for you."

Female Police Officers Save Lives

OPINION | BY AMY STEWART | JULY 26, 2016

A HUNDRED YEARS AGO this week, Georgia Ann Robinson joined the Los Angeles police force, making her, to the best of anyone's knowledge, the nation's first African-American policewoman.

At first she worked for no pay, with no official uniform, and, as The Los Angeles Times reported, her duties were limited to caring for "delinquents of her own race." Before entering law enforcement, she had founded civic groups for African-American women, and pressured homes for unwed mothers and orphanages to accept African-Americans.

"In my present position I expect to accomplish much good," she told the newspaper. "In fact, so much has already been done through this new office that there is no end to its possibilities."

In 1916, police departments were changing because citizens demanded it. Officer Robinson and her pioneering sisters insisted that adding women to the police force would make for better, safer policing. A century later, they've been proved right.

Studies show that female officers are significantly less likely to be involved in instances of excessive force or police brutality. Policewomen are also one-third to one-fourth as likely to fire their weapons, probably saving many lives: In New York and Los Angeles, policewomen commit roughly 5 percent of shootings, while making up just under 20 percent of sworn officers.

Women make up only about 12 percent of sworn officers nationwide. Katherine Spillar, the executive director of the Feminist Majority Foundation, which runs the National Center for Women and Policing, pointed out that "80 percent to 95 percent of police work involves nonviolent, service-related activities and interactions with people in the community to solve problems — the kind of policing that appeals to women." Her organization has called for emphasizing conflict resolution and judgment over brute physical strength in police academy training programs. She also calls for more female-friendly recruitment practices, and an end to discrimination and harassment by fellow officers, a persistent problem in many departments.

If Georgia Ann Robinson were here today, she might well wonder why we haven't accomplished that already, considering how long we've been at it.

Women entered law enforcement in 1845, when the American Female Reform Society demanded the appointment of matrons to New York City's jail and insane asylum, with the goal of protecting female inmates from mistreatment by male guards.

In the early 20th century, police departments started sending out female employees to monitor dance halls and saloons, places where women might engage in prostitution or be preyed upon by men. Although they were granted the title "policewoman," they were rarely given arrest authority or job duties on par with their male counterparts.

The idea of a woman doing a man's job was met with ridicule: "Lily Pines for a 'Billy' " was the Washington Times headline when, in 1894, Lily Thompson applied to the Washington police department and demanded a job. (She was turned down.) Constance Kopp, a deputy sheriff in Hackensack, N.J., made headlines in 1915 for doing what male deputies did every day: She chased down a male suspect and threw the cuffs on him. The sheriff who had hired her faced fierce criticism for putting a woman in that position.

By 1930, there were only 1,534 women employed nationwide as law enforcement officers. By 1960, that number had inched up to 5,617 — 2.3 percent of officers. Some did move up the ranks: Violet Hill Whyte, Baltimore's first African-American policewoman, advanced to lieutenant in 1967. But most women were still treated as a sort of ladies' auxiliary to the police force. In 1966, the first women to graduate from Albuquerque's police academy were put to work in the records department, freeing up men for crime fighting.

VICTOR J. BLUE FOR THE NEW YORK TIMES

It wasn't until employment law changed in 1972 that female officers won the right to go out on patrol, make arrests and serve equally alongside men — which is to say that they could sue their employer if they were prohibited from doing so on the basis of gender. Those lawsuits started immediately and continue today: In 2011, Kathleen Green won a suit over the Los Angeles Airport police's failure to promote her to captain.

It shouldn't take a lawsuit, or (as was the case in 1845 and for many decades after) a committee of outraged wives and mothers, to bring more women into policing. Police departments shouldn't recruit or promote women just because a judge orders them to, or because of some abstract notion that diversity is a noble goal. The fact is that female officers save lives. They're good at the job, and have been proving it for 171 years.

AMY STEWART is the author of the novel "Lady Cop Makes Trouble," based on Constance Kopp, one of the nation's first female deputy sheriffs.

Supreme Court Considers a Thorny Question of Free Speech and Police Power

BY ADAM LIPTAK | NOV. 26, 2018

WASHINGTON — The Supreme Court considered on Monday whether to allow lawsuits claiming abuse of police power in retaliation for exercising free speech rights. The case concerned a claim for retaliatory arrest at a festival in a remote part of Alaska, but several justices seemed to have an array of controversies in mind.

"You can think of it," Justice Elena Kagan said, "as a case where an individual police officer, you know, decides to arrest for jaywalking somebody wearing a 'Black Lives Matter' T-shirt or, alternatively, a 'Make America Great Again' cap."

Some courts have said the existence of probable cause for the arrest — the person was, after all, jaywalking — is always enough to bar lawsuits claiming retaliation in violation of the First Amendment. Others have allowed juries to decide whether the officers involved intended to suppress protected speech.

The Supreme Court has been struggling to find a line separating two kinds of arrests, Justice Samuel A. Alito Jr. said, noting that "there are a range of cases."

At one extreme, he said, were people arrested after mouthing off to the police in heated and confusing settings. On the other, were serious abuses. "A journalist has written something critical of the police department," he said. Some time later, that hypothetical journalist, he said, was arrested for exceeding the speed limit by five miles per hour.

Justice Alito suggested that the Supreme Court would have a difficult time fashioning a standard that would bar the first kind of suit but allow the second one.

"Which of these unattractive rules should we adopt?" he asked.

The case argued Monday arose from an encounter at the Arctic Man ski and snowmobile event in the remote Hoodoo Mountains of interior Alaska. Chief Justice John G. Roberts Jr. suggested that the setting alone should give officers some leeway.

"You've got 10,000 mostly drunk people in the middle of nowhere and you've got eight police officers," he said.

The plaintiff, Russell P. Bartlett, was arrested after yelling at police officers and refusing to answer questions. Afterward, Mr. Bartlett said, one officer told him, "Bet you wish you would have talked to me now."

He was charged with disorderly conduct and resisting arrest, but prosecutors dropped the charges, saying it was too expensive to pursue them given the distances involved. Mr. Bartlett sued, saying he had been arrested for exercising his First Amendment rights.

Justice Alito suggested that Mr. Bartlett's statements were not especially worthy of protection.

"Did your client say anything that was of social importance?" Justice Alito asked Zane D. Wilson, a lawyer for Mr. Bartlett. "He's not protesting some social issue or making some important point. He's involved in a personal dispute with a police officer."

Mr. Wilson disagreed. "The right to criticize a police officer," he said, is "one of the distinguishing features between a police state and a free country."

The case, Nieves v. Bartlett, No. 17-1174, was the court's third attempt to answer the thorny question of whether the existence of probable cause was always enough to defeat a lawsuit claiming retaliatory arrest.

In June, the court ruled that Fane Lozman, a critic of a Florida city who was arrested at a City Council meeting, could pursue a case for retaliatory arrest, but only because the city appeared to have had an established and official policy of harassing him.

In 2006, the court ruled in Hartman v. Moore that government officials could not be sued under the First Amendment for retaliatory prosecutions where there was probable cause to pursue the prosecution. The question on Monday was whether the same rule should apply to arrests.

Justice Stephen G. Breyer seemed eager to find a compromise that would allow dismissal of many suits at an early stage but allow ones with substantial, objective proof that officers intended to retaliate.

Justice Breyer added that allowing such suits could have unpredictable consequences, among them the possibility that police officers "will be very careful and not arrest people whom they should arrest."

Barr Says Communities That Protest the Police Risk Losing Protection

BY KATIE BENNER | DEC. 4, 2019

The attorney general's comments drew criticism that he was conflating objections to police misconduct with a disrespect for the police.

WASHINGTON — Attorney General William P. Barr warned that communities and critics of policing must display more deference or risk losing protection, a stark admonition that underscored the Trump administration's support for law enforcement amid an ongoing national conversation about police brutality against minorities.

"They have to start showing, more than they do, the respect and support that law enforcement deserves," Mr. Barr said on Tuesday afternoon in comments at an awards ceremony for policing. "And if communities don't give that support and respect, they may find themselves without the police protection they need."

The speech immediately sparked criticisms that Mr. Barr was conflating protests of police misconduct with a disrespect for the police and that he was advocating lawlessness as a potential reprisal.

"The idea that the attorney general of the United States, the nation's chief law enforcement officer, is recommending abandoning communities as retribution for pushing for police reform or criticizing policing practices, is profoundly dangerous and irresponsible," said Vanita Gupta, the president and chief executive of the Leadership Conference on Civil and Human Rights and the former head of the Justice Department's civil rights division.

Mr. Barr's stance amounted to a call to support police officers even when they abuse their power, another critic said. Mr. Barr "fails to understand police are not a protection racket," Andrew Stroehlein of Human Rights Watch said on Twitter.

DOUG MILLS/THE NEW YORK TIMES

Attorney General William P. Barr echoed earlier statements in which he said there should be zero tolerance for resisting police.

At the ceremony, Mr. Barr likened criticisms of the police to the abuse that Vietnam War veterans — many of whom were drafted and had to fight — endured when they returned home. Those troops sometimes "bore the brunt of people who were opposed to the war," Mr. Barr said.

"The respect and gratitude owed them was not given," he said. "It took decades for the American people to finally realize that."

Mr. Barr lauded police officers for their "special kind of bravery" and noted that beyond protecting communities and fighting crime, they often do the work of mental health professionals and drug addiction specialists.

He lamented that police officers did not receive the kind of cheers and support that the public had afforded returning war veterans. "When officers roll out of their precincts, no crowds cheer them on," he said. "When you go home at the end of every day, there is no ticker-tape parade."

Mr. Barr also echoed President Trump's attacks on critics of police abuse and the use of deadly force. Mr. Trump has said that the N.F.L. should "fire or suspend" players who knelt during the national anthem to protest police brutality and that police officers should not be "too nice" while transporting suspects.

Some law enforcement officials denounced the president's comments as potentially encouraging the inappropriate use of force.

Mr. Barr's remarks reflected his calls earlier this year for zero tolerance for resisting the police and served as a reminder of his history as an ardent backer of aggressive law enforcement.

During his first stint as attorney general, in the early 1990s during the George Bush administration, Mr. Barr supported tough-on-crime policies that furthered the incarceration of millions of Americans. Under his watch, the Justice Department issued a memo titled "The Case for More Incarceration."

Mr. Barr has defended his work as partly responsible for an ensuing drop in violent crime. During his confirmation this year, Mr. Barr said that his push for more incarceration was in response to the burgeoning crack epidemic and noted that today's world may call for a different approach to drug addiction and violent crime.

But Mr. Barr has remained firm in his support of police officers and the need for them to be tough on crime. Earlier this year, he said, "In the final analysis, what stands between chaos and carnage on the one hand, and the civilized and tranquil society we all yearn for, is the thin blue line of law enforcement."

KATIE BENNER covers the Justice Department. She was part of a team that won a Pulitzer Prize in 2018 for public service for reporting on workplace sexual harassment issues.

CHAPTER 2

Assessing Racial Profiling and Bias

The relationship between the police and racial minority populations, particularly between police and black Americans, is particularly fraught throughout the country. Racial profiling, police brutality and deadly force are all urgent issues in communities of color that require more attention and resources if bias and bigotry are to be successfully eradicated from police forces. Police activity at protests and the personal activity of various officers on social media shed light on how deeply entrenched racial bias is in police culture.

What Racial Profiling? Police Testify Complaint Is Rarely Made

BY JOSEPH GOLDSTEIN | MAY 12, 2013

HE HAD NATURALLY HEARD the accusations of racial profiling, from civil rights organizations and some politicians. But in more than a decade as the top chief in the New York Police Department, Joseph J. Esposito said he never once heard a private citizen complain about a racially motivated stop-and-frisk encounter.

"I have not had anyone come and tell me, 'I was stopped because I was a person of color,' " Mr. Esposito recently testified in the continuing stop-and-frisk trial in Federal District Court in Manhattan.

This seemed to catch the judge by surprise, especially when Mr. Esposito went one step further: no local community group or tenant association had ever made a racial profiling allegation to him.

"Not a single stop?" Judge Shira A. Scheindlin asked. "Our kids are being stopped. You've never heard that from any community group?"

But over the course of the trial, which began in March, that claim has been repeated by other police commanders, leading city lawyers to suggest that racial profiling is largely a fiction created by the civil rights lawyers who brought the case.

The plaintiffs who brought the suit, however, have argued that this testimony suggests that the New York Police Department is being willfully ignorant of the potential for racial bias, and that even when citizens do complain about their experiences of being stopped, the department refuses to consider the possibility of a pattern of race-based stops.

On Tuesday, for instance, a plaintiffs' lawyer observed that police paperwork reported that one person stopped had exclaimed, "Why don't you stop other people?"

"Did this raise any flags with you that these remarks might constitute an allegation of racial profiling?" the lawyer, Kasey Martini, asked. The officer who conducted that stop was among the four officers with the highest stop activity in the entire city: over one three-month period in Fort Greene and Clinton Hill, he performed 134 stops, 95.5 percent of which involved blacks and Hispanics.

"No," the lieutenant, Charlton Telford, who supervised the officer responded. "Because it stated the demeanor of the person being stopped is angry. I don't know why he was angry."

"You know that even if a person does not specifically say that he or she believes she was stopped based on race, that race could have been a motivating factor in the incident, right?" a lawyer for the plaintiffs, Jenn Borchetta, asked a high-ranking police official.

"I guess," responded Deputy Commissioner Julie L. Schwartz, an internal police prosecutor responsible for seeking discipline for misconduct by police officers. "A lot of other things could be motivating factors."

HIROKO MASUIKE/THE NEW YORK TIMES

Joseph J. Esposito, left, a former police chief, with Commissioner Raymond W. Kelly in March.

When Mr. Esposito testified last month, the lead city lawyer, Heidi Grossman, asked him, "How do you know that racial profiling is not happening, in your view, in the Police Department?"

"Well, we don't get complaints about it," he answered. (In fact, a police inspector later testified that Mr. Esposito's office receives about 30 complaints from the public involving race each year, which are labeled under a broad category of "general dissatisfaction.")

Inspector Kenneth Lehr, the commanding officer of the 67th Precinct, which covers East Flatbush, Brooklyn, and encompasses a Caribbean-American community, said that in his interactions with the community, "racial profiling has not come up."

"Someone hasn't come up to me and said, 'Hey, you know what? The cops in the 67, they stopped me because they're profiling,' " he said.

Inspector Lehr did acknowledge that citizens had complained about being stopped. But the nature of the complaints, he testified, was

44 POLICE IN AMERICA

along the lines of "I was stopped for no reason or, you know, the officer didn't explain why I was being stopped and, you know, those types of scenarios."

"They haven't said, 'This officer stopped me because of a race issue,' " he said.

About 88 percent of stop-and-frisk encounters involve a black or Hispanic person, which the Police Department says reflects the neighborhoods where stops occur as well as the racial demographics of suspects for crimes.

But a lawyer for the plaintiffs, Gretchen Hoff Varner, suggested that Inspector Lehr was ignoring the obvious: "Has the person complaining about the stop been African-American or black?"

"Yes," Inspector Lehr said.

The plaintiffs' lawyers hope the judge finds significance in such moments.

They seek to prove not only that a pattern of race-based stops exist, but that department supervisors have acted with "deliberate indifference, the legal term for burying your head in the sand," Baher Azmy, legal director of the Center for Constitutional Rights, the organization which brought the lawsuit, said in an interview.

Judge Scheindlin, who is deciding the case, seems most interested in the testimony on this topic from precinct commanders and higher-ranking officials in the department.

Whenever a commander claims to have never received a racial profiling complaint, Judge Scheindlin rarely misses an opportunity to follow up with more questions on the topic.

But it is hard to gauge whether the judge is skeptical of the commanders' veracity or finds their claims convincing and wants to make sure she is not missing anything.

"My community is a vocal, intelligent, educated community," a recently retired Bronx precinct commander, Charles Ortiz, testified at one point.

"If there were issues about racial profiling and unlawful stops, I would know that from my community meetings."

He noted that he had an "open-door policy" with members of the community, adding, "my phone rings 24 hours a day, 7 days a week — you can ask my family — with people from the community."

Judge Scheindlin wanted to make sure that she had heard the commander correctly.

"Let me make sure I understand," she said, asking Mr. Ortiz to list the communities in the 43rd Precinct.

After Mr. Ortiz obliged, the judge asked: "With all those communities, you never heard anybody complain to you about bad stops or racial profiling?"

Mr. Ortiz acknowledged that he has heard complaints about stops.

"But it's not about the legality of the stop. It's how the officers, when they stop them, how the residents feel when they walk away."

She asked again: "Did anybody ever complain about racial profiling?"

"No, ma'am," Mr. Ortiz said.

Are Police Bigoted?

ANALYSIS | BY MICHAEL WINES | AUG. 30, 2014

IF ANYTHING GOOD has come out of this month's fatal shooting of Michael Brown in Ferguson, Mo., it is that the death of the black teenager shined a spotlight on the plague of shootings of black men by white police officers. And maybe now, the nation will begin to address the racism behind it.

That is the conventional wisdom, anyway, and maybe it is true. Only a fool would deny that racial bias still pervades aspects of American society. The evidence is clear that some police law-enforcement tactics — traffic stops, to cite one example — disproportionately target African-Americans. And few doubt that blacks are more likely than whites to die in police shootings; in most cities, the percentage almost certainly exceeds the African-American share of the population.

Such arguments suggest that the use of deadly force by police officers unfairly targets blacks. All that is needed are the numbers to prove it.

But those numbers do not exist. And because of that, the current national debate over the role of race in police killings is being conducted more or less in a vacuum.

Researchers have sought reliable data on shootings by police officers for years, and Congress even ordered the Justice Department to provide it, albeit somewhat vaguely, in 1994. But two decades later, there remains no comprehensive survey of police homicides. The even greater number of police shootings that do not kill, but leave suspects injured, sometimes gravely, is another statistical mystery.

Without reliable numbers, the conventional wisdom is little more than speculation. Indeed, some recent research suggests that it may not even be correct: One study of police data in St. Louis concluded that black and white officers were equally likely to shoot African-American suspects, while another experiment found that both officers and civilians in

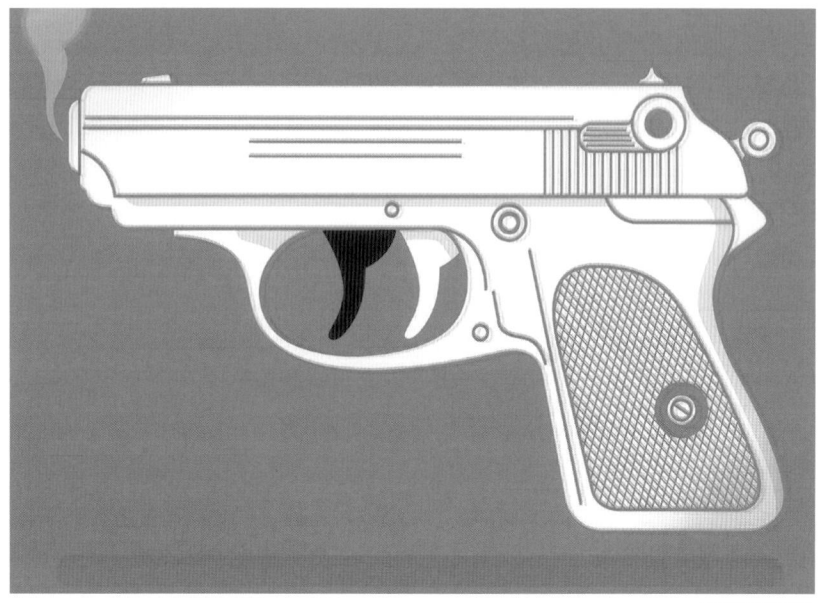

HARRY CAMPBELL

simulated situations hesitated significantly longer before firing at black suspects than they did at whites.

"It's shocking," said Geoffrey P. Alpert, a professor of criminology at the University of South Carolina. "For 20 years, we've been trying to get the government to do something. We don't have a clear picture of what's going on in the use of lethal force. Are young black males being shot at a rate disproportionate to their involvement in crime? Are white officers shooting black males in areas where they're not expected to have those sorts of interactions? Is this an aberration, a trend, routine, something going on for a long time? We don't know."

Not only do we not know the racial breakdown of police homicides, we don't know with any precision how many homicides occur, period.

The F.B.I.'s Uniform Crime Reporting Program tabulates deaths at the hands of police officers. So does the National Center for Health Statistics. So does the Bureau of Justice Statistics. But the totals can vary wildly.

By the F.B.I.'s figures, there were between 378 and 414 police homicides in the five years ending in 2012, the most recent year available. Those numbers, however, include only justifiable homicides without reference to race; mistaken or unjustified killings are not reported. Years of academic research indicate that the actual total is considerably higher.

A 2012 study by David A. Klinger, a former police officer and professor of criminology at the University of Missouri-St. Louis, compared 13 years of internal reports on homicides by Los Angeles police officers and sheriffs' deputies with the figures published by the F.B.I. The result: the 184 homicides reported by the F.B.I. were 46 percent fewer than the 340 logged by the departments themselves.

The lack of reliable data has ramifications that go well beyond merely keeping tabs on one's local police department. "There is a long list of important research questions — not arcane ones, or of mere interest to the academic research community — that we currently cannot study or systematically analyze because there is no data," said Richard Rosenfeld, another University of Missouri-St. Louis criminology professor.

Beyond measuring racial inequities, he said, researchers could use data to ferret out differences between homicides and nonlethal shootings, the nature of communities where shootings generally occur, and the character of police departments whose officers are more likely — or less — to be involved in shootings.

Whether or not racial bias is a significant factor in police homicides is very much an open question.

Studies have long concluded that police killings are more common in cities with more violent crime and larger minority populations, yet some researchers have found no positive association between race and killings. Others, however, have concluded that fewer black suspects were killed in cities with black mayors, and, in one city, that blacks made up a greater share of police homicide victims than of arrests overall.

But all those studies used the government's imperfect data and measured only homicides, excluding the greater number of shootings in which suspects survived. A more comprehensive analysis exists: Dr. Klinger and Dr. Rosenfeld, among others, examined all 230 instances over 10 years in which officers of the St. Louis police fired their weapons (the city's police, in contrast to the police in Ferguson involved in Mr. Brown's shooting).

Their conclusions, presented last November at the American Society of Criminology's annual meeting, were striking. Officers hit their targets in about half of the 230 incidents; in about one-sixth, suspects died. Of the 360 suspects whose race could be identified — some fled before being seen clearly — more than 90 percent were African-American.

But most interesting, perhaps, was the race of the officers who fired their weapons. About two-thirds were white, and one-third black — effectively identical to the racial composition of the St. Louis Police Department as a whole. In this study, at least, firing at a black suspect was an equal-opportunity decision.

In laboratory experiments, meanwhile, subjects who see pictures or videos of threatening activity, and then punch "shoot" or "don't shoot" buttons befitting their evaluations of the threat, consistently "shoot" black suspects more often than white ones.

But a different experiment last year at Washington State University in Spokane suggested that the opposite might be true: In realistic simulations of confrontations, subjects armed with laser-firing pistols acted in ways that left black suspects less likely to be shot at — not more.

The experiment's 102 subjects, a mixture of police officers, combat veterans and civilians, were run through a random sample of 60 scenarios drawn from actual police encounters. The scenarios, using white, black and Hispanic actors, were projected in life-size high-definition video on laboratory screens.

Whether officers, veterans or civilians, the subjects consistently hesitated longer before firing at black suspects and were much more likely to mistakenly shoot an unarmed white suspect, the researchers found. And when they failed to fire at an armed suspect — a potentially fatal mistake — the suspect was about five times more likely to be black than white. The study's 36 police officers were the lone exception in failing to fire: The suspect's race wasn't a factor in their decision not to shoot. "The findings were very unexpected given the previous experimental research," said Lois James, an assistant professor who conducted the research.

"The notion that cops want to shoot anybody is a lot of baloney," said Dr. Klinger, who has interviewed some 300 officers involved in shootings. "But white officers are much more reticent to shoot a black man than a white man because, all things being equal, they know the social context in which they're operating."

By that theory, officers are more careful when confronting black suspects because they know a fatal shooting will open them to controversy.

Which studies reflect reality? Hard to say. But perhaps the death of Michael Brown will help researchers find out.

MICHAEL WINES is a national correspondent for The New York Times.

ALAIN DELAQUÉRIÈRE contributed research for this article.

Class-Action Lawsuit, Blaming Police Quotas, Takes on Criminal Summonses

BY BENJAMIN WEISER | MAY 17, 2015

IN MARCH 2010, at age 19, Sharif L. Stinson was issued two criminal summonses in the Bronx: One ticket charged him with trespassing, and the other with disorderly conduct. Court records show that both were later thrown out by a judge for the same reason: "legally insufficient."

Mr. Stinson thus joined an unusual but hardly exclusive club in New York City: people who were stopped by the police and given a summons for a criminal offense, only to have it dismissed.

Indeed, records show, about one-fifth — or 850,000 — of the 3.8 million criminal summonses issued by the police between 2007 and 2014 were thrown out on grounds of legal insufficiency, which a federal judge has found was "tantamount to a decision that probable cause was presumptively lacking."

Summonses have long been heralded as a valuable law enforcement tool, not only for combating minor offenses like drinking in public or disorderly conduct, but also because an officer may demand identification and discover someone with an outstanding warrant for a more serious crime.

The Police Department's use of summonses has received renewed attention in the debate over police tactics, with the City Council speaker, Melissa Mark-Viverito, calling for lower-level offenders to be issued summonses rather than be arrested and charged with a crime. Under the law, the police must have probable cause to issue a summons, the same legal requirement for making an arrest.

But a class-action lawsuit, with Mr. Stinson, now 24, as the lead plaintiff, alleges that the city's officers, under the pressure of a Police Department quota system, have engaged in an illegal pattern and

RUTH FREMSON/THE NEW YORK TIMES

Sharif L. Stinson, 24, is the lead plaintiff in a class-action suit that accuses New York police officers of issuing summonses "in the absence of probable cause for offenses never committed."

practice of issuing summonses "in the absence of probable cause for offenses never committed." The lawsuit seeks damages and a change in the way summonses are issued.

In 2012, Judge Robert W. Sweet of Federal District Court in Manhattan, in granting class-action status to the suit, said it would cover all individuals who had been issued summonses that judges later dismissed for facial insufficiency, meaning they were legally insufficient on their face.

City lawyers, during the administrations of Mayors Michael R. Bloomberg and Bill de Blasio, have vigorously contested the lawsuit, denying in court papers that the police have quotas and arguing that the dismissals for legal insufficiency were not merit-based rulings on whether probable cause existed in particular cases. The city has also argued that such dismissals may be the result of mere "poor drafting by the issuing officer."

"When a piece of information is not included on a written summons," a Law Department spokesman, Nicholas Paolucci, said in a statement, "that does not mean that there was not probable cause to believe that an offense occurred. It simply means all of the legally required facts were not recorded on the face of the summons."

But Judge Sweet rejected that position when the city argued it in court last year. "The overwhelming majority of summonses dismissed at the facial sufficiency review stage were dismissed for want of probable cause," the judge found.

Summonses are reviewed in two stages. Court personnel initially screen them for defects, like a missing signature or an improper return date, which would invalidate them. The review for facial sufficiency is then conducted by judges, or in some cases retired judges sitting as judicial hearing officers.

Judge Sweet has ruled that individuals whose summonses were dismissed in the second review, for facial sufficiency, were "presumptive members of the class," although he said that the city could challenge an individual plaintiff to prove that a summons had been dismissed for other reasons.

Gerald M. Cohen, one of the lawyers representing the plaintiffs in the class action, said that the potential pool of class-action plaintiffs was now in the hundreds of thousands and was "constantly growing." Another plaintiff's lawyer, Elinor C. Sutton, added, "Clearly, the sheer numbers show that there is a citywide, systemic problem in the policies that are being used to police."

Mr. Stinson, the lead plaintiff, received the two summonses that were later dismissed as legally insufficient in early 2010. Joshua P. Fitch, another of the plaintiffs' lawyers, said the summonses were legally insufficient on their face.

The ticket for trespassing accused Mr. Stinson of entering and remaining in a building "without permission or authority" of its owner. But Mr. Stinson had his aunt's permission to be in the building, Mr.

Fitch said. Mr. Stinson, in a brief phone interview, said, "I go over there every week to visit her, to see how she's doing."

The disorderly conduct summons alleged that Mr. Stinson had used "obscene language and gestures, causing public alarm." But it did not specify what Mr. Stinson's behavior and obscene language had been, Mr. Fitch said. "Using foul language is not a crime," he said. "Anyone in New York knows that."

After Judge Sweet ruled in 2012 that the suit could proceed as a class action, city lawyers sought reconsideration of the order, arguing that a finding of facial insufficiency was "not a merits-based determination of whether an officer had probable cause to issue a summons." But Judge Sweet declined to change his position.

In 2014, the Law Department again asked the judge to reverse his ruling, and submitted a statement from Justin Barry, the chief clerk of the city's criminal courts, who said such dismissals might be the result of summonses that were poorly drafted.

"Facial sufficiency review may well be a test of the officer's narrative talents, rather than a reflection of the underlying facts," Mr. Barry wrote.

But Judge Sweet ruled that "the failure to provide requisite facts establishing the elements of a crime necessarily means that no reasonable cause existed to summons a person for any offense."

The judge has said that he will schedule the class-action suit for trial early next year.

A Struggle for Common Ground, Amid Fears of a National Fracture

BY JACK HEALY AND NIKOLE HANNAH-JONES | JULY 9, 2016

LONG AFTER HER two sons were in bed, Shanel Berry kept vigil in front of the television at her home in Waterloo, Iowa, watching the week's horror unfurl and obsessing over a single question: Was the gunman who killed five Dallas police officers black?

"I just thought, 'Please, please don't let him be black,' " because if he was, she worried that police shootings of black men could become easy to justify. Ms. Berry, an elementary-school teacher, said she hurt for the officers and their families. But when the gunman was identified and his photo flashed on the screen, she sank even lower.

"I told my boys, 'Now, this will make it even harder.' "

Fifteen hundred miles away, David Moody, a retired Las Vegas police officer, woke on Friday morning to fellow officers writing messages of anger and condolence on their Facebook pages, posting black-clad badges in solidarity with the Dallas Police Department. He had seethed at what he called the anti-police sentiment of protests over the deaths of two black men fatally shot by the police in Louisiana and Minnesota. And now this.

"The atmosphere that's out there right now," he said. "We don't get up in the morning thinking how can we violate somebody's rights today, how can we pick on this type of person. Every guy I know that's out there working is getting up every day and thinking he's going to make a difference."

Even as political leaders, protesters and law enforcement officials struggled to find common ground and lit candles of shared grief, there was an inescapable fear that the United States was being pulled further apart in its anger and anguish over back-to-back fatal shootings by police officers followed by a sniper attack by a military veteran who said he wanted to kill white police officers.

Just days after the United States celebrated its 240th birthday, people in interviews across the country said that the nation increasingly felt mired in bloodshed and blame, and that despite pleas for compassion and unity, it was fracturing along racial and ideological lines into angry camps of liberals against conservatives, Black Lives Matter against Blue Lives Matter, protesters against the police. Whose side were you on? Which victims did you mourn?

In a televised interview, the executive director of the National Association of Police Organizations blamed President Obama for waging a "war on cops." On social media, others confronted the discrepancies in the everyday lives of black and white Americans, hoping understanding would lead to conversations and action.

Along the Las Vegas Strip, a sunbaked cross-section of races, backgrounds and political views, tourists and workers said the relentless parade of violence during the week had left them mostly in shock and disbelief. They worried that more would follow.

Police departments across the country took precautions, ordering officers to double up in their patrol cruisers and to work in pairs or teams. Civilians were also on guard. Trey Jemmott, an incoming freshman at the University of Nevada, Las Vegas, said his mother warned him to be careful before he left for the gym the other night.

"She always told me, being an African-American, you already have strikes against you," he said. "I just feel like something's got to change. We thought we were over this."

At an outdoor food stand on the Strip, three co-workers — black, white and Asian — debated whether the bloodshed would lead to healing or deeper divisions as they talked about their own experiences with the police.

Martin Clemons, 28, said he and other black friends had been frisked for jaywalking across the Strip. Zach Luciano, 23, who is white, said he had never been stopped or had a negative run-in with law enforcement, and had considered becoming a police officer.

"There's more good cops than bad cops," Mr. Luciano said. "I wanted to be one of those good ones."

What the three co-workers shared was a grim view that the country's divides would not heal anytime soon.

"It's sad, but this is what the world's coming to," Mr. Luciano said.

In New York, Monifa Bandele has spent the past 17 years working to get citizens to video record police interactions, yet as the Facebook Live recording of Philando Castile's shooting in Minnesota coursed across social media on Wednesday night, she could not bring herself to watch.

"I literally thought I would have a stroke. I could feel my blood pressure going up," said Ms. Bandele, 45, a Brooklyn native. "I work day and night to end police brutality, and no matter how much responsibility I felt, I just couldn't do it."

Ms. Bandele and her husband, Lumumba, helped found Copwatch after the 1999 death of Amadou Diallo in a hail of bullets fired by New York City police officers who mistook a wallet in his hand for a gun. She is frequently called upon to comment on police killings, and so watching these videos is part of her work.

The night before the Castile video posted, Ms. Bandele had to watch the recording of a police officer in Baton Rouge, La., shooting Alton Sterling as he lay pinned to the ground. But the back-to-back videos, after what has felt like a constant cycle of videos of police killings of black Americans, proved too much.

"It was just a breaking. I have spoken to people who are broken, and they just can't take any more," Ms. Bandele said. "Those images visit me at night. The impact is emotional and it is physical."

Instead, she rushed upstairs to try to take the phones of her two teenage daughters before they could watch the video. But her oldest, Naima, 17, met her on the stairs, distraught, her eyes filled with tears. Ms. Bandele had to take off from work Friday to comfort her girls, to help them deal with the pain they were feeling.

Mr. Moody, the retired Las Vegas officer who also is the president of the Las Vegas Fraternal Order of Police, represents the reverse side of that vigilance. He said he spent much of his career patrolling the city on motorcycle, and now, when he comes across a traffic stop or a police cruiser flashing its lights, he pauses to watch out for the officers.

"You need citizens out there doing this kind of stuff," Mr. Moody said, "because you never know what's going to happen."

Ms. Berry, the teacher in Iowa, said she worked hard to raise her two boys, Dallas, 15, and Amari, 11, to make a good impression. Square your shoulders, she has always told them, look people in the eyes when they talk to you, and stand up for what is right. But that advice comes with a painful exception: Do none of these things if stopped by the police.

"That is the hurting part," said Ms. Berry, 37. "Because that is the part that Dallas doesn't quite get. 'Why are you telling me to comply if I am not doing anything wrong?' I am trying to teach them to be men and stand up for themselves, but at the same time I am telling them to back down and not be who they are."

This past week has only made that tightrope walk all the more difficult, trying to balance protecting her children's innocence with preparing them for what feels like an eventuality. She sat down with her sons to watch the news coverage of the shootings and said she struggled with how to simultaneously caution her boys and comfort them.

Dallas is about to turn 16, that age when the chests of teenage boys swell with bravado, when they obtain that quintessential American rite of passage — the driver's license.

"This is something we should be celebrating," Ms. Berry said, "but I am terrified."

DANIEL VICTOR contributed reporting.

Police and Protesters Clash in Minnesota Capital

BY MITCH SMITH | JULY 10, 2016

ST. PAUL — Police officers in riot gear clashed with protesters who blocked a major highway here for hours on Saturday night, marking a tense turn for the demonstrations that have continued almost nonstop since a black man, Philando Castile, was fatally shot by a suburban police officer during a traffic stop on Wednesday.

The protesters marched from the Minnesota governor's mansion onto Interstate 94, chanting refrains such as "We're peaceful, y'all violent" as the police urged them to leave. Officers struggled for more than four hours to disperse the crowd, at times deploying smoke and marking rounds in a standoff that stretched into early Sunday before snowplows cleared debris and the highway was reopened to traffic.

The police in St. Paul said at least five officers were injured by fireworks, rocks, bricks and glass bottles that they said were thrown by protesters. None of their injuries were believed to be serious. Officers said they made arrests, but did not provide information about the number of people in custody or the charges they might be facing.

The Minnesota protest was among several sizable demonstrations across the country on Saturday expressing outrage at the deaths of Mr. Castile and of Alton Sterling, another black man, who was killed by the police in Baton Rouge, La.

DeRay Mckesson, a well-known activist with a large Twitter following, was among more than 30 people arrested on Saturday outside the Baton Rouge Police Headquarters. A live stream via Twitter's Periscope service captured his arrest after a verbal confrontation with an officer who ordered him not to walk onto a street.

Protesters also blocked traffic on Saturday in New York, the local NBC station reported, and The Chicago Tribune said that a series of demonstrations in that city turned tense at times and led to arrests.

In Minnesota, the contentious highway shutdown marked a change in tack for the protesters who had occupied the area outside the governor's mansion for days but had remained almost entirely peaceful. On Friday night, the protest group had been stationary for the most part, listening to music and taking turns at the microphone outside the governor's residence discussing state laws and calling for changes to police tactics.

Earlier on Saturday, a separate group of peaceful protesters had gathered at a park in downtown Minneapolis and prepared to walk through the streets. Nekima Levy-Pounds, president of the Minneapolis NAACP, said organizers scheduled that march because "people are experiencing trauma after trauma after trauma as a result of what happened."

Ms. Levy-Pounds said many African-Americans here had still been coming to terms with the fatal shooting of Jamar Clark by the Minneapolis police in 2015 and the decision not to charge the officers involved. Protesters also blocked traffic on a Minnesota highway after Mr. Clark's death, and after the fatal shooting of Michael Brown by a Missouri police officer in 2014.

As protests continue here, much remains unknown about Mr. Castile's death. The Minnesota Bureau of Criminal Apprehension, which is investigating, has not said why he was pulled over or what happened during the traffic stop. A Facebook Live video of the shooting's aftermath prompted widespread attention and outrage, with Mr. Castile's girlfriend suggesting that he had been reaching for his identification when shot by Officer Jeronimo Yanez of the St. Anthony Police.

Thomas Kelly, a lawyer for Officer Yanez, said his client had been "reacting to the presence of a gun," though Mr. Castile's girlfriend said in the Facebook video that he was licensed to carry a weapon.

CHRISTIAAN MADER contributed reporting from Baton Rouge, La.

President Obama Urges Mutual Respect From Protesters and Police

BY MARK LANDLER AND NICHOLAS FANDOS | JULY 10, 2016

MADRID — President Obama on Sunday urged those protesting the recent shootings of black men by police officers to avoid inflammatory words and actions, which he said would worsen tensions and set back their cause.

"Whenever those of us who are concerned about fairness in the criminal justice system attack police officers, you are doing a disservice to the cause," said Mr. Obama, speaking in Spain after a meeting with the country's interim prime minister, Mariano Rajoy.

Mr. Obama's plea for a reasoned debate came on the last day of a trip to Spain and Poland. His visit was overshadowed, and abbreviated, by the wave of grief and anger convulsing the United States after the police shootings of black men in Louisiana and Minnesota, and the killing of five police officers by a black gunman in Dallas.

On Sunday, hours before he was to fly home a day earlier than planned, Mr. Obama found himself once again addressing this national tragedy, this time while sitting next to a European leader who was eager to talk about Spain's close ties to the United States.

One of the United States' great virtues, Mr. Obama said, is its openness to protest and efforts to speak truth to power. While that process is often messy, he warned that harsh language would drive people on opposing sides to their corners, hardening positions and stalling a difficult but necessary debate over racial bias in the criminal justice system.

Mr. Obama said the Black Lives Matter movement had grown out of a tradition that dated to the abolitionist movement, the women's suffrage campaign and the protests against the war in Vietnam.

In protest movements, he said, "there's always going to be some folks who say things that are stupid or imprudent or over-generalize, or are harsh."

While Mr. Obama said it was unfair to characterize an entire movement by a few dissonant voices, he said inflammatory words could hinder legitimate efforts to reform the justice system.

"Even rhetorically," Mr. Obama said, "if we paint police officers with a broad brush — without recognizing that the vast majority of police officers are doing a really good job and are trying to protect people, and do so fairly and without racial bias — if the rhetoric does not recognize that, then we're going to lose allies in the reform process."

Likewise, he urged police organizations to treat protesters respectfully and to treat their grievances seriously. He repeated an observation he made after arriving in Poland on Friday: that reliable statistics prove there is bias in the criminal justice system.

A respectful debate, Mr. Obama said, is "what's going to ultimately help make the job of being a cop a lot safer."

Mr. Obama also pledged again to bring together political leaders, civil rights advocates and law enforcement officials to try to devise solutions to this problem. He plans to travel on Tuesday to Dallas, where he will take part in an interfaith memorial service.

"I'd like all sides to listen to each other," he said.

Mr. Obama's secretary of homeland security, Jeh Johnson, echoed that message on Sunday as he appeared in a series of joint television interviews alongside New York City Police Commissioner William J. Bratton.

Addressing the anxieties of Americans shaken by the shootings last week, Mr. Johnson said that it was "a time for healing," but also a time to redouble efforts to build bridges between law enforcement and the communities they serve.

"It's a time to come together, to heal, to mourn, but to remember that the shooter is not reflective of the larger movement to bring about change that was out in Dallas to peaceably demonstrate," Mr. Johnson said on CBS's "Face the Nation." "And those who engage in excessive force in the law enforcement community are not reflective of the larger law enforcement community."

Mr. Johnson strongly rejected the suggestion made by some critics that Mr. Obama and his administration had helped incite violence against the police by supporting Black Lives Matter activists. He reiterated in personal terms the legitimacy of the activists' concerns while pledging continued federal support for local law enforcement.

"Well, I've obviously got some experience with this as a parent and as somebody who's been around," Mr. Johnson said on CNN's "State of the Union."

"I'm 59 years old now," he said, "and I've had my share of unpleasant encounters with law enforcement when I was much younger."

Pressed for more details of those experiences, Mr. Johnson largely demurred, saying, "Well, you know, the type of road encounters that others have talked about."

"But," he added, "they do not reflect the actions of law enforcement in general."

MARK LANDLER reported from Madrid, and **NICHOLAS FANDOS** from Washington.

When Police Officers Vent on Facebook

BY SHAILA DEWAN | JUNE 3, 2019

Emily Baker-White's systemic look at officers on social media found thousands of racist, Islamophobic or otherwise offensive posts. Here's how (and why) she did it.

"IT'S A GOOD DAY for a chokehold," one officer wrote. Another equated black people with dogs. Still another compared women in hijabs to trash bags.

These public posts on Facebook, written by police officers in eight departments across the country, were among those identified as offensive by the Plain View Project, a new database chronicling officers' use of social media. The departments were chosen to reflect a range of sizes and geographic regions: Dallas; Denison, Tex.; Lake County, Fla.; Philadelphia; Phoenix; St. Louis; Twin Falls, Idaho; and York, Pa.

The researchers began with about 14,400 names of officers. Of those, they were able to verify Facebook profiles for about 2,800 current officers and nearly 700 more people who had once worked for those eight departments. About one in five of the current officers, including many in supervisory roles, and more than two in five former officers, used content that was racist, misogynist, Islamophobic or otherwise biased, or that undermined the concept of due process, the project found.

A deeper look by Buzzfeed and Injustice Watch discovered that in Philadelphia, almost a third of the officers whose posts were flagged were the subject of civil rights and brutality complaints that ended in settlements or verdicts for the plaintiffs.

Police departments have long struggled to keep officers from using social media in a way that could undermine police-community relations. There have been episodes in which departments disciplined or tried to discipline officers for embracing Confederate flag imagery or using racist epithets.

The Plain View Project attempts to gauge the extent of the problem in departments across the country. It was the brainchild of Emily Baker-White, a lawyer, who explained in an interview what got her started. Her answers have been lightly edited for length and clarity.

Q: What made you want to do this?

A: Right after law school, I received a yearlong fellowship to work at the capital habeas unit in Philadelphia, and I was assigned to write and investigate a claim related to police brutality.

There was a claim that there was systemic police brutality in this neighborhood — it was a cop-killing case — and that, had the trial attorney presented information about that systemic brutality and how it affected my client, the jury might have chosen to give him a life sentence instead of a death sentence.

I stumbled upon the public profiles of several officers in that neighborhood, and I was stunned. I thought, "Oh my God, how can this information be public — why are these guys saying this stuff to the world?"

What was in those posts?

The first post that really struck me was a meme that I have seen numerous times since, that shows a police dog being restrained by an officer with its teeth bared, raring to chase after something. And the caption is, "I hope you run, he likes fast food."

If there was one, that was the image that made me think: I want to know how widespread this is.

And maybe it was the fact that it was a meme. I'm almost positive that that guy didn't create that meme, right; he got it from somewhere. And how many officers came by that meme and shared it? I still don't know the answer to that question.

How did you do the project?

The goal was to take a systemic look at a small number of departments. We went and got the roster, the publicly available roster of all the police officers in those jurisdictions.

Then we searched Facebook for folks that had the same name and location as folks on the rosters. Obviously, that wasn't enough — there are a whole lot of people with each of those names — so when we got a person who appeared to be an officer, we took that profile and looked specifically for some sort of verifying information.

The most common piece of verifying information was simply, "works at Philadelphia Police Department," "works at Dallas Police Department." A lot of people didn't list an employer. For those folks, the next most common way we verified someone was with a picture of that officer in uniform.

We made a list of all the people we verified, and we reviewed all of the public posts made by those people.

What were the criteria you used to determine whether or not a particular post or comment should be flagged?

The overarching question was, "Is this a post that might erode public trust in policing?" And there are a number of subcategories — obviously if a post appears to endorse or celebrate or glorify violence, either vigilante violence or excessive force used by officers — that, we think, would erode public trust in policing. Posts that show bias against a certain group of people, posts that use dehumanizing language, calling people animals or savages or subhuman, that would count.

What did you find out?

Critical mass means a lot of things, but there is enough of this that I can't see it as a bad apple problem anymore. I see it as a cultural problem.

One of the reasons that I don't think it's an individual problem is that these folks are talking to each other. There are a lot of posts that have eight comments underneath them, and three of those comments are by other police officers, and in those long comment threads you often see a kind of piling on. If one guy makes a comment that's sort of violent, another guy will say, "Oh, that's not enough, I would have hit him harder." "I would have shot him." "I would have killed him."

It creates a space where officers feel like this is what they should do or think, and I fear that leads more officers to do and think this stuff.

It's not a statistical sample; it's not a statistical study.

In the Buzzfeed article, there's a former police officer in Baltimore who says this language needs to be taken in the context of the job — it may just be expressions of officers who are recognizing the dangers of the profession and saying, "I have your back." What did you think of that?

I disagree with him on that. I think that, especially in posts that show some sort of bias against a group of people, it's hard for me to understand how that is showing that I have your back. It might show that "I have your back, you other white officer." But what does that say to everyone else?

Yes, police officers have an incredibly hard job. There's probably an incredible amount of PTSD; there's an incredible amount of stress. But it's not O.K. then to say, "Let's go get these animals tonight."

SHAILA DEWAN is a national reporter and editor covering criminal justice issues including prosecution, policing and incarceration.

'I Was Wrong,' Bloomberg Says. But This Policy Still Haunts Him.

BY EMMA G. FITZSIMMONS AND JOSEPH GOLDSTEIN
PUBLISHED JAN. 21, 2020 | UPDATED FEB. 19, 2020

After defending the stop-and-frisk policing tactic, the former mayor apologized. But black voters in the Democratic presidential race may not forgive him.

TWO MONTHS AFTER jumping into the presidential race, Michael R. Bloomberg has hired staff members in 35 states. He has poured $200 million into advertising. He has crisscrossed the country, visiting dozens of cities far from the standard campaign trail.

But one issue has dogged him the entire way: His use of stop-and-frisk policing as mayor of New York City and his late apology for the tactic, which targeted black and Latino men.

In the clearest sign yet of the threat that stop-and-frisk poses to his candidacy, Mr. Bloomberg traveled to Tulsa, Okla., on Sunday to deliver an unusually personal speech that attempted to show a greater awareness about race. After visiting a church with a largely black congregation, Mr. Bloomberg said at a nearby cultural center that being white likely helped propel his success and announced an economic plan to help black Americans.

But in making those remarks, Mr. Bloomberg is inevitably drawing attention to his record on stop-and-frisk. Its crushing impact on many minority New Yorkers remains a vulnerability for him in the Democratic race, where black voters are deeply influential.

"I think what he said was good, but it doesn't take stop-and-frisk off the table," the Rev. Al Sharpton said in an interview on Monday. "It just means there's more on the table to discuss. I want to hear a plan from every other candidate about how to close the black wealth gap."

Stop-and-frisk had been a staple of policing in the United States for decades before Mr. Bloomberg took office. But under him, New York

City drastically expanded its use: The number of stops multiplied sevenfold, surging to 685,724 in 2011 from 97,296 in 2002.

The practice grew even as evidence accumulated that the stops were disproportionately affecting minority residents. Across the city, a generation of young men felt harassed, humiliated and under surveillance.

And after the city lost a landmark case in 2013, in which a federal judge ruled that New York's use of stop-and-frisk violated the constitutional rights of minorities, Mr. Bloomberg was defiant, warning that the decision could lead to "a lot of people dying."

It took him more than seven years to reassess his position, apologizing for the practice at a black church in Brooklyn one week before declaring his bid for the Democratic nomination for president late last year.

His critics question whether that apology was genuine, suggesting that it was intended to mollify black voters, an important constituency in Super Tuesday voting, and left-leaning Democrats.

Mr. Bloomberg, who declined to be interviewed for this article, said in a statement that as he considered running, he kept hearing criticism over the policy and his defense of it.

"The more I listened, the more I began to accept what I had struggled to admit to myself: they were right, and I was wrong," he said in the statement. "I believe when you get something wrong, you stand up and admit it, and so I started working with my team on the speech."

Still, the issue keeps coming up, and Mr. Bloomberg trails other candidates among black voters. He was asked about stop-and-frisk in recent interviews with Stephen Colbert and on "The View." When Democratic-leaning black voters nationwide were asked which candidate they would "definitely not consider supporting," 17 percent named Mr. Bloomberg, according to a Washington Post-Ipsos poll this month. Only one candidate, Representative Tulsi Gabbard of Hawaii, had a higher level of disapproval.

Several prominent black leaders in New York City said in interviews that they believed that Mr. Bloomberg's apology was, as he has suggested, the result of a gradual shift. They said that they had, over time, tried to convince Mr. Bloomberg that the policy was far more harmful to young men than the mayor might have realized.

His supporters said that Mr. Bloomberg had viewed stop-and-frisk as part of his broader campaign to save lives, which included a ban on smoking in restaurants, a war on soda and salt, and attempts to get weapons off the streets through gun control measures, and that he trusted his police commissioner, Raymond W. Kelly.

During Mr. Bloomberg's 12 years in office, the New York City police made five million street stops.

THE ORIGINS OF STOP-AND-FRISK

The increase in street stops during the Bloomberg administration did not start with a clear order or written policy. It was more of an evolution of a strategy that took hold under Mr. Bloomberg's predecessor, Rudolph W. Giuliani.

The Police Department adopted new crime-control tactics, including a version of "broken windows" policing and a data-driven management ethos known as CompStat.

The department was under pressure to bring down crime and get guns off the streets. Leaders emphasized enforcement: more arrests, more tickets and more stops.

Police officers were given broad leeway to stop and question people. So-called furtive movements became a catchall reason for many stops, even if those movements were sometimes nothing more than fidgeting or looking back and forth repeatedly. People were frisked if officers said they noticed a bulge in a pocket — which was often a wallet or a phone.

Nonetheless, the stops became an important metric in the department's CompStat meetings, where top brass questioned subordinates if the numbers pointed the wrong way.

"Stops became the lingua franca of the department; this was the way that police officers gained currency," said Jeffrey Fagan, a Columbia Law School professor who was an expert witness in the 2013 case.

Crime continued to fall. The number of murders, for example, dropped from nearly 600 in 2002 to 335 in Mr. Bloomberg's final year in office, far below what many New Yorkers thought was possible in a city so large.

At the same time, however, street stops soared. In 2007, the Police Department released statistics revealing for the first time that the stops had increased rapidly to 500,000 in 2006 from just under 100,000 stops in 2002.

As the encounters rose, many in the city's poorest neighborhoods were left with the feeling that the police were an occupying force. Officers would detain young black men and pat them down, feeling around their waists and groins for weapons or drugs.

Guns were rarely confiscated. In 2003, officers found a gun for every 266 stops. By 2011, they found a gun every 879 stops.

The debate over stop-and-frisk grew more divisive over time. And Mr. Bloomberg's position hardened.

A VIGOROUS DEFENSE

Eric Adams, the Brooklyn borough president and a former police captain, recalled that he met with Mr. Bloomberg at Gracie Mansion during his third term as mayor and told him that the police were overusing stop-and-frisk. Mr. Bloomberg told him that he was going to trust Mr. Kelly.

"He really felt the commissioner was leading him down the right path," said Mr. Adams, who was then a state senator.

Mr. Bloomberg's rhetoric grew more provocative, even after the police had quietly begun to abandon the tactic. The number of stops plummeted in 2013, Mr. Bloomberg's last year as mayor, to 191,851 stops.

That April, in a speech at Police Headquarters, Mr. Bloomberg said there was "no doubt that stops are a vitally important reason why so many fewer gun murders happen in New York than in other major cities."

In August 2013, after a federal judge found that the practice equated to a "policy of indirect racial profiling," Mr. Bloomberg was unbowed. He accused the judge of denying the city a fair trial and promised an appeal.

There would be no change in policing tactics, Mr. Bloomberg said, because "I wouldn't want to be responsible for a lot of people dying."

Shira A. Scheindlin, the judge who ruled against stop-and-frisk, said it was difficult to watch Mr. Bloomberg and Mr. Kelly disparage her decision.

"That's always a fear that a judge has — as a result of a decision, something bad could happen," she said in a recent interview. "You always worry. But the validation is that when the stops plummeted, nothing bad happened."

The number of murders kept dropping, and New York grew safer.

In the 2013 mayoral race to replace Mr. Bloomberg, the eventual winner, Bill de Blasio, made stop-and-frisk a central issue on the campaign — and has returned to it now that Mr. Bloomberg is running for president.

"Michael Bloomberg had a stop-heavy, arrest-heavy, very punitive, very aggressive approach to policing," Mr. de Blasio said in an interview late last year with The Young Turks, "in a country, bluntly, that is still coming to grips with the reality of race-based policing."

A PRIVATE 'EVOLUTION'

Despite his staunch defense of the practice, Mr. Bloomberg had, at least privately, seemed to soften his position over the years.

At a renaming event for the Hugh L. Carey Tunnel in 2012, David A. Paterson, New York's first black governor, recalled that he chided Mr. Bloomberg over stop-and-frisk. Mr. Bloomberg acknowledged at the time that it was possible that research would prove it did not stop crime.

"He was weighing the possibility that he might be wrong," Mr. Paterson said.

Others, including Geoffrey Canada, a Harlem education leader, and Dennis Walcott, a deputy mayor and former schools chancellor under Mr. Bloomberg, helped change his mind, according to Mr. Bloomberg's campaign.

"I told him he was setting up a whole new generation of folks who think that the police were not there to serve them," said Mr. Canada, who said he had the conversation with Mr. Bloomberg during a breakfast in 2018.

Mr. Canada said that Mr. Bloomberg at the time did not offer a rebuttal, as he had in past conversations, but he was not sure he was ready to change his mind. Mr. Canada recently endorsed Mr. Bloomberg.

Last year, as he considered running, Mr. Bloomberg kept hearing about stop-and-frisk, according to Stu Loeser, a campaign spokesman. There were no internal polls; just Mr. Bloomberg and a speechwriter who carefully pored over several drafts of the apology.

In October, Mr. Bloomberg called the Rev. A.R. Bernard, the leader of a black megachurch, Christian Cultural Center, to talk about apologizing at his church. Mr. Bloomberg told him he had been considering the idea "over the last several months."

"I was wrong," Mr. Bloomberg said at the church. "And I am sorry."

Mr. Walcott, who attended the speech, said that he had spoken many times to Mr. Bloomberg about stop-and-frisk and how often his son was stopped during Mr. Bloomberg's mayoralty.

Mr. Walcott said he understood stop-and-frisk from "both sides of the fence" in terms of having a child who was stopped and who was also the victim of gun violence: His son was shot in the leg in Queens in 2006.

"What you heard at Christian Cultural Center," he said, "was the culmination of his evolution on stop-and-frisk."

Mr. Bernard believed the apology was important, even if some questioned Mr. Bloomberg's motives.

"I think the timing will be suspect no matter what you say and what you do — that's a given reality," Mr. Bernard said. "It's great you're willing to admit you were wrong, and you were right in owning it."

SUSAN BEACHY and **KITTY BENNETT** contributed research.

EMMA G. FITZSIMMONS is the City Hall bureau chief, covering politics in New York City. She previously covered the transit beat and breaking news.

JOSEPH GOLDSTEIN writes about policing and the criminal justice system. He has been a reporter at The Times since 2011, and is based in New York. He also worked for a year in the Kabul bureau, reporting on Afghanistan.

CHAPTER 3

Efforts at Reform: Examinations of Training, Principles and Practices

In order to reform police practices, law enforcement agencies must assess their training methods. If a training video promotes Islamophobic thinking, how will the exposed officers treat Muslim citizens? If officers are encouraged to use force over de-escalation techniques, how much more likely are they to involve themselves and others in deadly situations? Law enforcement leaders have made recommendations for reforming various practices, but what obstacles prevent them from enacting those changes? As police struggle to rebuild trust with different communities, deadly encounters — for both officers and civilians — stress the need for reform.

Police Training and Gun Use to Get Independent Review

BY CARA BUCKLEY | JAN. 5, 2007

RESPONDING TO THE shooting death of an unarmed Queens man by police officers nearly seven weeks ago, New York City's Police Department has commissioned a six-month independent review of its firearms training, of instances in which officers have fired their guns and of the phenomenon of so-called contagious shooting, the department's top official said yesterday.

The study, which police officials said was the first of its kind commissioned by the department, will be done by the RAND Corporation, a private nonprofit organization that has reviewed police practices in other major cities, Police Commissioner Raymond W. Kelly said. The announcement came amid continuing bitterness since the death of Sean Bell, who was killed in a hail of 50 police bullets in Jamaica, Queens, hours before his wedding on Nov. 25.

"Questions have arisen as to the quality and effectiveness of our training" Mr. Kelly said at a news conference. "We thought it would be appropriate to bring in a recognized world-renowned nongovernment organization to take a look at all of our firearms training."

Mr. Kelly said a team from RAND would assess five aspects of firearm use by police officers. They include initial, continuing and tactical firearms training, investigations of police-involved shootings, and situations in which shots fired by one officer spur other officers to shoot, a phenomenon that may have played a role in Mr. Bell's death.

The organization will delve into the details of shootings in which the police are involved, examining an officer's experience, the nature of the threat, the environment in which they fired their guns and other issues. Comparisons will be drawn to firearms training in other law enforcement agencies, Mr. Kelly said.

RAND will not be looking into the death of Mr. Bell, which is under review by a grand jury in Queens, Mr. Kelly said.

K. Jack Riley, the acting director of the RAND Center on Quality Policing, said the organization had previously evaluated training in the Los Angeles Police Department, investigated racial profiling among Oakland police officers, and examined ways to improve recruitment and retention among the police in New Orleans after Hurricane Katrina.

"This is a very proactive step the N.Y.P.D. is taking," Mr. Riley said. "I think there is an honest interest in having a dispassionate third party take an objective look at their training, and see if there's anything they're not getting right or can improve with regards to firearms training."

News of the New York study, which will cost about half a million dollars and be paid for by the New York City Police Foundation, a charity that supports the Police Department, drew mixed responses from experts in firearms and police tactics.

Thomas A. Reppetto, a former president of the Citizens Crime Commission, said that bringing in an outside organization like RAND would likely inspire more public confidence, which has wavered of late, than an in-house Police Department review would.

But Dean Speir, who writes about firearms and tactics, asked why the Police Department had not undertaken such a review before, citing the death of Amadou Diallo, the unarmed West African immigrant whom officers shot at 41 times. Another expert suggested that the money would be better spent on hands-on tactical training.

"If you talk to cops, they'll tell you people on the front line are starved for operational training," said Eugene O'Donnell, a professor of police studies at John Jay College of Criminal Justice.

But Paul J. Browne, a spokesman for the department, said that one purpose of the review was to determine whether the current training needed to be revamped. He also noted that Mr. Kelly was not the police commissioner during the Diallo shooting.

"What the commissioner wants is an independent assessment," Mr. Browne said. "If the training needs to be improved, he wants an independent assessment of what improvements are needed."

In Police Training, a Dark Film on U.S. Muslims

BY MICHAEL POWELL | JAN. 23, 2012

OMINOUS MUSIC PLAYS as images appear on the screen: Muslim terrorists shoot Christians in the head, car bombs explode, executed children lie covered by sheets and a doctored photograph shows an Islamic flag flying over the White House.

"This is the true agenda of much of Islam in America," a narrator intones. "A strategy to infiltrate and dominate America. ... This is the war you don't know about."

This is the feature-length film titled "The Third Jihad," paid for by a nonprofit group, which was shown to more than a thousand officers as part of training in the New York Police Department.

In January 2011, when news broke that the department had used the film in training, a top police official denied it, then said it had been mistakenly screened "a couple of times" for a few officers.

A year later, police documents obtained under the state's Freedom of Information Law reveal a different reality: "The Third Jihad," which includes an interview with Commissioner Raymond W. Kelly, was shown, according to internal police reports, "on a continuous loop" for between three months and one year of training.

During that time, at least 1,489 police officers, from lieutenants to detectives to patrol officers, saw the film.

News that police trainers showed this film so extensively comes as the department wrestles with its relationship with the city's large Muslim community. The Police Department offers no apology for aggressively spying on Muslim groups and says it has ferreted out terror plots.

But members of the City Council, civil rights advocates and Muslim leaders say the department, in its zeal, has trampled on civil rights, blurred lines between foreign and domestic spying and sown fear among Muslims.

"The department's response was to deny it and to fight our request for information," said Faiza Patel, a director at the Brennan Center for Justice at New York University Law School, which obtained the release of the documents through a Freedom of Information request. "The police have shown an explosive documentary to its officers and simply stonewalled us."

Tom Robbins, a former columnist with The Village Voice, first revealed that the police had screened the film. The Brennan Center then filed its request.

The 72-minute film was financed by the Clarion Fund, a nonprofit group whose board includes a former Central Intelligence Agency official and a deputy defense secretary for President Ronald Reagan. Its previous documentary attacking Muslims' "war on the West" attracted support from the casino magnate Sheldon Adelson, a major supporter of Israel who has helped reshape the Republican presidential primary by pouring millions of dollars into a so-called super PAC that backs Newt Gingrich.

Commissioner Kelly is listed on the "Third Jihad" Web site as a "featured interviewee." Paul J. Browne, the Police Department's chief spokesman, wrote in an e-mail that filmmakers had lifted the clip from an old interview. The commissioner, Mr. Browne said, has not asked the filmmakers to remove him from its Web site, or to clarify that he had not cooperated with them.

None of the documents turned over to the Brennan Center make clear which police officials approved the showing of this film during training. Department lawyers blacked out large swaths of these internal memorandums.

Repeated calls over the past several days to the Clarion Fund, which is based in New York, were not answered. The nonprofit group shares officials with Aish HaTorah, an Israeli organization whose officials have opposed a full return of the West Bank to Palestinians. The producer of "The Third Jihad," Raphael Shore, also works with Aish HaTorah.

Clarion's financing is a puzzle. Its federal income tax forms show contributions, grants and revenues typically hover around $1 million annually — except in 2008, when it booked contributions of $18.3 million. That same year, Clarion produced "Obsession: Radical Islam's War Against the West." The Clarion Fund used its surge in contributions to pay to distribute tens of millions of copies of this DVD in swing electoral states across the country in September 2008.

"The Third Jihad" is quite similar, in style and content, to that earlier film. Narrated by Zuhdi Jasser, a Muslim doctor and former American military officer in Arizona, "The Third Jihad" casts a broad shadow over American Muslims. Few Muslim leaders, it states, can be trusted.

"Americans are being told that many of the mainstream Muslim groups are also moderate," Mr. Jasser states. "When in fact if you look a little closer, you'll see a very different reality. One of their primary tactics is deception."

The film posits that there were three jihads: One at the time of Muhammad, a second in the Middle Ages and a third that is under way covertly throughout the West today.

This is, the film claims, "the 1,400-year war."

How the film came to be used in police training, and even for how long, was not clear. An undated memorandum from the department's commanding officer for specialized training noted that an employee of the federal Department of Homeland Security handed the DVD to the New York police in January 2010. Since then, this officer said, the video was shown continuously "during the sign-in, medical and administrative orientation process." A Department of Homeland Security spokesman said it was never used in its curriculum, and might have come from a contractor.

As it turned out, it was police officers who blew the whistle after watching the film. Late in 2010, Mr. Robbins contacted an officer who spoke of his unease with the film; another officer, said Zead Ramadan, the New York president of the Council on American-Islamic Relations, talked of seeing it during a training session the previous summer. "The officer was completely offended by it as a Muslim," Mr. Ramadan said. "It defiled our faith and misrepresented everything we stood for."

When the news broke about the movie last year, Mr. Browne called it a "wacky film" that had been shown "only a couple of times when officers were filling out paperwork before the actual course work began."

He made no more public comments. Privately, two days later, he asked the Police Academy to determine whether a terrorism awareness training program had used the video, according to the documents.

The academy's commander reported back on March 23, 2011, that the film had been viewed by 68 lieutenants, 159 sergeants, 31 detectives and 1,231 patrol officers. The department never made those findings public.

And just one week later, the Brennan Center officially requested the same information, starting what turned out to be a nine-month legal battle to obtain it.

"It suggests a broader problem that they refuse to divulge this information much less to discuss it," Ms. Patel of the Brennan Center said. "The training of the world's largest city police force is an important question."

Mr. Browne said he had been unaware of the higher viewership of the film until asked about it by The New York Times last week.

There is the question of the officers who viewed the movie during training. Mr. Browne said the Police Department had no plans to correct any false impressions the movie might have left behind.

"There's no plan to contact officers who saw it," he said, or to "add other programming as a result."

Obama Puts Focus on Police Success in Struggling City in New Jersey

BY JULIE HIRSCHFELD DAVIS AND MICHAEL D. SHEAR | MAY 18, 2015

CAMDEN, N.J. — President Obama came here on Monday to celebrate the progress a revamped police force has made in building trust between law enforcement and the people of Camden, a rare bright spot in what he has acknowledged is an otherwise troubled relationship between the police and black communities.

But as the presidential limousine passed through street after street of decrepit buildings, stopping at a community center so he could talk to young black men and police officers, Mr. Obama confronted a set of problems that have helped define his own complicated relationship with the police.

Ever since he said in 2009 that the police "acted stupidly" in arresting Henry Louis Gates Jr., a black Harvard professor who is a friend of Mr. Obama's, outside his Cambridge home, there has been a sense among at least some law enforcement officials that Mr. Obama is not on their side, and is suspicious of them and disdainful of their culture.

As racially tinged clashes between black men and police officers have cropped up in cities throughout the country, Mr. Obama has tried to strike a delicate balance in condemning inappropriate police practices without making a blanket condemnation of their profession. Law enforcement officials say he has often fallen short.

"I don't think there's a lot of trust," Chuck Canterbury, the national president of the Fraternal Order of Police, said in an interview.

Too often, Mr. Canterbury said, the president has been quick to assume — and to say publicly — that police officers acted inappropriately. He added that only recently had Mr. Obama begun to even acknowledge the troubling stew of poverty and lack of educational and employment opportunity that made police officers' jobs so difficult.

"There's been too many incidents where he has made comments or

DOUG MILLS/THE NEW YORK TIMES

President Obama on Monday in Camden, N.J., where he hoped to rebut the notion that he is insensitive to the plight of police officers on the front lines.

members of his administration have made comments without knowing the facts," Mr. Canterbury said. "He has certain views, and they're drawn from his personal experiences and from the advisers that he has around him, but it's a skewed view."

The strains surfaced late last year after the killing of a young black man by a white police officer in Ferguson, Mo., and again last month after the death of another black man who had been taken into police custody in Baltimore.

But they are nothing new for Mr. Obama, who came of age as a community organizer in Chicago, where the same toxic mix of poverty, racial tension and lack of opportunity often boiled over into hostility and violence. The president, who spent his childhood in Indonesia and Hawaii and attended elite schools, had a far different experience in his own youth, but he has talked about having felt racially profiled by the police as a young man.

From his earliest days in politics, as an Illinois state senator, Mr. Obama tried to forge close connections with law enforcement. Back then, he pushed for legislation to require videotaped police interrogations and prohibit racial profiling, managing to win the backing of police organizations for his efforts. Now, as he has watched the tensions boiling over in cities around the country, advisers say he is determined to find a way to speak to the root causes without scapegoating the police.

"Right now, police around the country are under an enormous amount of scrutiny and pressure, so emotions run high," Valerie Jarrett, a senior adviser to Mr. Obama, said in an interview.

"He has never put it all on the police," she continued. "He's responding because he appreciates the fact that law enforcement really does have the spotlight on them, so he doesn't want to create the impression that they alone can solve some of these structural problems."

Mr. Obama made the trip to Camden on Monday in part to rebut the notion that he is insensitive to the plight of police officers on the front lines of often-violent communities. The city attracted attention as a national model for better relations between the police and residents after replacing its beleaguered police force with a county-run system that prioritizes community ties.

"To be a police officer takes a special kind of courage," Mr. Obama said, echoing remarks he made on Friday at a memorial service for fallen police officers. "We can't ask the police to contain and control problems that the rest of us aren't willing to face or do anything about."

The president announced Monday that he was barring the federal government from giving certain types of military-style equipment to local police forces and sharply restricting others, and called for a broader shift in law enforcement practices across the country, in which community connections and transparency are the norms and mistrust and aggression are the exceptions.

But even here, the changes have attracted criticism. The American Civil Liberties Union's New Jersey branch expressed concern on

WHITNEY CURTIS FOR THE NEW YORK TIMES

Police officers in military-style equipment in Ferguson, Mo., last year. On Monday, President Obama banned the use of some military equipment by local police departments.

Monday that the shift in Camden has been toward more arrests and tickets for low-level offenses such as riding a bicycle without a bell or lights, disorderly conduct and failure to maintain lights on a vehicle. And of the 65 complaints last year accusing the police of using excessive force, about two-thirds were dismissed by the department.

"The significant increase in low-level arrests and summonses, combined with what appears to be the absence of adequate accountability for excessive force complaints, raise serious concerns," said Udi Ofer, the branch's executive director. Arresting more people for petty offenses, he added, "has the potential to create a climate of fear, rather than respect."

The criticism highlighted how hard it has been for Mr. Obama to find the right balance in his relationship with law enforcement, with civil rights activists always ready to criticize him as being too lax about police practices and with the police themselves defensive about being singled out.

Mr. Obama has often enjoyed the support of law enforcement organizations when it comes to his policy agenda, including his efforts to enact stricter gun safety laws and an immigration overhaul. He won praise for creating a policing task force last year after the unrest in Ferguson, and for holding scores of open hearings where police organizations weighed in with suggestions, although he was criticized for not including a rank-and-file police officer in the group.

Still, some law enforcement officials said they had always felt that Mr. Obama had a chip on his shoulder when it comes to the police.

David A. Clarke Jr., the sheriff of Milwaukee County in Wisconsin, said that he believed that Mr. Obama disdained the police and that it was because the president had grown up going to prestigious schools and did not understand the world that many police officers operate in daily.

"He is from that academic elite," Sheriff Clarke said. "They sit in those ivory towers not understanding what goes on at ground level in these often difficult situations."

That perspective has hung over much of what Mr. Obama has done since Ferguson. On Monday, as he announced the restrictions on military-style gear popularized after the terrorist attacks of Sept. 11, 2001, he said the equipment "can alienate and intimidate local residents, and send the wrong message."

Some police organizations heard a different message. Mr. Canterbury said the decision showed the president had a "naïve view of law enforcement."

"Putting those on restricted lists and making it so you're going to have to justify having that equipment gives the connotation that the police shouldn't have that protection," he said. "The fact is, a riot can happen in any city in America."

JULIE HIRSCHFELD DAVIS reported from Camden, and **MICHAEL D. SHEAR** from Washington.

Long Taught to Use Force, Police Warily Learn to De-escalate

BY TIMOTHY WILLIAMS | JUNE 27, 2015

SEATTLE — Officer Corey Papinsky was recently showing a group of Seattle police officers how to reduce the chance of using force against a citizen during a suddenly antagonistic encounter.

Approaching a civilian with your hands on a weapon or making too much eye contact with someone could unnecessarily escalate a situation, Officer Papinsky said. "Keep your hands visible at all times," he advised.

But he faced a tough crowd. "It seems good advice for the suspect," one officer said. "We want to see their hands."

Another officer had a different approach. "Last week, there was a guy in a car who wouldn't show me his hands," the officer said. "I pulled my gun out and stuck it right in his nose, and I go, 'Show me your hands now!' That's de-escalation."

Across the country, police departments from Seattle to New York and Dallas to Salt Lake City are rethinking notions of policing that have held sway for 40 years, making major changes to how officers are trained in even the most quotidian parts of their work.

The changes that departments are considering include revising core training standards and tactics, reassessing when and how to make arrests, and re-evaluating how officers approach and interact with members of the public during street and traffic stops.

At the forefront are de-escalation tactics, the variety of methods officers use to defuse potentially violent encounters, such as talking and behaving calmly and reasonably with sometimes unreasonable people.

But some of the officers' reactions in Seattle show just how hard it might be to change entrenched ideas about what their job involves.

For police departments, the question is whether today's standard model of aggressive policing — based in part on the broken windows theory of making arrests and issuing citations for even the most minor offenses — is compatible with a more progressive goal of simultaneously catching criminals and building greater trust within neighborhoods.

"I was trained to fight the war on crime, and we were measured by the number of arrests we made and our speed in answering 911 calls," said Kathleen O'Toole, the Seattle police chief, who is overseeing the department's changes as part of a consent decree with the Justice Department.

"But over time," she continued, "I realized that policing went well beyond that, and we are really making an effort here to engage with people, not just enforce the law."

The efforts nationwide are largely a response to a series of fatal police shootings of unarmed African-American men and boys during the past year, and to pressure from both the White House and the public for local law enforcement agencies to become more transparent in their operations. They are also a recognition that as the high crime rates of the 1980s and 1990s have ebbed, the country's appetite for a continuing war on crime seems to have diminished.

Officers at police academies have always been trained in de-escalation, but there has been less emphasis on such methods over the past 20 years. A recent Police Executive Research Forum survey of 281 police agencies found that the average young officer received 58 hours of firearms training and 49 hours of defensive tactical training, but only eight hours of de-escalation training.

The training regimens at nearly all of the nation's police academies continue to emphasize military-style exercises, including significant hours spent practicing drill, formation and saluting, said Maria R. Haberfeld, a professor of police science at the John Jay College of Criminal Justice in New York.

Many police officials now say that even while these approaches might have helped reduce crime, they have also impeded officers' ability to win the public's cooperation and trust.

"What is the collateral damage after that policing strategy?" asked Charles H. Ramsey, the police commissioner in Philadelphia, where

RUTH FREMSON/THE NEW YORK TIMES

Carmen Best, Seattle's deputy police chief, right, loaded ammunition before target practice with other members of the police department.

the department is also under a federal order to make extensive policy changes, including in training. "Have we alienated people? Yeah, you solved the problem and lowered the numbers, but if you've alienated people, have you served your purpose?"

Officials say that given the combination of lower crime and elevated public mistrust of the police, defusing heated situations is simply better policing.

"If we ask people instead of telling them, and if we give them a reason for why we're doing something, we get much less resistance," said Gary T. Klugiewicz, a retired Milwaukee County Sheriff's Office captain and former chairman of the now defunct American Society of Law Enforcement Trainers, who trains police in de-escalation techniques. "If we just started to treat people with dignity and respect, things would go much better."

Robert Haas, the police commissioner in Cambridge, Mass., said he teaches his staff that it is sometimes best for an officer to simply pause if his or her presence is causing unreasonable, but not necessarily illegal, behavior.

"If I back away and the person calms down and the situation resolves itself, then I've done what I came to do," Mr. Haas said. "We are telling officers, 'You don't have to be so assertive about it, hitting people over the head with your authority.' "

Still, talking alone may have its drawbacks, some trainers say.

"The concern we have is that hesitation might end up having an officer getting killed or assaulted," said Harvey Hedden, executive director of the International Law Enforcement Educators and Trainers Association.

"Sometimes using the least amount of force turns out to be a bad idea," he added. "It's a myth that officers want to use more force."

In Seattle, the new training was developed as part of the consent decree, which came after the Justice Department found in 2012 that the police here had engaged in a pattern of excessive force. The finding was underscored by the 2010 fatal shooting of a woodcarver who had been carrying a carving knife while walking down the street.

In the training, required for the department's 1,300 officers, the officers are taught to ask open-ended questions, paraphrase what a person has just said so that he or she knows the officer is listening, and make statements that connote empathy with the person's situation. If properly executed, these techniques will significantly decrease the need for officers to use force, police officials say.

But the changes have caused unease among many veteran officers, some of whom have filed a lawsuit challenging use-of-force guidelines required by the Justice Department. Other officers have abruptly retired.

"We've always been supposed to help people, but the emphasis has gone way farther the other way," said J Moyer, 52, a 28-year veteran of the Seattle department. "The emphasis now is that we're supposed to be social services, whereas it had been our job to look for bad guys.

We're not supposed to offend anybody, but the bad guys aren't playing by the same rules."

Some officers here and elsewhere also say the new policies can place officers in unnecessary danger.

"You can't de-escalate someone unwilling to establish rapport with you," said Chris Myers, 48, a 25-year veteran of the Seattle police force, after a training exercise last month.

But there have been notable successes.

One night late last month, a police officer confronted a man who was clutching a knife while walking down the middle of a residential street in North Seattle. When the officer ordered him to stop, the man responded with a vulgar gesture and kept going.

Over the next 30 minutes, the officer learned the man's name from his wife and used it, beginning an unconventional peripatetic monologue to try to persuade him to surrender. "Hey, Gregory," the officer said, "let me help you, brother!"

The man, disconsolate after an argument with his spouse, eventually dropped the knife. Instead of being arrested, he was taken to a hospital for a mental health checkup.

Still, officers say they have become more hesitant about confronting people they believe are acting suspiciously because the Justice Department now requires officers to write detailed reports when force is used or when someone is questioned during a street stop.

"Police work is very individualistic," said Ben Kelly, 44, a 10-year veteran. "There's 1,000 ways to do things, and you have to find a style that meshes with your personality."

The department, however, says that is precisely the problem. Officials say they want officers to perform in a standard way both to reduce discriminatory policing and to cut down on errors.

"We want to limit officers' discretion," said Lt. Scott Bachler, who oversees the de-escalation training program. "People say, 'I have a style of doing things.' We are saying: 'We don't want 25 ways of doing things anymore. We want it to be uniform.'"

Training Police in Social and Communication Skills

LETTER | THE NEW YORK TIMES | JULY 3, 2015

TO THE EDITOR:

"POLICE BEGIN STRESSING De-escalation Tactics, Despite Skepticism in the Ranks" (news article, June 27) promises a needed change away from hyperaggressive policing that harms individuals, undermines communities' ability to trust the police and has resulted in historic levels of attention and calls for reform in the last year.

In the course of our work training police officers, chiefs often tell me that the police academy typically spends 90 percent of its training on defensive tactics and 10 percent on communication skills. Unfortunately, the current community expectations of officers are just the reverse.

The most effective police officers and commanders understand that the best policing happens between the ears. Training officers how to understand people's reactions to distress, conflict and trauma is fundamental for equipping officers to de-escalate situations thoughtfully with minimum use of force.

Officers emerging from academies run like military boot camps seeing the world through the lens of suppression are ill equipped to serve their communities and the ideal of community policing.

Officers who view this as "social work" are in the wrong profession. By current estimates, between 70 and 80 percent of calls to 911 are requests for assistance because of unmet mental health needs, overtaxed families with no social safety net to turn to, or the conflict born of unrelenting poverty.

Law enforcement leadership needs to better align officer training with the current needs of communities, better equip officers with an array of social skills and knowledge, and increase partnerships with service providers to reflect the 21st-century demands of the communities they serve.

LISA H. THURAU
Cambridge, Mass.

The writer is the executive director of Strategies for Youth, which seeks to improve interactions between the police and youths.

Police Leaders Unveil Principles Intended to Shift Policing Practices Nationwide

BY AL BAKER | JAN. 29, 2016

WASHINGTON — Police officers should aid anyone they hurt immediately. They should abandon a so-called 21-foot rule, which in some encounters with emotionally volatile people can result in fatal shootings. And they should follow standards higher than those set by the United States Supreme Court for using force.

This week, a group of law enforcement leaders made these recommendations and others to inspire a shift in policing practices after two years of questions being raised about the American criminal justice system.

About 200 of those leaders gathered here on Thursday and Friday to unveil principles they want to spread to the country's more than 18,000 local, state and federal law enforcement agencies. They include ways to defuse volatile encounters and avoid violence, document and track the use of force, train officers in more effective communication and, ultimately, repair trust in communities.

"You're slowly starting to see a change in the direction of the ship," said Thomas J. Wilson, an official with the Police Executive Research Forum, a law enforcement policy group that wrote the principles with help from officers across the country.

"We've got to get to the point where the average American cop thinks a little bit more," Mr. Wilson added. "That's the bottom line."

The principles, 30 in all, come after nearly two years of research by the policy group, said its executive director, Chuck Wexler.

He surveyed 280 agencies last spring about training to de-escalate volatile situations. He brought a group of police leaders to Scotland in November to see how crime fighting is done by a mostly unarmed police force. And in December, he observed the tactics of New York Police Department's Emergency Service Unit. Pushing the principles across the country is an acknowledgment that "we can do better," said Allwyn Brown, the interim police chief in Richmond, Calif., who was on the Scotland trip.

No one knows precisely how often officers fire their weapons because that data is not kept uniformly. In New York City last year, there were 67 officer-involved shootings, a record low, with 33 of them considered "adversarial," said Inspector John J. Sprague, who commands the New York Police Department's Force Investigation Division. But policing has endured widespread condemnation and calls for reform since a series of deadly police encounters with unarmed black men and women, including the death of Eric Garner during an arrest on Staten Island, the death of Freddie Gray in police custody in Baltimore and new revelations about the fatal shooting of Laquan McDonald in Chicago.

Mr. Wexler on Friday showed photos and played videos of some of the most high-profile killings by police officers, which he warned were "hard to watch."

Collectively, they showed leaders the need for officers to "slow things down," Chief Brown said, and use levels of force more proportional to the threats they face.

"My experience in Scotland sort of changed my lens, in terms of how I look at force incidents today," he said. "Our cadence, leading up to the moment of truth, when force is used, seems like it can be a little fast."

Some principles are rooted in common sense. But putting them in writing was necessary, many leaders said.

Principle No. 7, "respect the sanctity of life by promptly rendering first aid," for instance, may seem routine for officers tending to someone injured as a result of their use of force — a baton blow, takedown or shooting. But it is not, as shown by a video of the fatal shooting last year of Walter L. Scott, an unarmed black man who was wounded and left unattended in North Charleston, S.C.

"Law enforcement doesn't look like we're trying to help people," said Jeff Cotner, a deputy chief of the Dallas Police Department. "Your soul tells you, 'I need to go up and help this person,' but your training says, 'No, you need to step back and preserve the crime scene.' We've got to change that, and we know that."

Other ideas are progressive. Principle No. 2 calls for use-of-force policies exceeding the legal standard of "objective reasonableness" outlined in the Supreme Court decision Graham v. Connor. Under the ruling, fatal shootings can be considered legal even if they are unnecessary or disproportional.

Asked by Mr. Wexler during a presentation on Friday about the push to go beyond the ruling, Vanita Gupta, the federal Justice Department's top civil rights prosecutor, told the leaders, "I think it is quite revolutionary or transformative to put that out there."

For decades, department guides have called for officers to create a "buffer zone" of 21 feet in the handling of emotionally disturbed persons armed with knives. But that concept, allowing for officers to use force if someone breaches that distance, can have fatal consequences.

"In many situations, a better outcome can result if officers can buy more time to assess the situation and their options, bring additional resources to the scene and develop a plan for resolving the incident without use of force," principle No. 16 says.

Many leaders said some of the new principles — like one borrowed from Britain's method of quickly analyzing and responding to volatile episodes — are already enmeshed in some ways in American policing.

"They talk about 'spinning the model,' " said Brian Johnson, the deputy chief of the Metropolitan Nashville Police Department, referring to the step-by-step process that Scottish officers use to assess situations. "Our guys are already doing that, but they just didn't know what to call it."

Lt. Sean Patterson, of New York's Emergency Service Unit, said that as he recently watched a video of Scottish constables managing a disorderly man, he turned to one of them, who was in the room with him, and mouthed the words, "It's the exact same thing."

"Now," he said, "we have to see how we can have our patrol officers nationwide adopt the same practices." His unit is an elite cadre, a small part of New York's 35,000-member force.

Many departments, including the one in St. Paul, and federal agencies are already weaving the ideas into their policies, said Mr. Wexler.

George T. Buenik, the executive assistant chief of the Houston Police Department, said one of his department's 24 police districts was poised to adopt the principles wholly, as part of a project to test them. Chief Brown said his entire force in Richmond, 185 officers, would give them a try.

Despite a familiarity with the ideas, and the enthusiasm of the leaders embracing them, there is bound to be resistance. Several officials said they expected police unions to fight the recommendations. Some of that reluctance would be born of the skepticism of national standards of any sort, whether in health care, education or policing, said Deputy Chief Johnson.

Next week, he is set to address the Tennessee Association of Chiefs of Police on what he has learned. Already, "the emails have come in to the executive director of the organization saying, 'We can't do this,' " he said. "And they haven't even heard what I have to say."

New York Police Illegally Profiling Homeless People, Complaint Says

BY NIKITA STEWART | MAY 26, 2016

ADVOCATES FOR HOMELESS PEOPLE filed a complaint with New York City's Civil Rights Commission on Thursday accusing the Police Department of targeting people living on the street, a practice they say violates a two-year-old law that prohibits "bias-based profiling."

In June 2015, police officers began issuing "move along" orders in the area around 125th Street in East Harlem, which had become a sprawling community of mostly homeless men, according the complaint.

The efforts grew more aggressive as up to 100 homeless people gathered in the area, turning a spotlight on the city's homelessness crisis. Police Commissioner William J. Bratton assigned a 38-officer unit to focus on the area, and the city later started Home-Stat, a program involving several different agencies working to move people off the streets and into shelters.

But advocates for homeless people say the city's efforts are discriminatory because people are being targeted simply for living on the street, even though they have not broken any laws. "We have the right to not have the police interrupt our daily lives," Alexis Karteron, a lawyer for the New York Civil Liberties Union, said. "It really just boils down to pure harassment."

The New York Civil Liberties Union and Picture the Homeless, a nonprofit in East Harlem, asked the Human Rights Commission to investigate the practice. The complaint says the police are violating the Community Safety Act, a law that took effect in 2014 with a goal of ending discriminatory profiling, including the widespread use of stop-and-frisk.

"Racial profiling was part of what was on people's minds," Donna Lieberman, executive director of the New York Civil Liberties Union, said of the law. But people pushing for the law always sought to use it to protect people of different backgrounds, she said. Profiling people because of "housing status," meaning if they have no fixed address, live in a shelter or are even perceived to be homeless, is also against the law.

In separate statements, Lt. John Grimpel, a police spokesman, and Monica Klein, a spokeswoman for the mayor's office, said the complaint would be reviewed when it was received.

Ms. Klein said the city "respects the rights of homeless New Yorkers and has put in place a new comprehensive plan to reduce homelessness."

Lieutenant Grimpel defended the Police Department. "The N.Y.P.D.'s outreach services and interactions involving the homeless are carried out in a lawful and appropriate manner," he said.

City Councilman Brad Lander, a Brooklyn Democrat who co-sponsored the legislation, said on Thursday, "There's plenty of room for a policy around homelessness that is effective, compassionate and within the law."

With few drop-in centers, concerns about safety in shelters and the dearth of affordable housing in the city, many homeless people preferred to stay on the streets. The East Harlem sidewalks had become a safe haven.

Jazmin Berges, a 32-year-old woman who now lives in transitional housing in the Bronx, said she was homeless for about three years and was a target of police profiling last summer when she was removed from Marcus Garvey Park in Harlem. She said her blankets, identification and clothes were scooped up and placed in a trash bin. "I was feeling helpless," she said. "I couldn't believe my property was being destroyed, and I didn't want to get arrested."

A Strategy to Build Police-Citizen Trust

OPINION | BY TINA ROSENBERG | JULY 26, 2016

First of two articles.

THE HORRORS OF the last few weeks — eight police officers assassinated, at least two more unarmed black men to add to a long list of those killed by police — have produced increasingly desperate calls for unity and understanding. How can Americans build empathy and trust between their police and their minority communities? How can they stop the killings? And is there a way to do this while reducing crime?

On July 17, Eric Jones, the police chief in Stockton, Calif., spoke at Progressive Community Church, an African-American church on Stockton's south side. On Sunday evening, people from three different churches gathered at Progressive to talk about police-community relations. The police department streamed the speech live on Facebook, where it has 94,000 followers.

Jones talked about the murdered police officers. But his real subject was black lives, not blue ones. "There was a time where police were used to be dispatched to keep lynchings 'civil,' " said Jones, who is white. "The badge we wear still does carry the burden, and we need to at least understand why those issues are still deep-rooted in a lot of our communities." And injustice continues, he said: "We know that there are disparities in arrests and shootings across the country."

Stockton was devastated in the 2008 recession. A quarter of the police force was laid off. The unemployment rate soared to over 20 percent by 2011, twice the national average. The city, with 300,000 people, has been one of America's 20 most violent ever since.

But the force, now back to nearly its former size, is known as one trying to do something — about crime, and about creating a different relationship with the community. These are related, said Jones, who became chief in 2012.

"Traditionally, we'd go into a neighborhood with a highly visible police patrol and zero-tolerance enforcement," Jones said in an interview. "That did reduce crime — but only for a brief time, and at great cost to community trust." He decided that winning trust was crucial.

"We will never impact violent crime the way we need to if we're not gaining community trust in the work we're doing," he said at the church. "It makes our job safer, we solve more crime and we are legitimate and credible in the eyes of the community."

Stockton is one of six American cities taking part in a new experiment funded by the Department of Justice. (The others are Birmingham, Ala.; Pittsburgh; Gary, Ind.; Fort Worth; and Minneapolis.) The cities are beginning programs to promote racial reconciliation; to address the racial biases all of us carry; and to gain the community's trust using an idea known as procedural justice.

Tom R. Tyler, now a professor at Yale Law School, first framed the idea in his 1990 book, "Why People Obey the Law." He wrote that people obey the law not because they fear punishment, as commonly thought. They obey it largely because they believe the authorities have the right to tell them what to do; in other words, the law has legitimacy.

And what gives the law legitimacy is how people are treated. "What people actually pay attention to when assessing behavior of people in legal authority is not how good they are in reducing crime or whether they get a ticket," said Tracey Meares, also a professor at Yale Law School and a leading researcher of, and advocate for, procedural justice. "What people care about is how they're treated and how they're treated in particular ways."

"All the research converges on the same basic points," said David M. Kennedy, a professor at John Jay College of Criminal Justice in New York City. The National Network for Safe Communities, which he co-founded and directs, runs the pilot project that includes Stockton. "People want to believe whatever action police and authorities are taking is being done for good reason — that it's equitable and fair rather than personal and prejudicial. They want to be treated with respect," he said. "And they want to have a chance to speak their piece."

"But you don't learn this in the first instance from social science literature," Kennedy continued. "You learn it from your mother."

Although it was not reflected in the Republican convention that nominated Donald J. Trump for president last week, Americans have been experiencing a rare moment of bipartisan convergence on the toxicity of maximum-force policing. Procedural justice has become one of the most important strategies for changing direction — perhaps the most important. In 2014, the White House convened the President's Task Force on 21st Century Policing, which published its report last year. Its first recommendation: build trust and legitimacy, using procedural justice. Now many major police forces, including New York City's, are starting to use it.

I talked to Sammy Nunez, the executive director of Fathers and Families of San Joaquin, and to Pastor Curtis Smith of People and Congregations Together. Both groups work with Stockton's most vulnerable communities — among other things, to track police abuse and campaign against it. Both men said that while problems remain, Jones was doing a good job as police chief. "It's a big change for me to say this," said Nunez, "but I believe we do have an opportunity to actually change the department in Stockton."

Jones began to try new approaches. The force began to work closely with clergy and the community. Then Jones learned about procedural justice. The Chicago Police Department had developed a course and was training all its officers. Stockton sent three officers to take the course, and then three more.

Stockton adapted Chicago's curriculum and began training officers, cadets in the police academy and other members of the community.

The course has had two parts so far (Part 3, on implicit bias, starts next month). Part 1 covers basic principles, and the effects on officers of a constantly hostile relationship with the community — the stress, burnout and cynicism. That lesson gets particularly high marks from trainees, said Capt. Scott Meadors, who runs the training.

Perhaps surprisingly, so does a lesson on the history of police-minority relations. There's a photo tour of law enforcement's hall of shame: lynchings, internment of Japanese-Americans in World War II, Stonewall, Rodney King and Abner Louima, among others. There's George Wallace on the steps of the Alabama capitol in 1963 shouting "segregation forever!" "And who's standing next to him?" said Meadors. "We are. Law enforcement. Most of our officers weren't born then, but we inherited that history, and we have to understand that."

Part 2 applies the idea to what police face on the job. For example: Police officers have typically dismissed residents trying to enter a blocked-off street with a terse "You can't go there." The course teaches them to say instead something like: "We've got a report of an armed person in the neighborhood. Let us sort this out and you can get back to your house. Sorry for the inconvenience."

The trainers also talk about something that happened to one of them, Sgt. Gary Benevides. A man having a mental health crisis had barricaded himself in a car and was revving the engine. Other police officers had been unable to persuade him to come out. Benevides, however, had met the man a few weeks before, and used that connection — forged in a brief but positive exchange — to get him to abandon the car.

I asked Meadors how the police would traditionally have handled the situation. "We would negotiate, negotiate and negotiate and create that connection," he said. "But sometimes it's very difficult if every encounter a person ever had with the police is negative."

Training is the easy part. It's much harder to integrate new ideas into the day-to-day running of the department. Stockton is trying. The department is overhauling its general orders and incorporating procedural justice, said Joseph Silva, the department spokesman. And officers' evaluations, which affect promotions and transfers, now include how well they use the strategy.

A neighborhood impact team of chaplains and officers now goes into a community the day after a traumatic or otherwise significant event, knocking on doors to talk to residents about what happened, and other community issues. Silva said that in addition to improving relations, such outreach has led to tips from residents who didn't want to be seen coming up to an officer at a crime scene.

The department also employs four strategic community officers, each assigned to a single neighborhood. One is Sonia Diaz, who spends her days in Sierra Vista, a public-housing project.

Diaz grew up about 40 miles from Stockton, in a largely Hispanic area where all the police were white and didn't speak Spanish. Her brothers were repeatedly stopped, she said. When she was 12 she was standing in front of her house with a friend, and a sheriff asked the girls if they were prostituting. "I didn't even know what it was," she said.

Diaz responds to calls about criminal activity in Sierra Vista, but her main job is building a relationship between the community and the police. She has time to talk to people. One morning last week, a group of children excitedly showed her their scooter tricks; she gave them stickers.

"When I started in January, nobody would talk to me," she said. "They wouldn't wave at me. I'd say, 'Hey, how are you guys doing,' and they would scatter. It took about four months to develop that relationship." She said that now, tenants stop her to ask for help with problems like child custody and a brother's mental health issues.

The research on procedural justice suggests that such changes could have significant impact. In minority communities, it is important in itself to reduce the sense that police are an army of occupation.

Meanwhile, studies show that the strategy can also lower crime rates. Domestic violence offenders who believe they were treated fairly during their arrest are less likely to offend again. Violent criminals whose encounters with the police are more positive are more likely to believe the law is legitimate, and are less likely to carry a gun. A program that aims to increase legitimacy is associated with less neighborhood-level crime and less individual recidivism. Other research indicates that procedural justice can lead to more community cooperation — and therefore cases solved — and less stress for cops.

Still, although Stockton is probably among the handful of police departments in the country that are doing the most thorough job of implementing procedural justice, it continues to have one of the country's highest rates of violent crime. (Unlike many other cities, however, it did not see a rise in homicides last year.) The training module used all over the country is known as the Chicago model. Yet the Chicago police department itself is a model for no one right now.

There is crime. There is police brutality. But that doesn't mean procedural justice is a failure, or not worth doing. We cannot yet see its impact at a city level. But many factors govern police behavior, and even more govern crime. Some of these are extraordinarily powerful and hard to change. I'll look at this next week.

TINA ROSENBERG won a Pulitzer Prize for her book "The Haunted Land: Facing Europe's Ghosts After Communism." She is a former editorial writer for The Times and the author, most recently, of "Join the Club: How Peer Pressure Can Transform the World" and the World War II spy story e-book "D for Deception." She is a co-founder of the Solutions Journalism Network, which supports rigorous reporting about responses to social problems.

Barriers to Reforming Police Practices

OPINION | BY TINA ROSENBERG | AUG. 2, 2016

Second of two articles.

LAST WEEK, BALTIMORE prosecutors dropped all remaining charges against three officers accused in the killing of Freddie Gray in April 2015. Gray died of a neck injury sustained while he was transported — shackled and handcuffed, but unbelted — in a police van, setting off weeks of protests and riots against police brutality, especially killings of unarmed black men. The latest acquittals mean that none of the six officers charged in the case will be punished.

Here's a paradox: Anthony Batts, the police chief when Gray was killed, was a star reformer, widely admired for the progressive, enlightened strategies he had used as chief in Oakland and Long Beach, Calif., ideas he was trying in Baltimore. One innovation Batts championed was procedural justice, the policing strategy I wrote about last week. It's based on the idea that people follow the law when they believe authorities have the right to tell them what to do, and authorities earn that right by treating the public fairly and with respect.

The thought may be counterintuitive, but much research shows that procedural justice works. It's a radical departure from maximum force policing; it argues that tactics the public widely perceives as unfair and demeaning actually create more crime, because they diminish the legitimacy of the law. Police departments throughout the country are starting to use it; it was the first recommendation of the President's Task Force on 21st-Century Policing last year.

Both Tom Tyler and Tracey Meares — Yale Law School professors who are the leading researchers and proponents of procedural justice — told me last year that Batts in Baltimore and Garry McCarthy in Chicago were among the police chiefs most dedicated to the strategy.

GABRIELLA DEMCZUK FOR THE NEW YORK TIMES

A Baltimore officer talked to a crowd about the not guilty verdict in the Freddie Gray case.

That was in April 2015. Three months later, Batts was out. McCarthy was fired in December. Gray's death and the killing of Laquan McDonald in Chicago in 2014, along with rising murder rates, have made Baltimore and Chicago national symbols of police brutality and incompetence. (And in Baltimore, continued impunity. We'll see about Chicago, where the man suspected of killing McDonald has been charged with murder.)

What does this say about procedural justice? If the idea is so transformative, why are Chicago and Baltimore so broken?

The short answer is that procedural justice is an important tool, but it works slowly. Much else needs to happen simultaneously if the police are to earn a community's trust and use that legitimacy to bring down crime.

Here's the long answer:

All institutions resist reform, but police forces are among the most difficult to change. "Those are relationships and attitudes between police and public that are literally hundreds of years in the making," said David M. Kennedy, a professor at John Jay College of Criminal Justice who directs the National Network for Safe Communities. "The idea that one can completely reset all of that in a year or a couple of months is not reasonable."

In other words, Batts might have been *too* progressive — he never gained the support of a distrustful rank and file. Reform doesn't happen in a straight line.

McCarthy, too, tried some good things. The department developed a multiday course in procedural justice and taught it to every Chicago police officer. Lieut. Bruce Lipman of the Chicago police, who has since retired, led it. Unusually for a training that doesn't involve firearms, 93 percent of officers trained rated it good or excellent. Wesley Skogan, a professor of political science at Northwestern University, studied the course's effects and found it had changed police attitudes.

But when I interviewed Lipman last year, he also said that department rules and norms didn't reflect the training. He said there was only one department policy, on gang control, that used procedural justice techniques. "That's the only place in any of the orders that it appeared," he said. "What are you doing in your department to show police officers this is the way to do business? Do you promote it? Have it written into your policy? Or are you still doing the stop-and-frisk police? You can say it, or you can do it."

McCarthy spoke often with minority communities. He was frank about abuses. He continued programs like Project Safe Neighborhoods and CeaseFire Illinois, both of which have been shown to reduce shootings and homicides in the neighborhoods where those policies are used.

In 2014, Chicago had the lowest levels of violence in half a century. But the next year, homicides rose by 12 percent, and so far this year they are up 50 percent from the 2015 rate.

Nevertheless, there is sustained progress on police shootings. Chicago's Independent Police Review Authority, a civilian agency, reports that this year police shootings have dropped, and complaints of excessive force are down. The department has provided more Tasers and training for police officers in using them, increasing their use of Tasers instead of shooting in many cases. Officers are also taught how to de-escalate confrontations without violence.

Still, the latest killing was just last Thursday, when two officers shot an 18-year-old man who had sideswiped their vehicle in a stolen Jaguar. There was no report that the man was armed. The Chicago Tribune reported a witness statement that he was killed while running away from the police.

The CeaseFire and Safe Neighborhoods programs have brought down crime, in the neighborhoods using them, and Safe Neighborhoods have been shown to lower recidivism among its participants. But only very rarely can any such program show a citywide effect.

In many departments, procedural justice risks becoming one more in a series of halfhearted reform efforts; the police force institutes training and some rule changes, but makes no real attempt to integrate the programs into broader practices.

And even if a force did employ it fully, crime rates would be unlikely to fall quickly.

Meares compares it to fighting obesity. Imagine a successful, proven strategy to get people to lose weight by eating more fruits and vegetables. Now imagine that two years after that strategy began, many people using it were still obese. We wouldn't declare it a failure. We would recognize that obesity is a complex and long-term problem with multiple causes that requires many successful strategies at once. So we might even see a need to expand its use.

That's even more true of crime. Many things affect crime rates, and there is no agreement among experts about which factors have been most important in the two-decade drop in crime we are still enjoying. Common sense and decency tell us that procedural justice is a step in the right direction. We can't go back to treating entire communities as felonious.

Police abuses are a different matter. Forces that use procedural justice well — teach it to their entire force, integrate it into rules, consider it in evaluations and promotions — can expect to see less everyday mistreatment.

But other department policies also affect police behavior and community trust. Few are as harmful as widespread stop-and-frisk. In 2011 the New York Police Department carried out 650,000 such stops. More than 90 percent of those stopped were nonwhite. And a vast majority of stops were a waste of time: In 88 percent, the police found nothing. They found guns in just one of every 500 stops, according to the New York Civil Liberties Union.

That was the peak, a decade into the mayoralty of Michael R. Bloomberg; but then it began a decline that accelerated in 2013 after a federal judge found such stops discriminatory. The judge ordered changes that included oversight by a federal monitor. Last year, instances of stop-and-frisk in the city dropped to 23,000 — less than 4 percent of the 2011 number. And major crime hit another historic low, even though the most serious crimes, such as homicide, rape and robbery, rose slightly. (Homicides and shootings have resumed dropping this year.)

Baltimore and Chicago have used stop-and-frisk far more intensively than New York. At the peak of "zero tolerance" in 2005, the Baltimore police made 108,000 arrests — one for every four residents, but highly concentrated in young black men. A vast majority of those arrested were never charged; the purpose was purely to intimidate. In April, Batts's replacement as commissioner, Kevin Davis, told Baltimore's WYPR that zero-tolerance policing "didn't work and arguably led in part to the unrest that we experienced in 2015."

And in the summer of 2014, Chicago was stopping people at four times the rate of New York City at its peak, according to an American Civil Liberties of Illinois analysis of police data on stops that did not end in arrest. (Stops have dropped since, as a result of a lawsuit and public outrage over other abuses.)

Last year, Skogan led a survey of a representative sample of Chicagoans. He found that 68 percent of young black men reported being stopped in the past year. Minorities were more likely than whites to report being treated badly during investigative stops — handcuffed, roughed up or threatened. For African-Americans, that treatment included physical force or threats to use a weapon about half the time. Officers reported being pressured by their superiors to come back daily with more and more stops — what Skogan called "round up the usual suspects" policing.

Skogan also asked people how much they trusted the police. For whites, trust in the police was at the same high level for people who had been stopped and those who hadn't. But black people's trust was 25 percentage points lower than whites if they hadn't been stopped, 50 points lower if they had. That's a major blow to the legitimacy of the law. Procedural justice proponents would argue that stop-and-frisk could create more crime than the stops prevent.

Procedural justice is designed to improve the everyday interactions between the police and the public. But it can't touch the most serious abuses, such as shootings of unarmed men, which are carried out by a small number of the worst cops — who are then often shielded by their departments.

In October 2014, a Chicago policeman shot 17-year-old Laquan McDonald 16 times. McDonald was walking away, posing no threat, and he was shot several times after he was already down. The police stood by false statements by the shooter that McDonald tried to attack him, and the department held on to the damning dash-cam video for 13 months until a court ordered its release.

The first-degree murder charges brought against the shooter, Jason Van Dyke, were the first such charges brought since 1980; the Chicago police who kill people are almost never disciplined in any way.

Meanwhile, in Baltimore, where no one will be found guilty for Gray's death, the state's attorney, Marilyn Mosby, argued that the cases failed because she had to rely on the police to investigate their own. Her office "could try this case 100 times and cases just like it, and we would still end up with the same result," she said at a news conference.

Procedural justice won't help here; what's needed is accountability.

Jamie Kalven is a Chicago writer and activist with a long history of investigating police abuses. He uncovered a man who said he witnessed the McDonald shooting, and the damning autopsy report showing that McDonald was shot 16 times. He also founded a journalism production company, the Invisible Institute, which holds conversations with minority teenagers about their interactions with the police.

"Young black men say repeatedly that when they have an encounter with the police, mostly random stops, they know two things going into the encounter," said Kalven. "First, the police have all the power. And second, if anything happens, they won't be believed. They have no means of curbing that power, addressing grievances, no means of being heard when something happens.

"The procedural justice stuff is fine in itself," Kalven said. "But accountability should have priority. If people don't have confidence there are limits to police power, the absence of that confidence just undermines initiatives like procedural justice — if it doesn't impeach them altogether."

TINA ROSENBERG won a Pulitzer Prize for her book "The Haunted Land: Facing Europe's Ghosts After Communism." She is a former editorial writer for The Times and the author, most recently, of "Join the Club: How Peer Pressure Can Transform the World" and the World War II spy story e-book "D for Deception." She is a co-founder of the Solutions Journalism Network, which supports rigorous reporting about responses to social problems.

Changes in Policing Take Hold in One of the Nation's Most Dangerous Cities

BY JOSEPH GOLDSTEIN | APRIL 2, 2017

It's a sort of Hippocratic ethos: Minimize harm, and try to save lives. And in Camden, N.J., residents are noticing the results.

CAMDEN, N.J. — Every few months, the police chief here asks which officers wrote the most tickets.

Elsewhere, this might lead to praise, but in Camden — where 40 percent of residents live below the poverty line, the murder rate compares to that of El Salvador and one of the most interesting experiments in American policing is underway — Chief J. Scott Thomson sees aggressive ticket writing as a sign that his officers don't get the new program.

"Handing a $250 ticket to someone who is making $13,000 a year" — around the per capita income in the city — "can be life altering," Chief Thomson said in an interview last year, noting that it can make car insurance unaffordable or result in the loss of a driver's license. "Taxing a poor community is not going to make it stronger."

Handling more vehicle stops with a warning, rather than a ticket, is one element of Chief Thomson's new approach, which, for lack of another name, might be called the Hippocratic ethos of policing: Minimize harm, and try to save lives.

Officers are trained to hold their fire when possible, especially when confronting people wielding knives and showing signs of mental illness, and to engage them in conversation when commands of "drop the knife" don't work. This sometimes requires backing up to a safer distance. Or relying on patience rather than anything on an officer's gun belt.

And Chief Thomson has told officers that when they respond to shootings — or after the police open fire — they should carry the

TODD HEISLER/THE NEW YORK TIMES

Officers Vidal Rivera, left, and Tyrrell Bagby in North Camden, a neighborhood that has undergone seismic changes since the police started walking the beat.

wounded into their cruisers and rush to the hospital, rather than wait for an ambulance.

Such changes were shaped partly by headlines and YouTube videos from far beyond Camden, a city of some 80,000 that for decades has been synonymous with blight and decline.

The unrest in Ferguson, Mo., after a police officer shot and killed an unarmed black teenager, Michael Brown, in 2014, and the video from Staten Island of a dying Eric Garner gasping through a police chokehold, ignited a national dialogue about policing and race. Police departments were pressured to reconsider their policies for using force. Nationwide, many departments responded by issuing body-worn cameras; turning to "de-escalation" training in an effort to shoot fewer people; and paying more attention to how the police are perceived by black residents.

Across the country, the political momentum for police reform has slowed over the last year, even before the election of President Trump, whose administration has taken the position that federal efforts to make the police more accountable have made them less effective. Ambush attacks in Dallas and Baton Rouge, La., last year left eight officers dead, shifting the national discussion away from excessive force and toward the dangers officers face.

But not in Camden, where changes have been openly received and are taking hold within the department.

"The old police mantra was make it home safely," said Tyrrell Bagby, 25, an affable second-generation Camden police officer. "Now we're being taught not only should we make it home safely, but so should the victim and the suspect." Officer Bagby has saved 22 lives since joining the force in 2014 by administering naloxone, a drug that reverses opioid overdoses.

An early sign that Chief Thomson's message was taking hold among his officers came on Nov. 9, 2015, when a 48-year-old man walked into a Crown Fried Chicken, behaved menacingly toward customers and employees, brandished a steak knife and left. Outside, officers ordered him to drop the knife, according to video from police body cameras. But the man began walking away, slashing the knife through the air as he went.

For several minutes, the officers formed a cordon around the man and walked with him for a few blocks, trying to clear traffic ahead and periodically instructing him to drop the knife.

The crisis ended when the man did just that. Had the episode taken place a year before, "we would more than likely have deployed deadly force and moved on," Chief Thomson said.

The chief said he had stressed to his officers that the department "does not treat repositioning as retreating," and that backing up to put a car between a suspect and an officer "is not an act of cowardice."

Few videos like it have emerged in the annals of American policing.

Another lifesaving initiative in Camden, actually a mandate, is for officers to drive gunshot victims to a hospital if waiting for an ambulance would cause a delay. The policy, known as "scoop and go," was modeled after a longstanding Philadelphia policy. But in much of the country, officers view picking up victims as the ambulance crews' job.

Sgt. Angel Nieves, 45, a 17-year Camden officer, said the policy "stunned" him when it was put into effect in November 2015. He had been taught to "keep your distance — you don't know what these guys have," alluding to H.I.V.

Then he thought of "what happened in places like Ferguson," where officers had left Mr. Brown's body on the street, provoking outrage. "In light of what happened there," he said, "any department that doesn't go with a 'scoop and go' policy is just asking for it" — that is, asking for trouble.

Chief Thomson, 45, who leads the department of 400 officers, is president of a prominent police research group and has emerged as a significant voice in American policing.

But he is an unlikely reformer. A Camden officer since 1994, he became chief in 2008 mainly because he was next in a fast-moving line. The department had gone through five chiefs in five years.

"They looked at me and said, 'Well, he looks like he won't get indicted in the next six months — he'll do," Chief Thomson recalled.

The force was, he said, "apathetic, lethargic and corrupt," and yet still the "most effective government agency in Camden."

The city, across the Delaware River from Philadelphia, was once a manufacturing powerhouse — this is where Campbell's invented condensed soup in a can and where RCA built many of the nation's first television sets. But the city fell into a long decline.

Today there are glimmers of optimism. The Philadelphia 76ers opened a training facility here, and a few major companies are moving to Camden. But it is still a contender for the poorest and most dangerous city in America.

Grandmothers warn children, "Play in the streets, die in the streets." The streets are not meant as a metaphor. Just being outside is considered dangerous.

A Roman Catholic nun in Camden, Sister Helen Cole of Guadalupe Family Services, a social services agency, periodically hears from suburban friends offering to donate bicycles. "I don't take them, because our kids in this community, they will not ride bikes outside," she said.

The number of homicides in Camden has dropped significantly since 2012, when the city recorded 67, the most on record; last year, the total was 44. In 2013, the remnants of the Camden force — half had been laid off — were disbanded. A new department was formed, again with Chief Thomson at its helm. It was a maneuver that lowered salaries and pension obligations. It allowed the chief to bring on new officers and a new culture.

The improvements in public safety since then are particularly strong in North Camden, a neighborhood 10 blocks long and about that many wide, full of single-family homes, many long abandoned. Addicts from the suburbs often drove there to buy heroin from street dealers.

In 2013, police officers were sent to walk patrols in the neighborhood for 12 hours. They were told to knock on doors and introduce themselves. If they needed to use a bathroom, they had better make some friends. The city razed abandoned homes. Drug dealers were arrested or pushed indoors or out of the neighborhood. Initially, at least, residents were discouraged from congregating outdoors.

In interviews, several residents who had been stopped by the police, or even arrested, grudgingly conceded that things were better.

"Metro came out beasting — they locked everybody up," recalled Tee Tee Nobles, 28.

Since then, however, he has felt it safe enough to let his daughters, ages 8 and 2, run around outdoors. Before, he said, "you don't let them outside."

I'm a Police Chief. We Need to Change How Officers View Their Guns.

OPINION | BY BRANDON DEL POZO | NOV. 13, 2019

Why do we teach them that a person with a knife is always a lethal threat?

FEW THINGS ARE more harrowing than watching a video of a police officer confront a person in emotional crisis armed with a knife or other similar object. The officer almost always points a gun at that person and yells, "Drop it!" If staring down the barrel of a gun isn't enough to give a person pause, yelling at him or her is unlikely to make a difference.

If that person advances on the police officer, gunfire often results. Each year, American police officers shoot and kill well over 125 people armed with knives, many of them in this manner.

The public has grown impatient with seeing the same approach produce a predictably tragic result. In response, Chuck Wexler, the director of the Police Executive Research Forum, has released a guide to reducing the frequency of such incidents. At a national conference for chiefs of police in Chicago recently, he showed three videos to drive the point home: desperate people with knives met by officers who pointed guns and yelled in return.

In each case, the person grew more distressed, advanced out of a desire to be shot and was shot. Everyone suffers when this happens: the person in crisis who gets shot and may well die; the officer who will experience lifelong trauma and doubt, and his or her family and loved ones; and a community that feels it failed to help a person in need.

One of the problems is that we teach our police officers to lead with the gun. We tell officers that a knife or a shard of glass is always a lethal threat and that they should aggressively meet it with a lethal threat in return. But doing so forecloses all of the better ways to communicate with a person in crisis. There are alternatives.

Imagine being an unarmed police officer — like the ones in Iceland or Britain — in the same scenario. Barking orders as you stand there empty-handed would not only seem unnatural but also absurd. Your instincts would tell you to stay a safe distance away, try to contain the person, and calm the situation.

American police leaders can learn from their unarmed colleagues. Police academies should ingrain a wide range of skills, drills and responses in trainees before they ever handle a firearm. Training should start by sending officers into scenarios where they have to solve problems without recourse to lethal force.

Unarmed officers will cultivate an instinct to de-escalate: They will keep a safe distance, they will try to assess the true level of threat rather than see a weapon as a cue to rapidly escalate, and they will communicate in ways that reach people. There is good psychological research on what type of communication stands the best chance of calming people in distress, regardless of what is in their hands. And it is certainly not yelling at them or threatening their lives.

Only during the final phase of a police academy should trainees be presented with a firearm and taught how to use it. Officers should be taught that their weapons protect not only themselves and the public but also the life of the person who is armed and in distress, because they provide a means to stay safe if a calm and reassuring approach fails. By the end of academy, the officers will have learned that yelling at a person as you threaten to shoot is a panicked, last-ditch effort, not a sign of competence.

I lead the police force in Burlington, Vt., one of the nation's most progressive cities. One of our City Council members recently suggested that we should explore ways to disarm our city's police because it would prevent them from killing people and force them to approach crises differently.

In America, this idea is a non-starter. Police officers being rendered helpless to respond to mass shootings and other gun violence puts a community in danger. But if the police profession doesn't want politicians broaching these ideas, we owe the public a commitment to doing everything we can to respect the sanctity of life. We should fundamentally change the way police officers view their guns.

America's abhorrent rate of gun violence means that the police need the equipment and training to meet even the most lethal threats. But we have the opportunity to stop this mind-set from infecting their approach in other situations. Our nation's police departments should read Mr. Wexler's guide and take its recommendations seriously.

Going further by training officers to act as if their weapons are insurance policies, rather than persuasive devices, will transform the nation's police work. Every American will be made safer by police officers whose first instinct is to communicate with the people they encounter and whose success lies in getting the psychology of persuasion right.

BRANDON DEL POZO became the chief of police of Burlington, Vt., in 2015, after serving 19 years in the New York Police Department.

CHAPTER 4

The Tech Side: Body Cams, Data and Surveillance

In the 21st century, surveillance is not limited to traffic cameras and security footage: Social media, facial recognition software and GPS are only a few of the tools at law enforcement's disposal. Body cameras show an effort toward transparency in police activity, while the use of drones in some areas could allow officers to safely assess a dangerous situation before getting involved. With new tools comes the promise of streamlining procedure; however, there is also the opportunity to abuse those tools.

Police Use Surveillance Tool to Scan Social Media, A.C.L.U. Says

BY JONAH ENGEL BROMWICH, DANIEL VICTOR AND MIKE ISAAC | OCT. 11, 2016

A CHICAGO COMPANY has marketed a tool using text, photos and videos gleaned from major social media companies to aid law enforcement surveillance of protesters, civil liberties activists say.

The company, called Geofeedia, used data from Facebook, Twitter and Instagram, as well as nine other social media networks, to let users search for social media content in a specific location, as opposed to searching by words or hashtags that would be less likely to reveal an exact location.

Geofeedia marketed its abilities to law enforcement agencies and has signed up more than 500 such clients, according to an email obtained by the American Civil Liberties Union. In one document posted by the organization, as part of a report released on Tuesday, the company appears to point to how officials in Baltimore, with Geofeedia's help, were able to monitor and respond to the violent protests that broke out after Freddie Gray died in police custody in April 2015.

Geofeedia appears to have used programs that Facebook, Twitter and other social media companies offered that allow app makers or advertising companies to create third-party tools, like ways for publishers to see where their stories are being shared on social media.

Facebook, Twitter and Instagram say they have cut off Geofeedia's access to their information. But civil liberties advocates criticized the companies for lax oversight and challenged them to create better mechanisms to monitor how their data is being used.

"These platforms should be doing more to protect the free speech rights of activists of color," Matt Cagle, a lawyer with the A.C.L.U. in Northern California, said in an interview. "When they open their feeds to companies that market surveillance products, they risk putting their users in harm's way."

Instagram and Facebook terminated Geofeedia's access to their data in September, while Twitter shut off access on Tuesday. The response from the companies suggested that Geofeedia was using data from the companies in a way that was not allowed under their developer agreements.

Jodi Seth, director of policy communications at Facebook, said that Geofeedia had access to data that had been made public on the social network, and that access was subject to the limitations in its platform policy. That policy asks developers to "provide a publicly available and easily accessible privacy policy that explains what data you are collecting and how you will use that data."

It also asks that they "obtain adequate consent from people before using any Facebook technology that allows us to collect and process data about them."

Twitter said that based on the information found by the A.C.L.U., it was "immediately suspending Geofeedia's commercial access to Twitter data."

Phil Harris, chief executive of Geofeedia, said in a statement that his company "provides some clients, including law enforcement officials across the country, with a critical tool in helping to ensure public safety while protecting civil rights and liberties." He said the firm has policies to prevent "inappropriate use of our software."

Mr. Harris added that the company understands that given how quickly digital technology changes, Geofeedia "must continue to work to build on these critical protections of civil rights."

In addition to law enforcement agencies, the company has marketed its services to journalists as a way to find people at breaking news events for interviews and social media content. The New York Times used Geofeedia on a trial basis, but has not had access since 2015.

The A.C.L.U. said it first learned about the agreements with Geofeedia from responses to public records requests to 63 law enforcement agencies in California. Those records, the organization said, revealed a significant expansion of social media surveillance.

"Posts on social media platforms can reveal information about our location, our religion, the people we associate with," Mr. Cagle said. "Users of social media websites do not expect or want the government to be monitoring this information. And users should not be at risk of being branded a risk to public safety simply for speaking their mind on social media."

New York Police Say They Will Deploy 14 Drones

BY ASHLEY SOUTHALL AND ALI WINSTON | DEC. 4, 2018

LAW-ENFORCEMENT AGENCIES across the country have adopted aerial drones to map crime scenes, monitor large events and aid search-and-rescue operations. But the high-flying devices have also triggered backlash over fears they will be used to spy on law-abiding citizens.

The New York Police Department on Tuesday unveiled plans to deploy 14 of the unmanned fliers and to train 29 officers to operate them, opening an intense debate about whether an agency previously criticized for illegally surveilling citizens should possess such powerful technology.

Senior police officials said the drones would be used for monitoring giant crowds, investigating hazardous waste spills, handling hostage situations and reaching remote areas in crime scenes, among other tasks. They will not be used for routine police patrols, unlawful surveillance or to enforce traffic laws, the officials said. Nor will they be equipped with weapons.

"Drone technology will give our cops and their incident commanders an opportunity to see what they're getting into before they go into harm's way," Chief of Department Terence A. Monahan said. "For this reason alone, it would be negligent for us not to use this technology."

He added, "Let me be clear: N.Y.P.D. drones will not be used for warrantless surveillance."

But lawyers specializing in civil liberty cases who reviewed the department's proposed drone policy said it did not go far enough in preventing the police from misusing the devices. Advocates for police reform expressed alarm about the department's growing surveillance capacity. Aside from drones, the police have thousands of cameras in public places, license plate readers and devices that can siphon information from cellphones by mimicking cellphone towers.

Christopher Dunn, the associate legal director of the New York Civil Liberties Union, said police officials rejected recommendations that would have required the department to regularly disclose how often they use the drones and why.

The N.Y.P.D. will voluntarily report aggregate data regarding the drone program, said Devora Kaye, a department spokeswoman.

The department's policy also allows the use of drones for any "public safety" reason the Chief of Department deems necessary. That leaves room for the police to use the drones however they want, with no public oversight, Mr. Dunn said.

"I understand why they want us to bless it, but we're not going to bless it," he said.

Other critics, including public defenders and elected officials, have also raised concerns the drones might be used to spy on black and Hispanic neighborhoods that have long been targets of aggressive policing practices. These detractors also have raised the possibility the video from the drones could also be exploited by the Trump administration to target immigrants.

Dan Gettinger, the co-director of the Center for the Study of the Drone at Bard College, said privacy concerns are likely to grow as the technology becomes more widespread and the capabilities of the machines increase. More than 900 law enforcement agencies currently use them, he said.

"Drones are a very dynamic platform," he said. "They're one thing today, but the technology is going to evolve and sensors are going to become more sophisticated."

The use of drones by police departments soared after the federal government eased licensing requirements in 2016. The Las Vegas police have used them to monitor New Year's Eve festivities on The Strip, and the police in Cleveland have used them to pursue suspects.

But protests surfaced over their use in Los Angeles, and in Seattle, where public pressure forced the police to ground their drones in 2013.

The New York State Police have 18 drones, which troopers use for tasks like finding missing people and projecting flood depths. "It's easier to use a drone than to launch one of our helicopters, and it's less expensive," Beau Duffy, a spokesman, said.

Police officials in New York City said they were considering using drones in 2014, and last year the department ordered three for testing. By June, the department had purchased 14. The program cost about $480,000.

Many police departments have started drone programs without the blessing of local authorities, purchasing the devices with federal funds, private donations or through loopholes in procurement processes. The New York Police Department, however, consulted with local elected leaders, among others, on a policy for using drones before they were deployed, officials said.

Officials demonstrated the devices at a closed-door meeting with a few City Council members on Sept. 27 at Police Headquarters, then met with the civil liberties lawyers to discuss the policy on Oct. 5.

Donovan Richards, a Democrat and the chairman of the City Council's Committee on Public Safety, said the police were right to seek outside input before launching the drones.

Although Mr. Richards said he understood the potential value of the flying devices, he said he would seek to fast-track legislation requiring the police to report on how often the department uses drones and why, and establishing privacy safeguards.

"What we want to avoid is 'mission creep,' where you start with the use of drones for traffic and before you know it, it's being used for surveillance," Mr. Richards said.

But some critics said the secrecy surrounding the program has fueled skepticism of the agency's willingness to operate transparently.

"Drones are serious surveillance tools that can be weaponized," said Joo-Hyun Kang, the director of Communities United for Police Reform, an umbrella coalition. The lack of public input and oversight in developing the drones program "reflects a dangerous antidemocratic pattern of the de Blasio administration and the N.Y.P.D. that disregards the perspectives of communities most impacted by police abuses," she added.

The Police Department bought the drones between April and June from DJI Technology, a company based in China. Eleven of the devices are Mavic Pro quadcopters, which measure less than two feet in diameter. Two of them are M210 RTK quadcopters, which are larger, weather-resistant models equipped with powerful camera lenses capable of thermal and three-dimensional imaging. The police also bought a DJI Inspire quadcopter for training pilots.

Each drone is flown by a two-person team from the Technical Assistance Response Unit: One officer mans the controls, while the second monitors the device while it is in flight.

At a demonstration at Fort Totten in Queens, police drone pilots demonstrated several scenarios in which the devices could be helpful. One drone was used to provide an overview of a scene meant to resemble a fatal car crash. In the second scenario, two drones were flown to take pictures of a mock hazardous materials leak involving a van.

The larger drone provided thermal imaging of the smoking car while the smaller drone flew close enough to get a vantage on the vehicle's open doors. The final drill involved using a drone to find a person posing as a lost child in a city park.

Cleveland Police Officer Contacted 2,300 Women Using Work Computer, Authorities Say

BY JACEY FORTIN | MARCH 19, 2019

A POLICE SERGEANT in Cleveland was charged this week with using government property and a police database to find information about two women, and to send social media messages to about 2,300 women over the course of eight months.

The charges against the sergeant, Michael Rybarczyk, 58, stemmed from an earlier investigation in which he was charged in February with soliciting prostitution. He had been placed on restricted duty, doing work that did not put him in direct contact with the public.

On Monday, after the new charges were brought against him, he was suspended without pay.

The new charges against Sergeant Rybarczyk, who has been with the Cleveland Division of Police for nearly three decades, included two counts that allege that he used his access to a police database to find personal information about, and photographs of, two women.

A third count alleges that he "used a social media platform to send non-work related, written messages to approximately 2,300 females" from June 2018 through January, and that he did so on a computer owned by the city.

At least some of the messages were sent while Sergeant Rybarczyk was on duty, the authorities contend, saying that the city suffered a "loss of services" worth $1,000.

The Division of Police began an internal affairs investigation of Sergeant Rybarczyk in January, which culminated in 11 misdemeanor counts of soliciting prostitution being brought against him in February in Cleveland Municipal Court, according to a statement from the police.

Sergeant Rybarczyk has pleaded not guilty to those charges.

The statement added that further investigation led to the new felony charges, which were filed in the Cuyahoga County Criminal Court.

Sergeant Rybarczyk could not be reached for comment on Tuesday.

Earlier this month, a police officer in Florida was accused of using his access to a police database to find women he wanted to date and reaching out to them via social media, telephone calls and in-person visits.

Also this month, a detective with the Police Department in Columbus, Ohio, was arrested on charges that he kidnapped two women under the guise of arrest and forced them to have sex with him to gain their freedom.

Police Body-Cam Video Appears to Show Willie McCoy Sleeping Before He Was Fatally Shot

BY JACEY FORTIN | MARCH 31, 2019

WILLIE MCCOY APPEARED to be asleep in his car at a Taco Bell drive-through in Vallejo, Calif., when police officers, responding to a 911 call, arrived to check on him.

Minutes later, Mr. McCoy, 20, was shot and killed. The police said he had woken up and was reaching for a gun on his lap, but Mr. McCoy's friends and family members demanded more transparency.

On Friday, the Vallejo Police Department released footage from the body-worn cameras of six officers who fired their weapons during the shooting, which occurred Feb. 9.

The footage showed that Mr. McCoy appeared to be asleep for at least several minutes, and that he was shot about 10 seconds after he began to move. It was unclear whether he was reaching for a gun.

The police said in a statement last week that the Solano County district attorney's office was investigating the episode, adding that the department was releasing the videos because it wanted "to address the questions that have been raised to help the public digest both the media reports and to facilitate a community dialogue about the facts of this incident."

Since the shooting, relatives of Mr. McCoy have questioned the police version of events. "Willie was shot a whole lot of times," David Harrison, a cousin of Mr. McCoy's who saw his body after the shooting, said in an interview in February. "Our belief is that Willie was executed, like a firing squad."

On Sunday, Melissa Nold, a lawyer for the family, said the video footage had confirmed the family's fears. "We intend to file a federal civil rights lawsuit shortly," she said. "Based on the videos, it looks like the officers violated basic safety principles and made no real efforts to preserve human life."

The officers involved had been placed on administrative leave, but Ms. Nold said that they were back on duty within weeks of the shooting. Neither the police department nor the district attorney's office immediately responded to requests for comment on Sunday.

The half-hour video released by the police included footage from six body cameras, as well as an audio recording of the 911 call that ultimately brought officers to the Taco Bell drive-through.

"I have a person unresponsive to car horn honks in my drive-through," a Taco Bell employee could be heard saying, adding: "He's unresponsive. I've already had, like, people try to knock on the window. I have no idea what's going on."

A dispatcher could then be heard calling for officers to do a "wellness check."

Shortly after arriving, one officer could be heard saying: "Gun. Gun. Call it out. There's a gun in his lap."

About four minutes passed while the officers tried to open the car door and moved their patrol cars to box in Mr. McCoy's vehicle. In the videos, which were partly obscured by the officers' drawn weapons and outstretched arms, there was no indication that the police tried to awaken Mr. McCoy, although they were shining their flashlights into his car.

Referring to a gun on Mr. McCoy's lap, one officer could be heard saying that the magazine appeared to be detached from the weapon and noting that if Mr. McCoy fired the gun, he would be able to shoot only once. But in a caption added to the footage, the police said that "in fact, the gun was loaded with an extended 14-round magazine, extending past the grip."

At one point in the video footage, officers could be heard making a plan to open the car door, seize the gun and pull Mr. McCoy out of the car. "If he reaches for it," said one of the officers, nodding.

"Yup," said another. But they found the door locked, and Mr. McCoy appeared to remain asleep.

Eventually, Mr. McCoy could be seen beginning to stir, using his right hand to scratch at his left shoulder. "He's moving, he's moving," an officer said. "He's not up yet."

Then the officers began yelling at Mr. McCoy to raise his hands. Less than 10 seconds after Mr. McCoy scratched his left shoulder, he could be seen moving his left arm, and six officers opened fire.

"To respect the privacy of the decedent and his family, we are withholding the portions of the videos showing officers rendering medical aid," the police said in their statement Friday.

The police first showed body camera footage to a few relatives of Mr. McCoy on March 13. Last Monday, Open Vallejo, a local news outlet, made a public records request for the footage. It was released to the public four days later.

"I'm glad that the video was released and everyone can see it because, just like anything else, when there's something out there that's dangerous in the community, we want to know about it," Mr. Harrison, Mr. McCoy's cousin, said at a news conference on Friday. "We just happen to have police officers who are rogue out here."

Tracking Phones, Google Is a Dragnet for the Police

BY JENNIFER VALENTINO-DEVRIES | APRIL 13, 2019

The tech giant records people's locations worldwide. Now, investigators are using it to find suspects and witnesses near crimes, running the risk of snaring the innocent.

WHEN DETECTIVES IN a Phoenix suburb arrested a warehouse worker in a murder investigation last December, they credited a new technique with breaking open the case after other leads went cold.

The police told the suspect, Jorge Molina, they had data tracking his phone to the site where a man was shot nine months earlier. They had made the discovery after obtaining a search warrant that required Google to provide information on all devices it recorded near the killing, potentially capturing the whereabouts of anyone in the area.

Investigators also had other circumstantial evidence, including security video of someone firing a gun from a white Honda Civic, the same model that Mr. Molina owned, though they could not see the license plate or attacker.

But after he spent nearly a week in jail, the case against Mr. Molina fell apart as investigators learned new information and released him. Last month, the police arrested another man: his mother's ex-boyfriend, who had sometimes used Mr. Molina's car.

The warrants, which draw on an enormous Google database employees call Sensorvault, turn the business of tracking cellphone users' locations into a digital dragnet for law enforcement. In an era of ubiquitous data gathering by tech companies, it is just the latest example of how personal information — where you go, who your friends are, what you read, eat and watch, and when you do it — is being used for purposes many people never expected. As privacy concerns have mounted among consumers, policymakers and regulators,

ALEX WELSH FOR THE NEW YORK TIMES

Jorge Molina in Goodyear, Ariz. Detectives arrested him last year in a murder investigation after requesting Google location data. When new information emerged, they released him and did not pursue charges.

tech companies have come under intensifying scrutiny over their data collection practices.

The Arizona case demonstrates the promise and perils of the new investigative technique, whose use has risen sharply in the past six months, according to Google employees familiar with the requests. It can help solve crimes. But it can also snare innocent people.

Technology companies have for years responded to court orders for specific users' information. The new warrants go further, suggesting possible suspects and witnesses in the absence of other clues. Often, Google employees said, the company responds to a single warrant with location information on dozens or hundreds of devices.

Law enforcement officials described the method as exciting, but cautioned that it was just one tool.

"It doesn't pop out the answer like a ticker tape, saying this guy's guilty," said Gary Ernsdorff, a senior prosecutor in Washington State who has worked on several cases involving these warrants. Potential suspects must still be fully investigated, he added. "We're not going to charge anybody just because Google said they were there."

It is unclear how often these search requests have led to arrests or convictions, because many of the investigations are still open and judges frequently seal the warrants. The practice was first used by federal agents in 2016, according to Google employees, and first publicly reported last year in North Carolina. It has since spread to local departments across the country, including in California, Florida, Minnesota and Washington. This year, one Google employee said, the company received as many as 180 requests in one week. Google declined to confirm precise numbers.

The technique illustrates a phenomenon privacy advocates have long referred to as the "if you build it, they will come" principle — anytime a technology company creates a system that could be used in surveillance, law enforcement inevitably comes knocking. Sensorvault, according to Google employees, includes detailed location records involving at least hundreds of millions of devices worldwide and dating back nearly a decade.

The new orders, sometimes called "geofence" warrants, specify an area and a time period, and Google gathers information from Sensorvault about the devices that were there. It labels them with anonymous ID numbers, and detectives look at locations and movement patterns to see if any appear relevant to the crime. Once they narrow the field to a few devices they think belong to suspects or witnesses, Google reveals the users' names and other information.

"There are privacy concerns that we all have with our phones being tracked — and when those kinds of issues are relevant in a criminal case, that should give everybody serious pause," said Catherine Turner, a Minnesota defense lawyer who is handling a case involving the technique.

Investigators who spoke with The New York Times said they had not sent geofence warrants to companies other than Google, and Apple said it did not have the ability to perform those searches. Google would not provide details on Sensorvault, but Aaron Edens, an intelligence analyst with the sheriff's office in San Mateo County, Calif., who has examined data from hundreds of phones, said most Android devices and some iPhones he had seen had this data available from Google.

In a statement, Richard Salgado, Google's director of law enforcement and information security, said that the company tried to "vigorously protect the privacy of our users while supporting the important work of law enforcement." He added that it handed over identifying information only "where legally required."

Mr. Molina, 24, said he was shocked when the police told him they suspected him of murder, and he was surprised at their ability to arrest him based largely on data.

"I just kept thinking, You're innocent, so you're going to get out," he said, but he added that he worried that it could take months or years to be exonerated. "I was scared," he said.

A NOVEL APPROACH

Detectives have used the warrants for help with robberies, sexual assaults, arsons and murders. Last year, federal agents requested the data to investigate a string of bombings around Austin, Tex.

The unknown suspect had left package bombs at three homes, killing two people, when investigators obtained a warrant.

They were looking for phones Google had recorded around the bombing locations.

The specific data resulting from the warrants in the Austin case remains sealed.

After receiving a warrant, Google gathers location information from its database, Sensorvault, and sends it to investigators, with each device identified by an anonymous ID code.

Investigators review the data and look for patterns in the locations of devices that could suggest possible suspects. They also look for devices that appear in multiple areas targeted by the warrant.

They can then get further location data on devices that appear relevant, allowing them to see device movement beyond the original area defined in the warrant.

After detectives narrow the field to a few devices they think may belong to suspects or witnesses, Google reveals the name, email address and other data associated with the device.

Austin investigators obtained another warrant after a fourth bomb exploded. But the suspect killed himself three days after that bomb, as they were closing in. Officials at the time said surveillance video and receipts for suspicious purchases helped identify him.

An F.B.I. spokeswoman declined to comment on whether the response from Google was helpful or timely, saying that any question about the technique "touches on areas we don't discuss."

Officers who have used the warrants said they showed promise in finding suspects as well as witnesses who may have been near the crime without realizing it. The searches may also be valuable in cold cases. A warrant last year in Florida, for example, sought information on a murder from 2016. A Florida Department of Law Enforcement spokeswoman declined to comment on whether the data was helpful.

The approach has yielded useful information even if it wasn't what broke the case open, investigators said. In a home invasion in Minnesota, for example, Google data showed a phone taking the path of the likely intruder, according to a news report and police documents. But detectives also cited other leads, including a confidential informant, in developing suspects. Four people were charged in federal court.

According to several current and former Google employees, the Sensorvault database was not designed for the needs of law enforcement, raising questions about its accuracy in some situations.

Though Google's data cache is enormous, it doesn't sweep up every phone, said Mr. Edens, the California intelligence analyst. And even if a location is recorded every few minutes, that may not coincide with a shooting or an assault.

Google often doesn't provide information right away, investigators said. The Google unit handling the requests has struggled to keep up, so it can take weeks or months for a response. In the Arizona investigation, police received data six months after sending the warrant. In a different Minnesota case this fall, it came in four weeks.

But despite the drawbacks, detectives noted how precise the data was and how it was collected even when people weren't making calls or using apps — both improvements over tracking that relies on cell towers.

"It shows the whole pattern of life," said Mark Bruley, the deputy police chief in Brooklyn Park, Minn., where investigators have been using the technique since this fall. "That's the game changer for law enforcement."

A TROVE OF DATA

Location data is a lucrative business — and Google is by far the biggest player, propelled largely by its Android phones. It uses the data to power advertising tailored to a person's location, part of a more than $20 billion market for location-based ads last year.

In 2009, the company introduced Location History, a feature for users who wanted to see where they had been. Sensorvault stores information on anyone who has opted in, allowing regular collection of data from GPS signals, cellphone towers, nearby Wi-Fi devices and Bluetooth beacons.

People who turn on the feature can see a timeline of their activity and get recommendations based on it. Google apps prompt users to enable Location History for things like traffic alerts. Information in the database is held indefinitely, unless the user deletes it.

"We citizens are giving this stuff away," said Mr. Ernsdorff, the Washington State prosecutor, adding that if companies were collecting data, law enforcement should be able to obtain a court order to use it.

Current and former Google employees said they were surprised by the warrants. Brian McClendon, who led the development of Google

Maps and related products until 2015, said he and other engineers had assumed the police would seek data only on specific people. The new technique, he said, "seems like a fishing expedition."

UNCHARTED LEGAL TERRITORY

The practice raises novel legal issues, according to Orin Kerr, a law professor at the University of Southern California and an expert on criminal law in the digital age.

One concern: the privacy of innocent people scooped up in these searches. Several law enforcement officials said the information remained sealed in their jurisdictions but not in every state.

In Minnesota, for example, the name of an innocent man was released to a local journalist after it became part of the police record. Investigators had his information because he was within 170 feet of a burglary. Reached by a reporter, the man said he was surprised about the release of his data and thought he might have appeared because he was a cabdriver. "I drive everywhere," he said.

These searches also raise constitutional questions. The Fourth Amendment says a warrant must request a limited search and establish probable cause that evidence related to a crime will be found.

Warrants reviewed by The Times frequently established probable cause by explaining that most Americans owned cellphones and that Google held location data on many of these phones. The areas they targeted ranged from single buildings to multiple blocks, and most sought data over a few hours. In the Austin case, warrants covered several dozen houses around each bombing location, for times ranging from 12 hours to a week. It wasn't clear whether Google responded to all the requests, and multiple officials said they had seen the company push back on broad searches.

Last year, the Supreme Court ruled that a warrant was required for historical data about a person's cellphone location over weeks, but the court has not ruled on anything like geofence searches, including a technique that pulls information on all phones registered to a cell tower.

Google's legal staff decided even before the 2018 ruling that the company would require warrants for location inquiries, and it crafted the procedure that first reveals only anonymous data.

"Normally we think of the judiciary as being the overseer, but as the technology has gotten more complex, courts have had a harder and harder time playing that role," said Jennifer Granick, surveillance and cybersecurity counsel at the American Civil Liberties Union. "We're depending on companies to be the intermediary between people and the government."

In several cases reviewed by The Times, a judge approved the entire procedure in a single warrant, relying on investigators' assurances that they would seek data for only the most relevant devices. Google responds to those orders, but Mr. Kerr said it was unclear whether multistep warrants should pass legal muster.

Some jurisdictions require investigators to return to a judge and obtain a second warrant before getting identifying information. With another warrant, investigators can obtain more extensive data, including months of location patterns and even emails.

MIXED RESULTS

Investigators in Arizona have never publicly disclosed a likely motive in the killing of Joseph Knight, the crime for which Mr. Molina was arrested. In a court document, they described Mr. Knight, a 29-year-old aircraft repair company employee, as having no known history of drug use or gang activity.

Detectives sent the geofence warrant to Google soon after the murder and received data from four devices months later. One device, a phone Google said was linked to Mr. Molina's account, appeared to follow the path of the gunman's car as seen on video. His carrier also said the phone was associated with a tower in roughly the same area, and his Google history showed a search about local shootings the day after the attack.

After his arrest, Mr. Molina told officers that Marcos Gaeta, his mother's ex-boyfriend, had sometimes taken his car. The Times found a traffic ticket showing that Mr. Gaeta, 38, had driven that car without a license. Mr. Gaeta also had a lengthy criminal record.

While Mr. Molina was in jail, a friend told his public defender, Jack Litwak, that she was with him at his home about the time of the shooting, and she and others provided texts and Uber receipts to bolster his case. His home, where he lives with his mother and three siblings, is about two miles from the murder scene.

Mr. Litwak said his investigation found that Mr. Molina had sometimes signed in to other people's phones to check his Google account. That could lead someone to appear in two places at once, though it was not clear whether that happened in this case.

Mr. Gaeta was arrested in California on an Arizona warrant. He was then charged in a separate California homicide from 2016. Officials said that case would probably delay his extradition to Arizona.

A police spokesman said "new information came to light" after Mr. Molina's arrest, but the department would not comment further.

Months after his release, Mr. Molina was having trouble getting back on his feet. After being arrested at work, a Macy's warehouse, he lost his job. His car was impounded for investigation and then repossessed.

The investigators "had good intentions" in using the technique, Mr. Litwak said. But, he added, "they're hyping it up to be this new DNA type of forensic evidence, and it's just not."

MICHAEL LAFORGIA contributed reporting. **KITTY BENNETT** contributed research.

Police Data and the Citizen App: Partners in Crime Coverage

FEATURING ALI WATKINS
PUBLISHED OCT. 2, 2019 | UPDATED OCT. 3, 2019

On her New York City law enforcement beat, Ali Watkins mines CompStat for trends and crowdsourcing for breaking news. You can, too.

HOW DO NEW YORK TIMES *journalists use technology in their jobs and in their personal lives? Ali Watkins, who covers crime and law enforcement in New York, discussed the tech she's using.*

What are your go-to tech tools for work?

I'll be the first to admit: I'm a curmudgeon when it comes to tech. I like printing out and reading documents (and recycling them!) and mapping out stories on paper. But some organizational tech tools have become critical for me to keep track of stories.

I was a begrudging, late adopter of Slack, but it's been a godsend in the midst of breaking news. We can immediately create channels and pull in coverage lines for fast-moving stories like Jeffrey Epstein's death.

My reporting gets organized in the Google suite: Docs, Sheets and Drive. I'm probably too millennial with voice recording — I record interviews on my iPhone, email the voice memos directly to myself and use iTunes to review them. I carry a recorder with me in case of an emergency, but rarely use it.

As far as reporting on the police and the city, there is a whole library of tech and data tools that I use. One of the most valuable is CompStat, which is the Police Department's crime data hub. I've never seen such a user-friendly police data tool at any other department. Anyone has access to the CompStat website, which is produced by the department (and therefore needs to be taken with appropriate skepticism) but, on its face, is a wealth of data and story ideas.

If you want to compare shooting rates in a specific precinct in the Bronx over a decade, CompStat gets you those numbers in seconds. It saves us so much time on research, and has provided us with story leads and ideas. For example, if you start to see clusters of a certain crime in a precinct or neighborhood, that could be an interesting story.

I also use the Citizen app, which is essentially a crowdsourcing tool for crime and emergency incidents. We don't rely on Citizen to report facts, but it becomes important for us during breaking news, when initial wire reports are often wrong or confusing. Citizen allows anyone with a user profile to post what he or she is seeing, and even live-stream from a crime scene.

Say a report comes across the wire that a shooting happened in Brooklyn. Details are sparse: multiple shots fired, one victim in unknown condition. Someone could be dead — or someone's arm might have just been grazed. I'll check Citizen and see if anyone is streaming from the scene to decide if I should flag for the desk and head to the scene, or just monitor the situation remotely.

I do keep an old-school police scanner at home (passed down from my editor, Jim McKinley). Sometimes I'll turn it on and listen to traffic, usually for nearby precincts. But it's pretty clunky and not very efficient.

How does New York City's criminal justice system use technology? And how is it changing?

The city's embrace of tech is manic. There are elements of New York's criminal justice system that are up to date and streamlined, like electronic court records and crime data. CompStat, for example, was a watershed development in data policing.

But police use of technology is fraught. We're not talking about a private entity embracing a new interoffice communication system. We're talking about a very powerful institution — the New York City

Police Department — using extremely powerful technology in ways that affect people's lives (and have a disproportionate impact on brown and black lives).

In some of the cases we know about, like the N.Y.P.D.'s use of facial recognition software, the technology is too new to inspire full confidence, and it is so new that the tech industry isn't even sure what a coherent law enforcement policy should look like. It's fertile reporting ground, but it should give pause to both departments and the people who are covering them.

You've written about the mafia, high-profile criminal suspects, celebrities gone awry. Is tech increasingly figuring in the cases that you cover?

The importance of tech is magnified in these kinds of incidents, but it's probably an extension of how tech is increasingly having a role in every story.

As soon as I get a name associated with a crime, I scrub social media. If a victim, did he or she post anything before the crime that would give us a lead? Did friends post any cryptic Instagram story, or tweet something strange? What about perpetrators?

Sometimes it's still surprising to me how much of a narrative we can piece together just by going through people's social media accounts. In many cases, we're looking at the same open-source material the police are looking at.

What are some of your tech best practices for protecting the confidentiality of sources?

Burner phones are the only way I ever feel remotely confident, and even those aren't fail-safe. You could do everything right with a burner — buy it in cash, register it under a different name, keep any identifying information off it — and the second it plugs into the Wi-Fi in the office, it's toast.

My best advice is to go as old school as you can. Meet sensitive sources in person. Before you go, look at everything you're carrying, everything you're wearing, and don't take anything that has electronic components. (Smart watch? Take it off.) Don't Uber. If you have to drive, take a cab and pay in cash. (License plate readers? E-ZPass? Don't chance it.) Never pay with a credit card.

Reverse engineer every sensitive meeting: If I were an institution and wanted to find out about this, what electronic trail would I be able to follow? Nothing is too paranoid.

Outside of work, what tech do you love, and why?

My list is pretty short (give me a Bluetooth speaker and a record player and I'll be happy), but I just recently downloaded the language app Babbel to learn French. I'm late to the language app world, but what a game changer. I know it's not perfect, but the Babbel lessons are approachable and simple. I love that I can knock out a lesson on my morning commute.

How do you unplug from tech?

I love unplugging. Everyone should do it, as often and responsibly as possible. I make semiregular efforts to go places where there is zero cell service, just so I'm not tempted to check Twitter.

I'll use GPS to get wherever I'm going, and I use an offline GPS tracker when I'm out somewhere remote alone (a request from my mother), but that's it. I've actually found that unplugging helps clarify my reporting instincts. It's such a critical reminder that as journalists, so much of our worldview is shaped by the weird media bubble the algorithms create for us. Getting outside of that can be productive.

ALI WATKINS is a reporter on the Metro desk, covering crime and law enforcement in New York City. Previously, she covered national security in Washington for The Times, BuzzFeed and McClatchy Newspapers.

How the Police Use Facial Recognition, and Where It Falls Short

BY JENNIFER VALENTINO-DEVRIES | JAN. 12, 2020

Records from Florida, where law enforcement has long used the controversial technology, offer an inside look at its risks and rewards.

AFTER A HIGH-SPEED CHASE north of Orlando, Fla., sheriff's deputies punctured the tires of a stolen Dodge Magnum and brought it to a stop. They arrested the driver, but couldn't determine who he was. The man had no identification card. He passed out after stuffing something into his mouth. And his fingerprints, the deputies reported, appeared to have been chewed off.

So investigators turned to one of the oldest and largest facial recognition systems in the country: a statewide program based in Pinellas County, Fla., that began almost 20 years ago, when law enforcement agencies were just starting to use the technology. Officers ran a photo of the man through a huge database, found a likely match and marked the 2017 case as one of the system's more than 400 successful "outcomes" since 2014.

A review of these Florida records — the most comprehensive analysis of a local law enforcement facial recognition system to date — offers a rare look at the technology's potential and its limitations.

Officials in Florida say that they query the system 4,600 times a month. But the technology is no magic bullet: Only a small percentage of the queries break open investigations of unknown suspects, the documents indicate. The tool has been effective with clear images — identifying recalcitrant detainees, people using fake IDs and photos from anonymous social media accounts — but when investigators have tried to put a name to a suspect glimpsed in grainy surveillance footage, it has produced significantly fewer results.

The Florida program also underscores concerns about new technologies' potential to violate due process. The system operates with little oversight, and its role in legal cases is not always disclosed to defendants, records show. Although officials said investigators could not rely on facial recognition results to make an arrest, documents suggested that on occasion officers gathered no other evidence.

"It's really being sold as this tool accurate enough to do all sorts of crazy stuff," said Clare Garvie, a senior associate at the Center on Privacy and Technology at Georgetown Law. "It's not there yet."

Facial recognition has set off controversy in recent years, even as it has become an everyday tool for unlocking cellphones and tagging photos on social media. The industry has drawn in new players like Amazon, which has courted police departments, and the technology is used by law enforcement in New York, Los Angeles, Chicago and elsewhere, as well as by the F.B.I. and other federal agencies. Data on such systems is scarce, but a 2016 study found that half of American adults were in a law enforcement facial recognition database.

Police officials have argued that facial recognition makes the public safer. But a few cities, including San Francisco, have barred law enforcement from using the tool, amid concerns about privacy and false matches. Civil liberties advocates warn of the pernicious uses of the technology, pointing to China, where the government has deployed it as a tool for authoritarian control.

In Florida, facial recognition has long been part of daily policing. The sheriff's office in Pinellas County, on the west side of Tampa Bay, wrangled federal money two decades ago to try the technology and now serves as the de facto facial recognition service for the state. It enables access to more than 30 million images, including driver's licenses, mug shots and juvenile booking photos.

"People think this is something new," the county sheriff, Bob Gualtieri, said of facial recognition. "But what everybody is getting into now, we did it a long time ago."

YOSHI SODEOKA

A QUESTION OF DUE PROCESS

Only one American court is known to have ruled on the use of facial recognition by law enforcement, and it gave credence to the idea that a defendant's right to the information was limited.

Willie Allen Lynch was accused in 2015 of selling $50 worth of crack cocaine, after the Pinellas facial recognition system suggested him as a likely match. Mr. Lynch, who claimed he had been misidentified, sought the images of the other possible matches; a Florida appeals court ruled against it. He is serving an eight-year prison sentence.

Any technological findings presented as evidence are subject to analysis through special hearings, but facial recognition results have never been deemed reliable enough to stand up to such questioning. The results still can play a significant role in investigations, though, without the judicial scrutiny applied to more proven forensic technologies.

Laws and courts differ by state on what investigative materials must be shared with the defense. This has led some law enforcement officials to argue that they aren't required to disclose the use of facial recognition.

In some of the Florida cases The Times reviewed, the technology was not mentioned in initial warrants or affidavits. Instead, detectives noted "investigative means" or an "attempt to identify" in court documents, while logging the matters as facial recognition wins in the Pinellas County records. Defense lawyers said in interviews that the use of facial recognition was sometimes mentioned later in the discovery process, but not always.

Aimee Wyant, a senior assistant public defender in the judicial circuit that includes Pinellas County, said defense lawyers should be provided with all the information turned up in an investigation.

"Once the cops find a suspect, they're like a dog with a bone: That's their suspect," she said. "So we've got to figure out where they got that name to start."

Law enforcement officials in Florida and elsewhere emphasized that facial recognition should not be relied on to put anyone in jail. "No one can be arrested on the basis of the computer match alone," the New York police commissioner, James O'Neill, wrote in a June op-ed.

In most of the Florida cases The Times reviewed, investigators followed similar guidelines. But in a few instances, court records suggest, facial recognition was the primary basis for an arrest.

Last April, for example, a Tallahassee police officer investigating the theft of an $80 cellphone obtained a store surveillance image and received a likely match from the facial recognition system, according to the Pinellas list. The investigator then "reviewed the surveillance video and positively identified" the suspect, she wrote in a court document.

A police department spokeswoman suggested that this step provided a check on the facial recognition system. "What we can't do is just say, 'Oh, it's this guy,' and not even look at it," she said, adding that in this instance "it was a very clear photo." The case is proceeding.

NO MORE 'NAME GAME'

Pinellas County's Face Analysis Comparison & Examination System, or FACES, was started with a $3.5 million federal grant arranged in 2000 by Representative Bill Young, a Florida Republican who led the House Appropriations Committee.

Earlier tests with law enforcement agencies elsewhere had produced meager results, including systems in California that had led to one arrest in four years. Still, the potential was tantalizing. Pinellas's first planned use for facial recognition was in the local jail's mug shot system. After Sept. 11, the program was expanded to include the airport. Eventually, sheriff's deputies were able to upload photos taken with digital cameras while on patrol.

The program received more than $15 million in federal grants until 2014, when the county took over the annual maintenance costs, now about $100,000 a year, the sheriff's office said.

The first arrest attributed to the Florida program came in 2004, after a woman who was wanted on a probation violation gave deputies a false name, local news outlets reported.

The number of arrests ticked up as the system spread across the state and the pool of images grew to include the driver's license system. By 2009, the sheriff's office had credited it with nearly 500 arrests. By 2013, the number was approaching 1,000. Details on only a small number of cases were disclosed publicly.

The latest list, of more than 400 successes since 2014, which The Times obtained after a records request, is flawed: Not all successful identifications are logged, and questionable or negative results are not recorded. Still, together with related court documents — records were readily available for about half the cases — the list offers insights into which crimes facial recognition is best suited to help solve: shoplifting, check forgery, ID fraud.

In case after case on the list, officers were seeking ID checks. "We call it the name game," Sheriff Gualtieri said. "We stop somebody on the street, and they say, 'My name is John Doe and I don't have any identification.' "

In about three dozen court cases, facial recognition was crucial despite being used with poorer-quality images. Nearly 20 of these involved minor theft; others were more significant.

After a 2017 armed robbery at an A.T.M. in nearby Hillsborough County, the Pinellas records show, investigators used facial recognition to identify a suspect. They showed the A.T.M. surveillance video to his girlfriend, who confirmed it was him, according to an affidavit. He pleaded guilty.

Instances of violent crime in which the system was helpful — such as the F.B.I.'s tracking a fugitive accused of child rape — typically involved not surveillance images but people with fake IDs or aliases.

In nearly 20 of the instances on the Pinellas list, investigators were trying to identify people who could not identify themselves, including Alzheimer's patients and murder victims. The sheriff's office said the technology was also sometimes used to help identify witnesses.

The most cutting-edge applications of facial recognition in the area — at the airport, for instance — never showed significant results and were scrapped.

"For me it was a bridge too far and too Big Brother-ish," Sheriff Gualtieri said.

GARBAGE IN, GARBAGE OUT

"It comes down to image quality," said Jake Ruberto, a technical support specialist in the Pinellas County Sheriff's Office who helps run the facial recognition program. "If you put garbage into the system, you're going to get garbage back."

The software for FACES is developed by Idemia, a France-based company whose prototype algorithms did well in several recent tests by the National Institute of Standards and Technology.

But the systems used by law enforcement agencies don't always have the latest algorithms; Pinellas's, for example, was last overhauled in 2014, although the county has been evaluating other, more recent, products. Idemia declined to comment on it.

The gains in quality of the best facial recognition technology in recent years have been astounding. In government tests, facial recognition algorithms compared photos with a database of 1.6 million mug shots. In 2010, the error rate was just under 8 percent in ideal conditions — good lighting and high-resolution, front-facing photos. In 2018, it was 0.3 percent. But in surveillance situations, law enforcement hasn't been able to count on that level of reliability.

Perhaps the biggest controversy in facial recognition has been its uneven performance with people of different races. The findings of government tests released in December show that the type of facial recognition used in police investigations tends to produce more false positive results when evaluating images of black women. Law enforcement officials in Florida said the technology's performance was not a sign that it somehow harbored racial prejudice.

Officials in Pinellas and elsewhere also stressed the role of human review. But tests using passport images have shown that human reviewers also have trouble identifying the correct person on a list of similar-looking facial recognition results. In those experiments, passport-system employees chose wrong about half the time.

Poorer-quality images are known to contribute to mismatches, and dim lighting, faces turned at an angle, or minimal disguises such as baseball caps or sunglasses can hamper accuracy.

In China, law enforcement tries to get around this problem by installing intrusive high-definition cameras with bright lights at face level, and by tying facial recognition systems to other technology that scans cellphones in an area. If a face and a phone are detected in the same place, the system becomes more confident in a match, a Times investigation found.

In countries with stronger civil liberties laws, the shortcomings of facial recognition have proved problematic, particularly for systems intended to spot criminals in a crowd. A study of one such program in London, which has an extensive network of CCTV cameras, found that of the 42 matches the tool suggested during tests, only eight were verifiably correct.

Current and former Pinellas County officials said they weren't surprised. "If you're going to get into bank robberies and convenience store robberies, no — no, it doesn't work that well," said Jim Main, who handled technical aspects of the facial recognition program for the sheriff's office until he retired in 2014. "You can't ask, like: 'Please stop for a second. Let me get your photo.'"

KITTY BENNETT contributed research.

JENNIFER VALENTINO-DEVRIES is a reporter on the investigative team, specializing in technology coverage. Before joining The Times, she worked at The Wall Street Journal and helped to launch the Knight First Amendment Institute at Columbia University.

New Jersey Bars Police From Using Clearview Facial Recognition App

BY KASHMIR HILL | JAN. 24, 2020

Reporting about the powerful tool with a database of three billion photos "troubled" the state's attorney general, who asked for an inquiry into its use.

NEW JERSEY POLICE OFFICERS are now barred from using a facial recognition app made by a start-up that has licensed its groundbreaking technology to hundreds of law enforcement agencies around the country.

Gurbir S. Grewal, New Jersey's attorney general, told state prosecutors in all 21 counties on Friday that police officers should stop using the Clearview AI app.

The New York Times reported last week that Clearview had amassed a database of more than three billion photos across the web — including sites like Facebook, YouTube, Twitter and Venmo. The vast database powers an app that can match people to their online photos and link back to the sites the images came from.

"Until this week, I had not heard of Clearview AI," Mr. Grewal said in an interview. "I was troubled. The reporting raised questions about data privacy, about cybersecurity, about law enforcement security, about the integrity of our investigations."

His order to prosecutors was reported earlier by NJ.com.

In a promotional video posted to its website this week, Clearview included images of Mr. Grewal because the company said its app had played a role last year in Operation Open Door, a New Jersey police sting that led to the arrest of 19 people accused of being child predators.

"I was surprised they used my image and the office to promote the product online," said Mr. Grewal, who confirmed that Clearview's app had been used to identify one of the people in the sting. "I was troubled they were sharing information about ongoing criminal prosecutions."

Mr. Grewal's office sent Clearview a cease-and-desist letter that asked the company to stop using the office and its investigations to promote its products.

"We've received the attorney general's letter and are complying," said Tor Ekeland, Clearview's lawyer. "The video has been removed."

The video also included a claim that the New York Police Department had used Clearview's app to identify a man who was accused of planting rice cookers made to resemble bombs around the city. As reported by BuzzFeed, the Police Department said the app had played no role in the case.

"There is no institutional relationship between the N.Y.P.D. and Clearview," said Devora Kaye, a spokeswoman for the department. "The N.Y.P.D. did not rely on Clearview technology to identify the suspect in the Aug. 16 rice cooker incident. The N.Y.P.D. identified the suspect using the department's facial recognition practice, where a still image from a surveillance video was compared to a pool of lawfully possessed arrest photos."

Some officers in the Police Department are said to be using the Clearview app without official authorization, The New York Post reported on Thursday.

In addition to placing a moratorium on the Clearview app, the New Jersey attorney general's office has asked the state's Division of Criminal Justice to look into how state law enforcement agencies have used the app. Mr. Grewal wants to know which ones are using "this product or products like it," and what information those companies are tracking about police investigations and searches.

An earlier episode in which police officers received calls from the company after uploading a photo of a Times reporter to the app indicated that Clearview has the ability to monitor whom law enforcement is searching for.

Mr. Grewal said that his office would not have to preapprove use of a tool like Clearview AI by the police, but that maybe it should. His office reviews, for example, new forms of less-than-lethal ammunition to make sure that it's a "safe tool to have out there."

"I'm not categorically opposed to using any of these types of tools or technologies that make it easier for us to solve crimes, and to catch child predators or other dangerous criminals," Mr. Grewal said. "But we need to have a full understanding of what is happening here and ensure there are appropriate safeguards."

This week, Clearview also received questions from United States senators, as well as a letter from Twitter demanding that the start-up stop scraping photos from its site.

KASHMIR HILL is a tech reporter based in New York. She writes about the unexpected and sometimes ominous ways technology is changing our lives, particularly when it comes to our privacy.

Have a Search Warrant for Data? Google Wants You to Pay

BY GABRIEL J.X. DANCE AND JENNIFER VALENTINO-DEVRIES | JAN. 24, 2020

The tech giant has begun charging U.S. law enforcement for responses to search warrants and subpoenas.

FACING AN INCREASING NUMBER of requests for its users' information, Google began charging law enforcement and other government agencies this month for legal demands seeking data such as emails, location tracking information and search queries.

Google's fees range from $45 for a subpoena and $60 for a wiretap to $245 for a search warrant, according to a notice sent to law enforcement officials and reviewed by The New York Times. The notice also included fees for other legal requests.

A spokesman for Google said the fees were intended in part to help offset the costs of complying with warrants and subpoenas.

Federal law allows companies to charge the government reimbursement fees of this type, but Google's decision is a major change in how it deals with legal requests.

Some Silicon Valley companies have for years forgone such charges, which can be difficult to enforce at a large scale and could give the impression that a company aims to profit from legal searches. But privacy experts support such fees as a deterrent to overbroad surveillance.

Google has tremendous amounts of information on billions of users, and law enforcement agencies in the United States and around the world routinely submit legal requests seeking that data. In the first half of 2019, the company received more than 75,000 requests for data on nearly 165,000 accounts worldwide; one in three of those requests came from the United States.

Google has previously charged for legal requests. A record from 2008 showed that the company sought reimbursement for a legal

JOHN TAGGART FOR THE NEW YORK TIMES

The headquarters of Google in Manhattan.

request for user data. But a spokesman said that for many years now, the tech firm had not systematically charged for standard legal processes.

The money brought in from the new fees would be inconsequential for Google. Just last week, the valuation of its parent company, Alphabet, topped $1 trillion for the first time. Alphabet is scheduled to report its latest financial results on Feb. 3.

The new fees could help recover some of the costs required to fill such a large volume of legal requests, said Al Gidari, a lawyer who for years represented Google and other technology and telecommunications companies. The requests have also grown more complicated as tech companies have acquired more data and law enforcement has become more technologically sophisticated.

"None of the services were designed with exfiltrating data for law enforcement in mind," said Mr. Gidari, who is now the consulting privacy director at Stanford's Center for Internet and Society.

Mr. Gidari also said it was good that the fees might result in fewer legal requests to the company. "The actual costs of doing wiretaps and responding to search warrants is high, and when you pass those costs on to the government, it deters from excessive surveillance," he said.

In April, The Times reported that Google had been inundated with a new type of search warrant request, known as geofence searches. Drawing on an enormous Google database called Sensorvault, they provide law enforcement with the opportunity to find suspects and witnesses using location data gleaned from user devices. Those warrants often result in information on dozens or hundreds of devices, and require more extensive legal review than other requests.

A Google spokesman said that there was no specific reason the fees were announced this month and that they had been under consideration for some time. Reports put out by the company show a rise of just over 50 percent in the number of search warrants received in the first half of 2019 compared with a year earlier. The volume of subpoenas increased about 15 percent. From last January through June, the company received nearly 13,000 subpoenas and over 10,000 search warrants from American law enforcement.

Google will not ask for reimbursement in some cases, including child safety investigations and life-threatening emergencies, the spokesman said.

Law enforcement officials said it was too early to know the impact of the fees, which Google's notice said would go into effect in mid-January.

Gary Ernsdorff, a senior prosecutor in Washington State, said he was concerned that the charges for search warrants would set a precedent that led more companies to charge for similar requests. That could hamper smaller law enforcement agencies, he said.

"Officers would have to make decisions when to issue warrants based on their budgets," he said.

Mr. Ernsdorff said there was a potential silver lining, noting that the time it takes for Google to respond to warrants has significantly increased in the past year. Other law enforcement officers also said the time they had to wait for Google to fulfill legal requests had grown.

"If they are getting revenue from it, maybe this will improve their performance," Mr. Ernsdorff said.

Other law enforcement officials said the effects of the reimbursement fees would be minimal.

"I don't see it impacting us too much," said Mark Bruley, a deputy police chief in Minnesota. "We are only using these warrants on major crimes, and their fees seem reasonable."

Telecommunication companies such as Cox and Verizon have charged fees for similar services for years. At least one of Google's biggest peers, Facebook, does not charge for such requests. Microsoft and Twitter said they were legally allowed to request reimbursement for costs but declined to explicitly address whether they charged law enforcement for such requests.

MICHAEL H. KELLER contributed reporting.

GABRIEL DANCE is the deputy investigations editor. He was previously interactive editor for The Guardian and was part of the team awarded the 2014 Pulitzer Prize for Public Service for coverage of widespread secret surveillance by the N.S.A.

JENNIFER VALENTINO-DEVRIES is a reporter on the investigative team, specializing in technology coverage. Before joining The Times, she worked at The Wall Street Journal and helped to launch the Knight First Amendment Institute at Columbia University.

CHAPTER 5

Abuse, Deadly Force and Accountability

What is the appropriate response to cases of police abuse? Efforts to reform practices tackle the bigger issue of systemic prejudice in police culture, but cases of abuse and deadly force toward members of vulnerable communities, such as black people and transgender people, continue to happen as these efforts are being made. Failure to investigate complaints of police misconduct or to comply with court orders are obstacles to resolution for police forces and affected civilians alike. The final story of this chapter details the long fight for reform on quotas in the N.Y.P.D. spearheaded by Lt. Edwin Raymond.

Activists Wield Search Data to Challenge and Change Police Policy

BY RICHARD A. OPPEL JR. | NOV. 20, 2014

DURHAM, N.C. — One month after a Latino youth died from a gunshot as he sat handcuffed in the back of a police cruiser here last year, 150 demonstrators converged on Police Headquarters, some shouting "murderers" as baton-wielding officers in riot gear fired tear gas.

The police say the youth shot himself with a hidden gun. But to many residents of this city, which is 40 percent black, the incident fit a pattern of abuse and bias against minorities that includes frequent searches of cars and use of excessive force. In one case, a black female Navy veteran said she was beaten by an officer after telling a friend she was visiting that the friend did not have to let the police search her home.

Yet if it sounds as if Durham might have become a harbinger of Ferguson, Mo. — where the fatal shooting of an unarmed black teenager by a white police officer led to weeks of protests this summer — things took a very different turn. Rather than relying on demonstrations to force change, a coalition of ministers, lawyers and community and political activists turned instead to numbers. They used an analysis of state data from 2002 to 2013 that showed that the Durham police searched black male motorists at more than twice the rate of white males during stops. Drugs and other illicit materials were found no more often on blacks.

After having initially rejected protesters' demands, the city abruptly changed course and agreed to require the police, beginning last month, to obtain written consent to search vehicles in cases where they do not have probable cause. The consent forms, in English and Spanish, tell drivers they do not have to allow the searches.

"Without the data, nothing would have happened," said Steve Schewel, a Durham City Council member who had pushed for the change.

The protests in Ferguson — which may return in force when a grand jury decides whether to indict the police officer — may yet help rewrite the relationship between the police and communities there and in other cities. But what quietly played out in Durham may provide another model for activists: using stop and search data collected by an increasing number of cities and states to galvanize supporters and pressure departments to change policies.

The use of statistics is gaining traction not only in North Carolina, where data on police stops is collected under a 15-year-old law, but in other cities around the country.

Austin, Tex., began requiring written consent for searches without probable cause two years ago, after its independent police monitor reported that whites stopped by the police were searched one in every 28 times, while blacks were searched one in eight times.

In Kalamazoo, Mich., a city-funded study last year found that black drivers were nearly twice as likely to be stopped, and then "much more likely to be asked to exit their vehicle, to be handcuffed, searched and arrested."

As a result, Jeff Hadley, the public safety chief of Kalamazoo, imposed new rules requiring officers to explain to supervisors what "reasonable suspicion" they had each time they sought a driver's consent to a search. Traffic stops have declined 42 percent amid a drop of more than 7 percent in the crime rate, he said.

"It really stops the fishing expeditions," Chief Hadley said of the new rules. Though the findings demoralized his officers, he said, the reaction from the African-American community stunned him. "I thought they would be up in arms, but they said: 'You're not telling us anything we didn't already know. How can we help?'"

The School of Government at the University of North Carolina at Chapel Hill has a new manual for defense lawyers, prosecutors and judges, with a chapter that shows how stop and search data can be used by the defense to raise challenges in cases where race may have played a role.

In one recent case, the public defender representing a Hispanic man on cocaine trafficking charges in Orange County, N.C., got a dismissal after presenting the prosecutor with evidence that Hispanics — while only 8 percent of the local population — had received more than half of the hundreds of warnings issued by the sheriff's deputy who had made the arrest. The deputy had testified that he stopped the man's truck for a minor traffic infraction. The prosecutor said multiple factors led to the dismissal.

Defense lawyers' raising the issue "is gathering steam," said Alyson Grine, a lecturer at U.N.C. who trains defenders and is an author of the new manual. Several North Carolina police chiefs, she added, have even begun to use the data to sit down with individual officers and examine their search patterns as part of routine management.

Traffic stop data is so powerful a tool for analyzing police behavior that many police departments have begun participating in such studies. More than 50 departments have expressed a desire to take part in a database of traffic stop and search data by the Center for Policing Equity.

Phillip Atiba Goff, a professor at the University of California, Los Angeles, and visiting scholar at Harvard who is compiling the database, said he hoped that by standardizing how the data is collected, police departments that serve economically and demographically similar communities could compare their patterns of behavior to national trends.

The U.N.C. political science professor who processed and analyzed much of the data used by activists in Durham, Frank R. Baumgartner, was careful to make it clear that the figures by themselves were not proof of profiling or intent, though the disparities in searches were so large they called out for investigation. In the spring, the city's own human relations commission found "the existence of racial bias and profiling present in the Durham Police Department practices." Other national experts say traffic stop numbers alone do not account for departments that understandably spend more time in high-crime areas, or for commuter demographics significantly different from the composition of neighborhoods.

Durham, home to Duke University, has a rich history of civil rights and social movements, a legacy reflected in the well-organized coalition that pushed for changes. Activists agreed not to call for the resignations of any police or city officials, who could be replaced with more politically savvy executives who might still resist changes. They pressed instead for systemic changes no matter who was in charge. Written consent to search, they said, would reduce disparities and end coercive tactics that the police used to search even in the absence of true, willing consent.

"We were shaming them, and saying, 'We're tired of you all talking about how progressive Durham is,' " said Ian A. Mance, a lawyer for the Durham-based Southern Coalition for Social Justice, part of the broader group that pushed to reduce the imbalance in searches.

In city hearings and at news conferences, the activists paired abuse allegations with the search data.

"We started with the anecdotes, and then added the scholarship," said the Rev. Mark-Anthony Middleton, pastor of Abundant Hope Christian Church and one of the leaders of a prominent community group, the Durham Congregations, Associations & Neighborhoods. "We didn't allow the conversation to devolve into one person's job."

Pastor Middleton said community groups remained prepared to work with the chief of police, Jose L. Lopez Sr. "But he has to understand who runs the city," he added. "He sure does now."

Chief Lopez remains frustrated at the data's effects. He believes it was widely misinterpreted to demonstrate something far worse than the numbers showed. City leaders had instructed the police over the last decade to focus more attention on high-crime areas, which in many cases were predominantly black. So of course, police supporters said, blacks were subjected to stops at a higher rate.

"Think about this," Chief Lopez said. "You have a Puerto Rican police chief in the City of Durham, and you are going to accuse him of racism?"

What is clear, he says, is that departments will have to learn to crunch numbers in order to deflect charges of bias as community groups use their own data presentations to press leaders to curtail police tactics, just as in Durham.

"The pendulum has swung from 'We trust the police' to 'We don't trust what you say, and you better prove it to us,' " Chief Lopez said. "Every police department right now is either putting together data or looking for ways to enhance it, or looking for funding, in order to get on the metric bandwagon as a way of being able to explain what they do and why they do it, and also to prove they're not doing what they are accused of doing."

Activists Say Police Abuse of Transgender People Persists Despite Reforms

BY NOAH REMNICK | SEPT. 6, 2015

NEW YEAR'S REVELERS clamored outside the window of Shagasyia Diamond's apartment in the Bronx the day she was arrested.

Newly into 2014, she was in the midst of a dispute with her husband when officers showed up at her front door, placed her in handcuffs and escorted her to a nearby precinct. It was there, Ms. Diamond recalled, that the violations began.

Although the New York Police Department amended its patrol guide in 2012 to require respectful treatment of transgender people, Ms. Diamond, who is a transgender woman, said she was subjected to a strip search by a male officer. Two other officers watched from a few feet away, gawking as she spread her legs. Officers then placed Ms. Diamond in a cell for men, she said, where she cowered in the corner as other inmates heckled her and used the exposed toilet in her presence. When she expressed her discomfort to an officer, he replied, "You know you like it in there with all the men."

Officers snickered at Ms. Diamond throughout the process, she said, calling her a "he-she," "tranny" and "it."

"I felt totally voiceless," Ms. Diamond, who is 37 and now divorced, said recently through tears. "Like I wasn't even human. Like my safety didn't even matter."

When the patrol guide reforms were issued, advocates for transgender people lauded the changes as groundbreaking, if overdue. Officers now were required, among other provisions, to refer to people by their preferred names and gender pronouns, to allow people to be searched by an officer of their requested gender, and to refrain from "discourteous or disrespectful remarks" regarding sexual orientation or gender identity.

TODD HEISLER/THE NEW YORK TIMES

Shagasyia Diamond, 37, who is transgender, was arrested in 2014 during a domestic dispute in the Bronx. She said she was put in a cell with men and was subjected to slurs by police officers.

But in interviews with more than 20 transgender and gender nonconforming New Yorkers who have been arrested or had other contact with the police, as well as activists and lawyers representing them, they charge that three years since the regulations were adopted, police officers regularly flout them. Even as transgender visibility surges in the news media and in popular culture, and government agencies develop more sensitive policies, many transgender people continue to report that they are mocked in the most degrading terms by officers, searched roughly and inappropriately and placed in holding cells that do not correspond with their gender identity, all violations of the reforms enacted to address those very indignities.

"We're hearing the same sorts of things today that we heard five years ago," said Sharon Stapel, the executive director of the New York City Anti-Violence Project, an advocacy group for lesbian, gay, bisexual and transgender people. "Trans people are still targeted and harassed by the police for being trans."

Some activists and elected officials are calling on the Police Department's inspector general to audit the department's adherence to the reforms. At a meeting in late July with Commissioner William J. Bratton, members of the commissioner's L.G.B.T. Advisory Panel, made up of leaders in the lesbian, gay, bisexual and transgender community, also asked for an audit. Mr. Bratton showed reluctance, according to people present at the meeting, but eventually referred the group to the department's quality assurance division.

"It's one thing to make a reform on paper, but it takes a greater commitment of resources to make the necessary cultural changes," said Councilman Ritchie Torres, a Bronx Democrat who is formally requesting an audit.

"The N.Y.P.D. is a deeply intransigent, conservative institution," Mr. Torres added. "It's going to take extensive retraining for officers to fully live up to the spirit and letter of the 2012 changes."

Detective Tim Duffy, the department's liaison to the lesbian, gay, bisexual and transgender community, said the department had begun a variety of programs to address the concerns. Among other measures, he said, newly promoted sergeants, lieutenants and captains now undergo two hours of training meant to guard against profiling and other forms of mistreatment. The training familiarizes officers, for example, with police forms that now have space for a preferred name and preferred gender pronouns. He noted that in the past several years, two police officers and one school safety officer underwent gender transitions.

Although Detective Duffy said the department has had "no reports of any issues with officers not following the guidelines," he acknowledged some resistance. "Just like any big group, everybody may not agree with the policy," he said, "but we have to do our jobs."

The reforms followed years of complaints about police mistreatment, including one from 2010 in which a transgender woman who was arrested on suspicion of prostitution said an officer stomped on her head three times, breaking a tooth and a bone near her eye. Her skirt rode up, exposing her genitals, which she said the officer then twisted and squeezed. She filed a lawsuit against the city, which was settled for around $80,000.

But in 2013, a year after the guidelines were changed, Crystal Sheridan, a transgender woman arrested on suspicion of prostitution, was called a "whore" and a "man" by police officers, she said, as they took her to a Queens precinct, where she remained for several days.

"It was like I was being bullied for no reason," recalled Ms. Sheridan, 30, who said the charges were dropped by a judge.

Often rejected by their families and stymied in their pursuit of jobs, transgender people — particularly women who are members of racial minorities — experience high rates of poverty, homelessness and violent crime. They also sometimes resort to illegal activity as a means of survival. Ms. Diamond, who was arrested in the Bronx, spent 10 years in prison for robbing a gas station, she said, to get money for sex-reassignment surgery after her family in Flint, Mich., turned their backs on her.

Such circumstances, activists said, have contributed to a form of profiling. Just as African-Americans complain of being stopped for "driving while black," transgender people claim they are singled out by the police for "walking while trans," activists say.

At a transgender forum this July in the Bronx, the roughly 200 people in attendance were asked, Have you ever felt profiled or mocked by the police? Nearly every hand shot up. Have you ever complained? Nearly every hand came down.

Tasha Hodges, a 33-year-old transgender woman from East New York, Brooklyn, kept her grievances to herself after officers referred to her by a bevy of insulting titles, she said, after a 2013 arrest for trespassing. "I've learned to accept the disrespect," Ms. Hodges explained.

Mina Malik, the executive director of the city's Civilian Complaint Review Board, which investigates complaints against the police, said the organization had collected grievances from transgender people since the reforms were instituted, but that she could not provide any data.

"The C.C.R.B. is only as effective as its reputation in the community allows it to be," said Andrea Ritchie, a lawyer with the nonprofit group Streetwise and Safe. "People's experience with the C.C.R.B. is that they don't feel heard."

Ms. Malik said the review board has "historically not had the best reputation" among transgender people, which she said explained in part why "underreporting is a chronic problem" in that community. "We are working to improve it," Ms. Malik added.

Some transgender defendants have gotten redress by calling Ms. Ritchie. She said clients had phoned her from jail in anguish after being placed in cells for a different gender. Ms. Ritchie has then had to explain the new regulations to the officers in charge, often referring them to the exact page in their guides.

Detective Duffy said that officers faced a natural learning curve. "Just like the general public is learning about the trans community and learning about trans people by people coming out like Chaz Bono and Caitlyn Jenner, so are we," he said.

After her experience in the Bronx stationhouse, Ms. Diamond slipped into an intense depression, she said, during which she lost 60 pounds. Even though the district attorney dropped the charges against her, she said she still has not filed a complaint against the police, out of fear and doubt that she would not be taken seriously.

"People used to tell me things were different in New York," said Ms. Diamond, a singer who left home in 2009. "But I know better now."

4 Years After Eric Garner's Death, Secrecy Law on Police Discipline Remains Unchanged

BY ASHLEY SOUTHALL | JUNE 3, 2018

THE LEGAL BATTLE over a New York City police officer's disciplinary records after the chokehold death of Eric Garner in 2014 cast an obscure statute into the spotlight.

The city's explanation that it could not disclose the disciplinary history of the officer, Daniel Pantaleo, because the statute made the records confidential fed a national debate over transparency and police accountability and prompted promises from City Hall and the state Capitol to push for the law to be changed or repealed.

But nearly four years after Mr. Garner's death on July 17, 2014, on Staten Island, the statute, Section 50-a of the State Civil Rights Law, is, if anything, stronger, its interpretation expanded at the insistence of Mayor Bill de Blasio's administration, even as the mayor has vowed more transparency.

Judges and lawyers' groups have joined criminal justice activists, public defenders and newspaper editorial boards in calling for the Legislature to act. But with the legislative session ending later this month, lawmakers, for the second consecutive year, have not taken up legislation to repeal or modify the law.

"If it's led to this much confusion, it's a badly written law," said Cynthia Conti-Cook, a staff lawyer at the Legal Aid Society, a nonprofit that sought Officer Pantaleo's records from the Civilian Complaint Review Board, a police oversight agency.

The push to lift the veil on officer discipline faces powerful opposition: The city's police and corrections unions, which have deep coffers, vocal leaders and influential allies. Indeed, the unions carry considerable sway among lawmakers in Albany, to whom they have given more than $1.3 million in donations over the past decade, according to data compiled by the National Institute on Money and Politics, a campaign finance watchdog. In recent years, lawmakers have passed legislation that would have given police unions more say in officer discipline.

The Assembly Speaker, Carl E. Heastie, a Bronx Democrat, has not taken a position on the statute. The Senate majority leader, John J. Flanagan, a Long Island Republican, opposes changing it.

While the Legislature has not moved on the statute, neither Gov. Andrew M. Cuomo nor Mayor Bill de Blasio has laid out a path forward.

Mr. Cuomo, though he has criticized Mr. de Blasio's expanded interpretation of the statute, did not include changing it among the legislative priorities in his current agenda. Mr. Cuomo, a Democrat, has moved further left as he faces a primary challenge in his bid for re-election, but as governor and previously as attorney general he has accepted tens of thousands of dollars from law enforcement unions and rarely pushed back against their interests.

Mr. de Blasio, also a Democrat, has called for removing the cloak on disciplinary records that critics blame on his administration, but he has not come up with legislative language or indicated support for any proposed measures. At a police briefing last month, he said his administration was making a "big push" to get the law changed by the end of June.

"The commissioner, his predecessor and I are united in wanting change in the law that will create the transparency everyone wants and once and for all settle the question," he said.

Those who want the law changed concede it is unlikely as long as Republicans control the Senate. But they are still making the rounds in Albany, with the expectation that if they are not successful in the next few weeks, the political climate could be more favorable after November if Democrats regain control of the upper chamber.

"Unless the leadership changes, or unless the governor decides he wants to get behind the legislation, I do not see it changing," State Senator Kevin S. Parker, a Brooklyn Democrat, said. Mr. Parker is the sponsor of a bill supported by the Police Department that will allow some records to be disclosed once disciplinary proceedings have concluded, a process that can take years in high-profile cases, including fatal police encounters with unarmed civilians like Mr. Garner.

Even if Democrats win control of the Senate, changing the statute will not be easy. Many lawmakers fear the dozens of police, fire and corrections unions across the state that have millions of dollars in resources to undermine a campaign or provide a financial boost.

Ed Mullins, the president of the Sergeants Benevolent Association in New York City, said it was important to preserve the statute because releasing disciplinary records could serve to prejudice public opinion against police officers.

"We've got to find a balance where the public's interest is at the forefront, but so are the rights of the individual police officers involved because we don't get a do-over," he said.

The statute was intended to shield officers from defense lawyers looking to discredit police testimony using unverified civilian complaints. It is one of the strictest laws of its kind in the country. It shields records that states such as Washington and Alabama routinely make public. Opponents say that the secrecy the law codifies hurts police efforts to mend ties in predominantly black and Latino communities.

The New York City Bar Association endorsed repealing the statute last month in a white paper describing how the statute stymies transparency. And activists under the umbrella of Communities United for Police Reform have begun descending on Albany by the busload to lobby lawmakers on both sides of the political aisle to repeal it.

Joo-Hyun Kang, the coalition's director, said repeal had become necessary because of legal precedents that were established over the past two years affirming the de Blasio administration's interpretation of the statute's protections.

"The body of case law and their public messaging promotes the idea that pretty much anything related to an officer should be kept confidential — it's just really irresponsible," she said. "It makes a segment of the public believe that we don't have the right to know about the people patrolling our neighborhoods who can use deadly force against us, and we should have that right."

Councilman Donovan J. Richards Jr., the chairman of the City Council's Committee on Public Safety, said he thought the Police Department was worried that the public would see that "the disciplinary measures don't match up to the cases that come before them." Mr. Richards, a Queens Democrat, noted that the police often release the names and pictures of officers to praise them for good work on potentially dangerous cases, like drug and gun busts.

Lawmakers' inaction on the statute has left it to state courts to parse the law's meaning in litigation brought by transparency advocates seeking fuller disclosure and police unions looking to apply it more broadly.

Tensions over the statute escalated in 2016, when the Police Department stopped making disciplinary summaries available to the news media. In a continuing lawsuit brought by the Legal Aid Society, city lawyers have argued that removing officers' identities from the summaries is not enough to comply with the statute.

The Police Department reversed course in March, when it announced that it would provide disciplinary summaries on its website with officers' names removed. But that plan has been put off because the Patrolmen's Benevolent Association, the city's largest police union, obtained a court order temporarily halting it.

The union has also taken the city to court over the Police Department's policy of releasing edited body camera videos at Commissioner James P. O'Neill's discretion. City lawyers defend the policy with the assertion that edited videos do not fall under the statute because they are not used to evaluate officers.

Councilman Rory I. Lancman, a Queens Democrat and the chairman of the Council's Committee on the Justice System, led the push for a law passed in 2016 requiring the Police Department to provide data on officers' use of force and related disciplinary outcomes by precinct.

But last month, the department's top legal official said in a letter that the statute precluded the department from fully complying — a position that was abruptly reversed by Commissioner O'Neill, who has framed his department's use of the law as an effort to balance transparency and safety.

"There are people out here that are looking to do police officers harm, and I know you know that," he said at a Council budget hearing. "So, you know, we just don't sit over in 1 Police Plaza making these decisions without careful consideration."

Mr. Lancman said in an interview that the shifting position on whether it could comply with the disclosure law showed that the Police Department had "no coherent policy for how 50-a should be interpreted and applied."

"It really amounts to a game of three-card monte," he added.

Officer Pantaleo is not expected face disciplinary charges stemming from the Garner case until the federal inquiry is finished. Charges were recommended by the Civilian Complaint Review Board, which has said he should be fired.

Assemblyman Daniel J. O'Donnell, a Manhattan Democrat, had not heard of the statute before Mr. Garner was killed. With career prosecutors in the United States Justice Department recommending civil rights charges against Officer Pantaleo, Mr. O'Donnell said it was beyond time for the Legislature to deal with the law and has offered bills to narrow or repeal it.

"Until we legislatively fix it," he said, "it's going to be the whims of any mayor or police department to do with it what they want."

DORIS BURKE and **ALAIN DELAQUÉRIÈRE** contributed research.

The Lawyers Protecting the N.Y.P.D. Play Hardball. Judges Are Calling Them Out.

BY ALAN FEUER | SEPT. 12, 2018

IN ONE CASE, lawyers for the City of New York missed several filing deadlines and disobeyed court orders. An angry federal judge said they had "blown off" instructions, which he said was "outrageous."

In another case, lawyers from the same legal unit never fully investigated an excessive-force complaint against the police and then neglected 14 orders to produce discovery evidence. A judge called their behavior "egregious."

In a third case, the city lawyers took more than a year to give a man who had sued the police a recording of his questioning from the day of his arrest. The prolonged delay, a judge remarked, was "negligent, if not grossly negligent."

All of the lawyers worked for what is known as the Special Federal Litigation Division, an elite team in the city's Law Department that deals with some of the most important and politically sensitive cases the city has to fight: allegations of police misconduct.

Special Fed, as the team is often called, has great success in defeating suits against the police and corrections officers. But it has also been repeatedly accused by civil-rights lawyers — and at least six federal judges — of engaging in a pattern of obstructionist behavior.

City officials note that Special Fed has received judicial censure in only a fraction of the 1,400 cases the unit is currently handling. Each of those cases is complex, they say, often including dozens of requests for discovery materials that can tax the roughly 100 lawyers on the team.

"The feedback this office has received from the federal judiciary has been overwhelmingly positive," said Nicholas Paolucci, a Law Department spokesman. "While we work diligently to meet our discovery obligations, the sheer volume of cases can lead to occasional unintended delays in production. The city has no interest in prolonging litigation unnecessarily."

Patricia Miller, who has run Special Fed since 2015, said in an interview that the unit had succeeded in its central mission of defending the police by fighting lawsuits more aggressively in recent years.

"For years, there was this idea that you could hang up a shingle, file a lawsuit and get a few bucks," Ms. Miller told The Chief, a municipal union publication. "Sue the Police Department, or sue the city in general, and we'll go from there. Those days are done."

This aggressive stance has led to courtroom victories and also warded off frivolous lawsuits, Ms. Miller said. Even at a moment of cultural and media scrutiny of the police, new misconduct suits have dropped by almost half in recent years, she noted, and her team won 88 percent of the 44 cases it took to trial last year.

Still, the unit's tactics have drawn the ire of several federal judges.

Take the case of Karen Brown, who sued a group of officers three years ago after her son, Barrington Williams, died in police custody in 2013.

Mr. Williams, 25, had been selling MetroCard swipes inside the Yankee Stadium subway station. When he fled the police, an officer gave chase and tackled him to the ground.

A lifelong asthma patient, Mr. Williams suddenly stopped breathing. He was dead 10 minutes later when an ambulance arrived.

Ms. Brown claimed in her suit that the officers involved in the arrest should have saved her son with CPR and used a defibrillator to restart his heart. One was stored at a stadium police post less than a minute away.

The suit was the sort of litigation the city might have settled in the past. But today, Ms. Brown is still engaged in a protracted legal fight with Special Fed.

First, court papers say, lawyers from the unit took their time providing discovery on the basic facts of the case, and also dragged their feet in making two firefighters who treated Mr. Williams available for depositions. There were further delays producing documents about the CPR training the officers had received.

This spring, when Ms. Brown's lawyers asked Special Fed if any of the officers had violated Police Department policies by not providing medical attention, lawyers from the unit first claimed the request wasn't "relevant." Then they filed an incomplete answer to the question, asked for more time to respond and eventually missed their own extended deadline. When they finally submitted a response — the officers hadn't violated any policy or procedure — they broke court procedure. The document was never formally signed by the defendants.

Last month, losing patience, a Manhattan judge ordered the lawyers to explain the delays in a formal memorandum, adding that they needed to get it personally signed by Ms. Miller to ensure "she has approved."

"There have been fights about the most unnecessary things," Joshua Moskovitz, one of Ms. Brown's lawyers, said. "There have been fights about things they know they can't win and fights where it seems like they're just fighting. It actually feels tactical at times. It happens too often to be coincidental."

Similar problems have plagued other cases. In July, for instance, a Brooklyn magistrate judge said he was considering referring a Special Fed lawyer to the court's grievance committee for a "very troubling" violation of professional rules. The lawyer had refused to let the plaintiff's lawyer in a police-misconduct lawsuit use the Law Department's phones to call the judge to question a line of inquiry during a deposition.

Last November, another Brooklyn judge excoriated Special Fed lawyers for ignoring their ethical obligations after it emerged that they knew a plaintiff had accidentally sued the wrong detective for malicious prosecution and moved to dismiss the case — instead of promptly telling the man of his mistake.

A few months earlier, a different Brooklyn judge sanctioned the city after one of the unit's lawyers "acted improperly" at an officer's deposition, objecting nearly 600 times to questions, even though many were deemed to be "relevant to the case."

Special Fed itself was born in 1998, when federal civil-rights lawsuits against the police were rising dramatically, spurred in part by Mayor Rudolph W. Giuliani's new zero-tolerance law-enforcement strategy. The suits had been traditionally handled by the Law Department's general litigation division.

More than a decade later, with no sign of police-related lawsuits slowing down, Police Department executives complained that the city was settling too many cases and did not have their officers' backs, plaintiffs' lawyers and city officials said.

"The Police Department was angry at the time," said Richard D. Emery, a veteran civil-rights lawyer who also once ran the city's Civilian Complaint Review Board. "They didn't feel represented by their own attorneys."

And so in 2011, the Law Department, under Mayor Michael R. Bloomberg, created what it called the Trial Initiative, a program in which Special Fed took more cases to trial and assumed a more aggressive posture in settlement negotiations. Ms. Miller was promoted to lead the effort, and the number of cases the city took to trial grew from about a dozen a year to sometimes more than triple that.

Four years later, in consultation with police officials and unions, Mayor Bill de Blasio bolstered the work of Special Fed by establishing a 40-person legal team inside the Police Department to help defend against civil-rights lawsuits. The new team, Mr. de Blasio noted at the time, was "a practical response" to the "cynical reality of lawyers trying to scam the system."

Ms. Miller said the two efforts had not only protected officers against so-called nuisance lawsuits, but also made the police more accountable. "Putting cases in front of a jury is how we hear from the public — it's like a focus group," she said.

But several plaintiff's attorneys said that after the city altered its approach, Special Fed lawyers stepped up delay and obstructionist tactics to make it harder for plaintiffs to prevail.

"They will use every trick in the book to prolong a case and wear down the plaintiff and the plaintiff's lawyers, delaying discovery and basically making fights over nothing," said Joel B. Rudin, a lawyer who has fought against the unit numerous times in his career.

Mr. Rudin said the unit's hardball tactics have continued under Mayor de Blasio, even though the mayor has a record of settling high-profile suits against the police. Mr. de Blasio agreed to pay up to $75 million to end litigation over the Police Department's stop-and-frisk strategy. He also settled the case of the Central Park Five, a suit brought by men wrongfully convicted of the 1989 rape of a jogger.

Eric Phillips, a spokesman for the mayor, said that Mr. de Blasio "demands city litigators be as principled and aggressive on high-profile cases as they are in the hundreds of more mundane cases they handle every day."

On Aug. 20, Special Fed filed its memo to Chief Magistrate Judge Gabriel W. Gorenstein, explaining what went wrong in the case of Karen Brown.

The city lawyers "sincerely" apologized for what they called a "failure to comply with the applicable court orders" but said the mistakes didn't ultimately affect the case. After receiving the memo, Judge Gorenstein acknowledged that their "delay and inaction" was "indicative of negligence, not willfulness."

Either way, Ms. Brown has been waiting years for her suit to be resolved.

"There's just no words," she said. "My heart can't take any more."

Fort Worth Officer Charged With Murder for Shooting Woman in Her Home

BY MARINA TRAHAN MARTINEZ, NICHOLAS BOGEL-BURROUGHS AND SARAH MERVOSH
OCT. 14, 2019

Aaron Dean, who killed Atatiana Jefferson while she was home with her nephew, resigned hours before he was going to be fired.

FORT WORTH — A former Fort Worth police officer who fatally shot a woman while she was at home playing video games over the weekend was arrested and charged with murder on Monday, the latest development in a case that has sparked national outrage and renewed demands for police accountability.

The officer, Aaron Y. Dean, who is white, resigned earlier on Monday, hours before the police chief had planned to fire him, amid growing anger and frustration in the community that the woman, Atatiana Jefferson, had become yet another black person killed by the police, this time in the safety of her own home.

Police officers were responding to a call from a concerned neighbor when Ms. Jefferson, 28, was shot through her bedroom window.

The case resulted in a rare murder charge against a police officer only hours after the interim Fort Worth police chief, Ed Kraus, announced that the department was conducting a criminal investigation into the officer's actions and had reached out to the F.B.I. about the possibility of starting a civil rights investigation.

"I get it," Chief Kraus said of the widespread public anger that followed the release of body camera video in the case. It showed that Ms. Jefferson had been given no warning that it was a police officer who had crept into her backyard, shined a light into her bedroom window and shouted, "Put your hands up! Show me your hands!" immediately before firing a single fatal shot.

"Nobody looked at that video and said there was any doubt that this officer acted inappropriately," the chief said.

The unusual and rapid developments, which followed a similar case in nearby Dallas where a black man had been shot by an off-duty police officer in his own apartment, highlighted longstanding tensions in Fort Worth, where residents have frequently complained about abuse at the hands of the police. Since June, Fort Worth officers have shot and killed six people.

"A murder charge and an arrest is a good start — it's more than we are used to seeing," S. Lee Merritt, a civil rights lawyer who is representing Ms. Jefferson's family, said on Monday night. But like many others, he said he was waiting to see how the case was prosecuted.

"Fort Worth has a culture that has allowed this to happen," he said. "There still needs to be a reckoning."

In interviews on Monday, community members recited prior episodes with authorities from memory: In 2009, a man with a history of mental illness died after he was Tasered by the Fort Worth police, which his family had called for help. In 2016, a mother called the police to report that a neighbor had choked her young son for littering, but the mother herself ended up getting arrested. In the video-recorded encounter, the mother, Jacqueline Craig, was forced to the ground and placed in handcuffs; her teenage daughters were also detained.

Community activists also cited the seven police shootings since early summer, six of them fatal, including the killing of a man who the police thought was carrying a rifle but was actually pointing a flashlight at officers after barricading himself inside a house.

"We're beyond anger," said the Rev. Kyev Tatum, a pastor at New Mount Rose Missionary Baptist Church in Fort Worth. "It's trauma now. It's unaddressed, toxic stress."

Mr. Dean had been with the Fort Worth Police Department since April 2018, after graduating from the police academy a month earlier, according to documents provided by the Texas Commission on Law Enforcement, a state regulatory agency.

LAURA BUCKMAN FOR THE NEW YORK TIMES

A vigil on Sunday for Atatiana Jefferson, who was shot and killed by a police officer over the weekend.

On Monday night, he was released from the Tarrant County jail after posting a $200,000 bond.

Ms. Jefferson had recently moved home with her mother, who was in declining health, and was selling medical equipment while she studied to enter medical school. She had been playing video games with her 8-year-old nephew in the early hours of Saturday morning when a neighbor called a police nonemergency line at 2:23 a.m., saying he was concerned that the front and side doors of Ms. Jefferson's house had been open for several hours.

The authorities said Mr. Dean did not identify himself as a police officer before firing a fatal shot at Ms. Jefferson through the window.

Ms. Jefferson died in her bedroom after officers tried to provide medical assistance, according to the Tarrant County medical examiner's office. Her nephew was in the room when the shooting occurred, the authorities said.

Chief Kraus said he regretted that the Police Department had released photographs of a gun found on the floor below the window in Ms. Jefferson's bedroom after she was killed — though he declined to say if she was holding it, or if the officer saw it before he shot her.

She had every right to have a gun in her bedroom, the chief said. "We're homeowners in the state of Texas," he said. "I can't imagine most of us — if we thought we had somebody outside our house that shouldn't be and we had access to a firearm — that we wouldn't act very similarly to how she acted."

A small group of neighbors and activists who had remained outside Ms. Jefferson's home on Monday night cheered when they learned of Mr. Dean's arrest. Some of them gathered to pray. But others remained skeptical, citing what they saw as a historical reluctance to prosecute and fairly punish police officers.

"You know what, this is Fort Worth," said Michael Bell, the senior pastor of the Greater St. Stephen First Church in Fort Worth, who said he was among those waiting to see how the case was prosecuted. "Our community has experienced so much. I don't want to go overboard and start any kind of celebration because I don't know how it's going to turn out."

Ms. Jefferson was killed less than two weeks after the conclusion of the case in Dallas, in which Amber R. Guyger, a white former police officer, was convicted of murder. Ms. Guyger shot her unarmed black neighbor, Botham Shem Jean, in his apartment last year, claiming she thought the apartment was her own. The former officer was sentenced to 10 years in prison this month after a highly publicized trial.

That case took place in a neighboring county under a different district attorney. Still, many who had been following it could not help but draw comparisons. Though Ms. Guyger was convicted, activists have complained about what they saw as a lenient sentence.

"After watching what happened to Botham Jean and 10 years for taking his life, how excited can we be?" Dr. Bell said.

In 2017, after the controversy that followed the arrest of Ms. Craig and her daughters, the Fort Worth City Council appointed a task force to examine issues of race and culture. The task force presented a series of recommendations last year, including an avenue to involve citizens in oversight of the Police Department and recommendations to diversify the police force.

The City Council in September took action on several of the task force recommendations, including creating a police monitor position, setting up a police cadet program and beginning a diversity and inclusion program.

Over the weekend, activists who earlier this month stood outside the Dallas County courthouse to demand justice in the case against Ms. Guyger came to Fort Worth for a vigil for Ms. Jefferson.

"I saw many of the same faces," said Omar Suleiman, an imam and activist in the Dallas area.

He said the latest shooting contributed to a feeling of exhaustion in the North Texas community, which experienced trauma anew with each new shooting, each new arrest and each new trial.

"We literally have not had a chance to recover," he said. "There is just this deep anger and hurt in the streets that you can't be safe in your apartment, you can't be safe in your home, you can't be safe in your car."

MARINA TRAHAN MARTINEZ reported from Fort Worth, and **NICHOLAS BOGEL-BURROUGHS** and **SARAH MERVOSH** from New York. **DAVE MONTGOMERY** contributed reporting from Austin, Texas.

Philadelphia Police Inspector Charged in Sexual Assaults of Officers

BY AIMEE ORTIZ | OCT. 27, 2019

At least three women filed complaints against Chief Inspector Carl Holmes, who has been suspended.

A SENIOR PHILADELPHIA police official has been charged with assault and suspended after three female officers accused him of forcing himself on them, according to prosecutors.

The official, Chief Inspector Carl Holmes, 54, had offered to mentor at least two of the women, the grand jury report said.

His high-ranking position "insulated him from any meaningful investigation" while the three officers were subjected to investigations by the Internal Affairs Division after they blew the whistle on him, the report said.

In grand jury testimony, the women described a Police Department culture that discouraged reporting abuse, as "doing so can leave you vulnerable, and on the wrong side of the blue line."

The women, whose names were redacted from the report, have left the police force. One of the women filed a lawsuit against the city, the Police Department and Inspector Holmes. That case was settled out of court and one condition of the settlement was that she had to resign, the report said.

A warrant for Inspector Holmes's arrest was issued on Wednesday and he turned himself in on Thursday, the Philadelphia District Attorney's Office said. Inspector Holmes was also suspended on Thursday, The Associated Press reported.

The 11 charges against him include three counts of aggravated indecent assault, a felony.

The charges come a little more than two months after the city's police commissioner, Richard Ross, abruptly resigned after he failed to stop the harassment and discrimination that had plagued the department for years.

"We need to have a city and a police department where women can go to work without fear of this nonsense," the district attorney, Larry Krasner, said on Saturday. "We need some sort of accountability coming from Internal Affairs that doesn't amount to retaliating."

Mr. Krasner said his office would not shy away from policing the police.

"Every prosecutor's office is responsible for holding people accountable," he said. "That means everybody in every job."

Calls to Inspector Holmes's home were not immediately returned. His lawyer declined to comment.

The reported assaults, which date between 2004 and 2007, were graphically described in the grand jury report and were nearly identical. In each case, the female officers were approached by Inspector Holmes, who then forced himself on them.

After the women reported his actions, they faced retaliation for coming forward, often being subjected to internal investigations, the report said.

One of the women testified that Inspector Holmes threatened her as he assaulted her, telling her that no one would believe her and that "he could make her disappear." She had initially come to him for help after being sexually harassed by an unidentified supervisor, she said.

The woman filed a complaint against her supervisor but not Inspector Holmes because "she thought that no one would believe her about both," the report said.

A few weeks after the complaint was filed, the woman became the subject of an internal investigation after an anonymous letter accused her of being involved with drug dealers, the report said.

The woman was "so fearful that she was being framed that she found an independent laboratory and submitted a blood and urine sample the same day, paying out of pocket to ensure that the police 'couldn't put anything in there and say I had a dirty urine,' " the report said.

It would be nearly three years before the investigation concluded that the allegations against her were unfounded.

Another assault detailed in the report occurred at a farewell party for Inspector Holmes, who was leaving for an F.B.I. training program for three months. After kissing and groping a female officer, Inspector Holmes grabbed her hand and used it to begin masturbating in his city-issued sport utility vehicle, the report said.

During an investigation into what happened at the party, officials found Inspector Holmes's semen on one of the seats in his vehicle, the report said.

The woman testified she did not immediately report him because "in our culture, you don't tell on cops which is why … I did not report it, for fear of how it would affect my career and also being known as a rat … You just don't tell on cops at all, even if they're wrong."

The grand jury found that Inspector Holmes created a toxic workplace environment and that he should be criminally charged.

"No one, no matter position, rank, or power, is above the law," the grand jury said in its report.

Police Officer Charged With Murder in Killing of Handcuffed Suspect in Maryland

BY NEIL VIGDOR, MARIEL PADILLA AND SANDRA E. GARCIA | JAN. 28, 2020

Michael Owen, a Prince George's County police corporal, shot William H. Green seven times while he was handcuffed in a patrol car, the authorities said.

A POLICE CORPORAL in Maryland was charged with second-degree murder on Tuesday in the fatal shooting of a suspect who had been handcuffed in the front passenger seat of his patrol car the previous night, the authorities said.

The corporal, Michael Owen Jr., a 10-year veteran of the Prince George's Police Department, shot William H. Green seven times after a traffic stop on Monday night in Temple Hills, Md., on the outskirts of Washington, Henry P. Stawinski III, the county police chief, said Tuesday evening at a news conference.

Corporal Owen and another officer had been responding to a series of motor vehicle accidents in which Mr. Green, 43, had hit several cars and was suspected of being under the influence of an unknown substance, the chief said.

The officers had been waiting for another officer to arrive to evaluate Mr. Green for drugs when Corporal Owen opened fire, according to the chief, who said Mr. Green's hands were cuffed behind his back at the time.

"I have concluded that what happened last night is a crime," Chief Stawinski said. "There are no circumstances under which this outcome is acceptable."

Corporal Owen was also charged with voluntary and involuntary manslaughter, first-degree assault and use of a firearm to commit a violent crime, said the authorities, who on Tuesday walked back an initial police account that witnesses told them a struggle had preceded the shooting.

"That was not corroborated," Chief Stawinski said.

The shooting of Mr. Green, a father of two who lived in Southeast Washington and whose family said he worked for Megabus, drew condemnation from the American Civil Liberties Union. It also recalled previous fatal shootings by the police in Prince George's County, where the majority of residents are black.

"There is no reason why a handcuffed person should ever be shot multiple times by a police officer, let alone shot multiple times inside a patrol car," Deborah Jeon, the legal director for the A.C.L.U. of Maryland, said in a statement on Tuesday.

Mr. Green's family said he was not a violent person.

"Since the day he was born he was the most gentle, sweetest, kindest," Mr. Green's cousin Juanita Sharma said in an interview on Tuesday. "He loved his mother and he loved his family," she said. "He showed love to his family."

Corporal Owen, who was placed on administrative leave, was taken into custody on Tuesday and is expected to appear in court for a bond hearing in the next few days. It was not immediately clear if he had a lawyer.

The president of Lodge 89 of the Fraternal Order of Police, which represents Prince George's County officers, did not immediately respond to requests for comment on Tuesday night.

Prince George's County officials said they were in the process of getting body cameras for police officers. Corporal Owen was not wearing one at the time of the shooting.

In 2011, the department placed Corporal Owen, an officer at the time, on administrative leave after he shot and killed a Landover, Md., man who the police said had pointed a gun at him. Corporal Owen had pulled over to the side of the road to check on the man, who was lying in the grass, police said.

In the early 2000s, the United States Department of Justice investigated the Prince George's County Police Department over a spate excessive force complaints and the department's canine unit procedures.

The parallel investigations led to a memorandum of understanding between the Justice Department and the county police, which agreed to create a review board for firearm discharge cases and a risk management system for officers' performance. The police department also agreed to investigate and review misconduct allegations.

During the news conference on Tuesday, a local resident confronted county officials about police shootings.

"We understand you're upset," Angela D. Alsobrooks, the Prince George's County executive, said. "We get it. I promise you we will not minimize it."

SHEELAGH MCNEILL contributed research.

NEIL VIGDOR is a breaking news reporter on the Express Desk. He previously covered Connecticut politics for the Hartford Courant.

MARIEL PADILLA is a reporter covering national breaking news for the Express desk, based in New York.

A Black Police Officer's Fight Against the N.Y.P.D.

BY SAKI KNAFO | FEB. 18, 2016

Edwin Raymond thought he could change the department from the inside. He wound up the lead plaintiff in a lawsuit brought by 12 minority officers.

EVERY MORNING BEFORE HIS SHIFT, Edwin Raymond, a 30-year-old officer in the New York Police Department, ties up his long dreadlocks so they won't brush against his collar, as the job requires. On Dec. 7, he carefully pinned them up in a nautilus pattern, buttoned the brass buttons of his regulation dress coat and pulled on a pair of white cotton gloves. He used a lint roller to make sure his uniform was spotless. In a few hours, he would appear before three of the department's highest-ranking officials at a hearing that would determine whether he would be promoted to sergeant. He had often stayed up late worrying about how this conversation would play out, but now that the moment was here, he felt surprisingly calm. The department had recently announced a push to recruit more men and women like him — minority cops who could help the police build trust among black and Hispanic New Yorkers. But before he could move up in rank, Raymond would have to disprove some of the things people had said about him.

Over the past year, Raymond had received a series of increasingly damning evaluations from his supervisors. He had been summoned to the hearing to tell his side of the story. His commanders had been punishing him, he believed, for refusing to comply with what Raymond considered a hidden and "inherently racist" policy.

Raymond checked in to the department's employee-management office in downtown Manhattan. Three other officers waited there with him, all dressed as though for a funeral or parade, all hoping they would be judged worthy of a promotion and a raise. One officer had gotten in trouble for pulling a gun on his ex-girlfriend's partner.

"Everyone was nervous," Raymond says. "I was the only one who was confident, because I knew I'd done nothing wrong."

Hours crawled by. Finally, a sergeant announced that the officials — "executives," as they're known in the department — were ready to see them. One by one, the officers entered a conference room. Raymond saluted the executives and stated his name. Then the executives began to speak. Beneath the stiff woolen shell of Raymond's dress coat, tucked away in his right breast pocket, his iPhone was recording their muffled voices.

OVER THE LAST two years, Raymond has recorded almost a dozen officials up and down the chain of command in what he says is an attempt to change the daily practices of the New York Police Department. He claims these tactics contradict the department's rhetoric about the arrival of a new era of fairer, smarter policing. In August 2015, Raymond joined 11 other police officers in filing a class-action suit on behalf of minority officers throughout the force. The suit centers on what they claim is one of the fundamental policies of the New York Police Department: requiring officers to meet fixed numerical goals for arrests and court summonses each month. In Raymond's mind, quota-based policing lies at the root of almost everything racially discriminatory about policing in New York. Yet the department has repeatedly told the public that quotas don't exist.

Since January 2014, the start of the two-year period during which Raymond made most of his recordings, the department has been led by Police Commissioner William Bratton, who has presided over a decline in summonses and arrests even as crime levels have remained historically low. He has revamped the department's training strategy and has introduced a new program that encourages officers to spend more time getting to know the people who live and work in the neighborhoods they patrol.

Chief of Department James O'Neill told me that the expectations of officers have changed. "Whatever arrests we make, whatever summonses we write, I want them connected to the people responsible for the violence and crime," he said. The department is now focused on the "quality" of arrests and summonses rather than the "quantity," he said.

Raymond and his fellow plaintiffs will try to prove otherwise. The suit accuses the department of violating multiple laws and statutes, including a 2010 state ban against quotas, and the 14th Amendment, which outlaws racial discrimination. It asks for damages and an injunction against the practice. Although plaintiffs in other cases have provided courts with evidence suggesting the department uses quotas, this is the first time anyone has sued the department for violating the 2010 state ban against the practice.

Black and Latino officers have long contributed rare voices of dissent within a department that remains predominantly white at its highest levels. Raymond has cultivated a friendship with Eric Adams, a former police captain and the current Brooklyn borough president, who founded, during his time on the force, 100 Blacks in Law Enforcement Who Care, an organization that advocates for law-enforcement professionals of color. Adams has had a hand in several recent policing reforms. As a state senator, he sponsored the bill that led, in 2010, to the New York ban against quotas for stops, summonses and arrests. Then, in 2013, he joined several current and former minority officers in testifying against the department in the landmark stop-and-frisk case Floyd v. City of New York, which culminated with a federal judge's ruling that the department had stopped and searched hundreds of thousands of minority New Yorkers in ways that violated their civil rights.

Between 2011 and 2013, the publicity surrounding the case prompted the department to all but abandon the tactic — the number of annual stops fell by more than two-thirds over two years — but, according to Raymond and others, the pressure to arrest people for minor offenses has not let up. "Every time I read the paper, I thought, Why do they think the problem is stop-and-frisk?" Raymond says. "Although stop-and-frisk is unlawful, and it's annoying, you're not going to not get a job because you've been stopped and frisked," he says. "You're going to get denied a job because you have a record."

The lawsuit claims that commanders now use euphemisms to sidestep the quota ban, pressuring officers to "be more proactive" or to "get more activity" instead of explicitly ordering them to bring in, say, one arrest and 10 tickets by the end of the month. "It's as if the ban doesn't exist," Raymond says. Other cops agree. At a Dunkin' Donuts in Ozone Park, Queens, a black officer who is not involved in the lawsuit (and who, fearing retribution, requested anonymity) spoke at length about the inconsistency between the department's words and actions, her anger building as she spoke, the tea cooling in her cup, until she concluded, bluntly, "It's like they're talking out of their ass and their mouth at the same time."

I recently spoke to Daniel Modell, a retired lieutenant who in 2014 testified to the grand jury in the case of Eric Garner, the Staten Island man who was killed during an encounter with the police. Modell, who is white, said the frustration is departmentwide. "It's not only black and Hispanic officers," he said. "The rank and file generally, they're utterly demoralized and critical of the department.

"But they don't have a voice," he added. "If they speak out, they get crushed."

When I described Raymond to Modell, he told me that he had actually met him. In September 2015, Modell spoke on a panel at the John Jay College of Criminal Justice. The topic was "bridging the gap" between minorities and the police. Raymond, who attended the seminar, made an impression. "He's a good guy," Modell said. "I could tell by the way he spoke, and the sincerity in his eyes. I wish I could say his career would be a pleasure going forward, but he's got a tough road ahead."

Raymond is not the first police officer to record his commanders. Adrian Schoolcraft, who became the primary stop-and-frisk whistleblower, was forcibly admitted into a psychiatric ward for six days after objecting to police practices in 2009. He recorded the whole incident. One of Raymond's fellow plaintiffs in the lawsuit, Adhyl Polanco, taped

CELESTE SLOMAN FOR THE NEW YORK TIMES

Lt. Edwin Raymond.

his superiors while complaining about stop-and-frisk and was banished to a desk deep in Brooklyn, two hours from his home. Look up their names on Thee Rant, an anonymous message board for police officers, and the epithets come pouring forth: "crybaby," "rat," "zero." Even some of Raymond's closest friends and confidants, people who admire his boldness and vouch for his integrity, have told him, quite frankly, that what he's doing is nuts. Raymond says he has lost sleep worrying about what might happen, but he can sound contemptuous of those who advise caution. "Everyone else, they're just so scared," he says. "My thing is, never be afraid to do what's right."

RAYMOND GREW UP in East Flatbush, a West Indian neighborhood of wood-frame houses and brick apartment buildings in Brooklyn. A few blocks from his building was a corner that residents nicknamed "the front page" because of the many murders that ended up in the papers. Raymond remembers stepping over a dead body, blood pooling on the floor of the building lobby, to get to school. His father, a Haitian immigrant who barely finished grade school, managed to keep the kids well fed for a while, but then, when Raymond was 3 and his brother was 4, their mother died of cancer, and then their father lost his job at a paper factory. He fell into a depression and never worked again. Raymond and his brother often went to bed hungry, a feeling Raymond remembers as "sadness mixed with a headache." Sometimes a neighbor, Florise, a single mother of two from Haiti, gave them something for dinner; Raymond came to see her as an aunt, and Billy Joissin and Melissa Baptiste, her children, as his cousins. Other mothers in the neighborhood occasionally helped care for Raymond. In a very real sense, the neighborhood raised him.

Starting at 14, he spent 45 hours a week bagging groceries and stocking shelves after school and on the weekends. Raymond saw what the crack trade had done to the neighborhood and wanted no part of it. His friends say he had a powerful, even rigid sense of morality, lecturing them about the dangers of drugs and gangs, refusing to try even a puff of weed. "We always tell him he's different," Baptiste says. Joissin noted wryly that Raymond was "not afraid to not be popular and to not be liked." His unwavering rectitude kept the gangs from bothering him. The police, however, were a different story. "As soon as I had a little hair on my chin, I was getting stopped almost once a week," he says.

One day at a Haitian street fair when he was 16, Raymond ran into a family friend who had become a police officer. To Raymond's surprise, his friend raved about the job — about the benefits and the pension and the possibility of being promoted. Raymond decided to enter the police academy as soon as he was old enough. Even then, he says, he had vague ambitions of becoming a different kind of officer — one who would go after actual criminals. But he mainly saw the job as a way to pay the bills. And that's how he might still see it if, about three years before he joined the force, a friend hadn't lent him a copy of "The Destruction of Black Civilization."

The book, a work of Afrocentric history by Chancellor Williams, is a classic of its genre. Raymond still recalls "the pride that rushed through your veins" as he realized, he says, that the history of black people didn't begin with slavery. In high school, his work schedule got in the way of his studies, and he had never liked reading. Now he couldn't get enough of it. He read Malcolm X and Marcus Garvey. He says he started an email correspondence with Tim Wise, an activist and writer known for his books on critical race theory. As he read that the slave patrols of two centuries ago had evolved into the police departments of today, it occurred to him that the cops who stopped him in his youth weren't intentionally racist; they were merely complying with the demands of a system that was "historically rooted in keeping you down." Then, in 2008, he joined the system himself.

At first, and for most of his career, Raymond worked out of Transit District 32, the division of the Transit Bureau responsible for policing the Brooklyn sections of the 2 and 3 lines and several other stretches of the subway system. Many of his colleagues spent their time writing tickets or arresting people for "theft of service" — a minor violation better known as turnstile hopping. (From 2008 to 2013, fare-beating arrests shot up to 24,747 from 14,681, according to a 2014 Daily News analysis of public data.)

Legally, individual officers have the power to decide how to deal with certain minor offenses. Some officers, trying to increase their totals of summonses and arrests for the month, hide in bathrooms and closets meant for subway employees, peeking out through vents so they can jump out at anyone foolish or desperate enough to vault the turnstiles. If the offender, typically a teenager, lacks an ID or has a criminal record, the officer can make an arrest. According to a recent analysis by the advocacy group the Police Reform Organization Project, 92 percent of those arrested for theft of service in 2015 were black, Hispanic or Asian. Those offenders who aren't arrested are generally summoned to court to pay a $100 fine. If they fail to pay it or forget the court date or miss an appearance for any reason, the judge signs an arrest warrant.

Raymond didn't hide on the job. At the academy, he says, future officers were trained to remain "present and visible" while working in uniform, partly so passengers could find a police officer when they needed one. On Oct. 8, 2015, for example, a group of teenage girls approached Raymond at the Pennsylvania Avenue stop in Brooklyn and pointed out a man who had been following them. Had Raymond been hiding, he says, they might never have found him. Raymond stopped the man, asked him some questions and ultimately arrested him for stalking.

"He does these honorable things," said Willie Lucas, one of the other black officers who worked in Raymond's district. "The first time I worked with him, we were doing patrol out in the East New York area. There was a mother, she may have been a teenager, and she was in some kind of distress, crying and really upset. Her baby may have been around 3 or 4 months old. I remember him going to talk to her and help her out. He was willing to ride with her to the Bronx, all the way out of his jurisdiction."

Raymond didn't shy away from confrontation when it was necessary. While he was still at the academy, the department awarded him a badge of honor for breaking up a street fight during one of his lunch breaks, grabbing a metal pipe from one of the brawlers and pinning him to the ground. "When it's time to get busy, I get busy," he says. He says he typically stopped about three people a day, mostly for little things like holding the doors at a station. But usually he let them go with a warning. He worried about how an arrest could follow a kid through life.

Raymond realized that his supervisors didn't approve of his approach. Some of them came right out and told him he was dragging down the district's overall arrest rate, and said they had been taking heat from their own bosses as a result. In the summer of 2010, a commander stuck him with the weekend shift at Coney Island, the sort of unwanted job that cops call a "punitive post." Other undesirable assignments followed: sitting around with psychotic prisoners in psychiatric emergency rooms, standing at "fixed posts" on specific parts of subway platforms with orders not to move, staring at video feeds of the tunnels from the confines of an airless booth called "the box." As the pressures intensified over the next few years, Raymond decided he needed to do something to protect himself — even though it could also put him at greater risk. Convinced that his supervisors were punishing him unlawfully, and fearing for his reputation, he started to record his conversations.

THE PRACTICES THAT Raymond opposes began as solutions to the problems of another era. In 1994, when William Bratton started his first tour as the head of the department, the department was reeling from corruption scandals, and officers were discouraged from spending too much time in high-crime neighborhoods, lest they succumb to bribery. In the absence of a strong police presence, drug dealers operated in the open, and residents who complained risked incurring their wrath. Crack vials littered schoolyards, and police officers were still "giving freedom of the streets to the drug dealers, the gangs, the prostitutes, the drinkers and the radio blasters," Bratton later wrote with one of his advisers in the conservative quarterly City Journal. The crack trade in East Flatbush was so rampant that Raymond and his brother would fall asleep counting gunshots.

Bratton's solutions to these problems would make him famous. A self-described innovator, he embraced the "broken windows" theory of policing — the idea that the police could cut down on serious crimes by making it clear that even the trivial ones wouldn't go unpunished. To hold officers accountable to this philosophy, especially in neighborhoods they had once neglected, Bratton tasked a transit lieutenant, Jack Maple, with developing a management system that kept careful track of arrest and crime statistics throughout the city. The system, called CompStat, short for "compare statistics," was often credited for the drop in crime that followed. By the time Bratton left New York in 1997, New York's murder rate had fallen by half. Cities from Chicago to Sydney hired Bratton and his protégés as police chiefs and consultants. Today, most large American cities use some form of CompStat.

Eli Silverman, a police-studies professor at John Jay College of Criminal Justice, was an early apostle. Silverman lauded CompStat in his

1999 book "N.Y.P.D. Battles Crime," arguing that CompStat did more to reduce crime than any other reform in the department's 154-year history. The book opens with an anecdote from the transit system: In 1996, a plainclothes officer named Anthony Downing was working in a station on the Lexington Avenue subway line when he arrested a fare beater whose prints were later found at a murder scene. Before the CompStat era, when no one was keeping track of minor offenses, Downing would have had little incentive to stop someone for jumping a turnstile, and the fare beater, it follows, might have gotten away with murder.

Silverman still calls himself a CompStat supporter, but by 2001, when he published a second edition of the book, a number of police officers had written to him to say that the "revolution in blue," as Silverman styled it, wasn't all it seemed. Intrigued by their claims, Silverman and a fellow criminologist and retired New York Police Department captain, John Eterno, set out to see if they could arrive at a more detailed understanding of how the system worked. In 2008 and again in 2012, they sent out questionnaires to retired members of the department. More than 2,000 wrote back. The results were clear: Officers who had worked during the CompStat era were twice as likely as their predecessors to say that they had been under intense pressure to increase arrests, and three times as likely to say the same about the pressure to increase summonses.

In the 2000s, as violent crime hit historic lows, Mayor Michael Bloomberg, Police Commissioner Raymond Kelly and other city officials kept pressuring the department to drive the crime rate even lower, an expectation that became harder and harder to meet. In districtwide CompStat meetings, executives interrogated commanders about their violent-crime statistics. Some commanders tried to protect themselves by underreporting or reclassifying major crimes. Others tried to show they were being "proactive"; invariably this meant more stops, more summonses, more arrests.

Most of this activity took place in minority neighborhoods. In predominantly black Bedford-Stuyvesant, Brooklyn, for example, officers issued more than 2,000 summonses a year between 2008 and 2011 to people riding their bicycles on the sidewalk, according to the Marijuana Arrest Research Project, a nonprofit that studies police policy. During the same period, officers gave out an average of eight bike tickets a year in predominantly white and notably bike-friendly Park Slope. All told, between 2001 and 2013, black and Hispanic people were more than four times as likely as whites to receive summonses for minor violations, according to an analysis by the New York Civil Liberties Union.

Raymond and other critics of the program don't deny that CompStat is useful, or even that it may have helped the department save lives. The question, for them, is how to use it. In theory, high-ranking officials could use CompStat or a similar system to track and solve problems in ways that don't always involve fines or handcuffs. But after more than three decades, the system is deeply entrenched. A captain who requested anonymity for fear of retaliation told me about a program he had heard of that reduced shoplifting. But instead of praising the officer who developed it for the drop in arrests, the chief told him to "get more numbers." That kind of thing happens all the time, he said. "You don't get recognized and rewarded for helping a homeless person get permanent housing, but you get recognized for arresting them again and again and again."

THE FIRST OF RAYMOND'S tapes begins with a warning. In January 2014, Lt. Wei Long, then in his first month at District 32, confronted Raymond about his relatively low "activity." Like other supervisors featured in the early recordings, he expressed sympathy for Raymond, admitting that the "department is all about numbers" and even acknowledging that this "sucks." Raymond challenged Long, as he did many of his superiors. "This is people's lives," he tells a captain on one of the tapes. "It's not a game."

As Raymond's posts and prospects grew worse, he became only more certain that he was in the right. Even as he handed out fewer summonses and made fewer arrests, few serious crimes were reported in the areas he patrolled, he says. He believed that if he could get out from under the lower-level supervisors, at least some officials at the highest levels of the department would recognize that he was the right kind of officer for New York. He decided to try for a promotion. In December 2012, he began studying for the exam given to aspiring sergeants. The results of the test, which he took in September 2013, could hardly have been more promising. Out of about 6,000 test takers, just 932 passed, and Raymond placed eighth.

Changes within the department itself also bolstered his hopes. On Dec. 5, 2013, Mayor Bill de Blasio, then newly elected, announced that he would be bringing Bratton back for a second tour as commissioner, saying, "He is going to bring police and community back together." Critics questioned whether the architect of CompStat was right for the job. But de Blasio, an unabashed progressive, had run on a platform that included reforming stop-and-frisk, and Bratton had espoused his commitment to that goal, saying he would unite the police and the public "in a collaboration of mutual respect and mutual trust." In a video shown to the officers at their roll call, Bratton promised to focus on "the quality of police actions, with less emphasis on their numbers and more emphasis on our actual impact."

A month into his term, Bratton began enlisting teams of thinkers from on and off the force to brainstorm ideas for improving the department. Oliver Pu-Folkes, a black captain who had met Raymond through a mutual friend and had been impressed, appointed Raymond to a team focused on building relationships in black and Hispanic communities. Raymond was the lone rank-and-file officer asked to participate. That fall, inspired by the work, he and a friend formed an organization of their own, PLOT (Preparing Leaders of Tomorrow), offering mentorship services to black teenagers in Brooklyn.

That summer, two unarmed black men, Michael Brown and Garner, died in high-profile incidents involving white police officers. A wave of protests spread through the country, and President Obama, responding to the public outcry, lamented the "simmering distrust that exists between too many police departments and too many communities of color." A Justice Department official who had heard about PLOT invited Raymond and his partner to attend a conference on race and policing in Washington. After so many years of being ignored or, as he saw it, punished for his ideas, Raymond was suddenly at the center of a conversation of national importance. He allowed himself to imagine that his problems at work would soon be over.

Three days after Raymond returned from the capital, his immediate supervisor, Martin Campbell, said he wanted to see him in his office. Raymond felt that something wasn't right. Raymond had previously gotten the impression that Campbell, a black sergeant from Trinidad, privately deplored the constant push for numbers, but he also believed that Campbell, who had been in his position for only a year, was under the same pressure to deliver the numbers as everyone else. Fearing another punitive assignment, Raymond waited for Campbell to step into the office. He took out his phone and turned on an audio-recording app, then slid the phone back into his pocket.

In his office, Campbell gestured toward his computer screen. Raymond saw that the sergeant had given him something called an interim evaluation. Officers typically receive four quarterly evaluations a year plus an annual every January, but in exceptional circumstances, supervisors will sometimes write an additional report, usually as a way of signaling to the command that the officer was caught doing something egregious, even committing a crime. Just getting one of these reports was bad enough. Now Raymond saw that out of a maximum score of five, he had received only a 2.5, an abysmal grade. A score that low could block his promotion or lead to his being fired.

On the recording, Campbell sounds as unhappy about the evaluation as Raymond. He insists that his direct superior told him what to write, and suggests that she, in turn, did so under orders from her own supervisor, Natalie Maldonado, the district commander. Although

Raymond hadn't yet heard of the lawsuit, he knew about other officers who had sued the department or had testified against it in court, among them Adrian Schoolcraft, whose secret recordings of his commanders were detailed in a five-part series in The Village Voice in 2010. Raymond knew his recordings wouldn't carry much weight unless he got his supervisors to call the banned practice by name.

"What is the issue with me?" he asked Campbell. "Just the activity, the quota?"

Campbell laughed. "What do you think, bro?"

"Man," Raymond said.

"Honestly, what do you think?"

"But it has to be more," Raymond said, "because technically, when it comes to numbers — "

"No, no, no," Campbell said. "There's not more. That's *it*."

And yet that wasn't it — at least, Raymond didn't think so. There were other officers in the district, not many, but some, whose numbers were even lower than his.

"You really want me to tell you what I think it is?" Campbell asked.

"Of course, because I need to understand this."

"You're a young black man with dreads. Very smart, very intelligent, have a loud say, meaning your words is loud. You understand what I'm saying by that?"

"Yeah."

"I never seen anything like this, bro," Campbell said.

RAYMOND FILED AN appeal of his evaluation right away, but before it could make its way to Maldonado's desk, she was transferred out of the Transit Bureau to a more coveted post. It was around this time, in the summer of 2015, that Raymond heard about the lawsuit, which had just been filed. Until then, Raymond had felt alone. Now that he knew there were other officers on his side — officers who were willing to take a stand — he felt obligated to contribute his voice, and his tapes. He still wanted to believe he could rise within the department, so he signed on quietly. Other than a few friends and his fellow plaintiffs, no one knew he had joined the suit, and no one, other than the lawyer, knew about his recordings.

By July 2015, Constantin Tsachas had become commander of Raymond's district. According to Raymond, Tsachas hadn't even moved all his boxes into the office when he began occupying himself with the problem of what do about the uncooperative officer in his command. On Aug. 3, Campbell told Raymond he had gotten a call from Tsachas at home.

"I was already convinced that they didn't want you to get promoted," Campbell says on the recording. "Well, it's clearer to me now."

Campbell says Tsachas told him to write yet another brutal interim evaluation, this time dropping Raymond's grade from a 2.5 to a two. Tsachas also told him to rewrite Raymond's annual evaluation for 2014. Tsachas would later tell Raymond that the original version, which Campbell gave Raymond at the start of 2015, was never finalized.

While the original evaluation, as Raymond remembers it, criticized him for his supposedly low "activity," the new one appeared to have been scrubbed of any language that could be recognized as code for failing to meet a quota. It was also harsher. Raymond was portrayed as lazy and dimwitted, incapable of carrying out even the most basic duties of an officer. It claimed he "does not demonstrate any ability to make sound conclusions," does "not take any initiative" and "needs constant supervision." (The New York Police Department declined to comment on the specifics related to Raymond's case.)

Raymond filed another appeal. In October, he sat down with Tsachas in his office, accompanied by Campbell, a third supervisor and a union delegate, Gentry Smith. Once again, Raymond's phone was recording. The meeting lasted an hour. Raymond spoke about his work on Bratton's brainstorming group and his visit to Washington, and he argued that the evaluation misrepresented him. In several ways, Raymond asked Tsachas to explain what he had done wrong; in several ways, Tsachas avoided saying anything explicit about Raymond's numbers. More than once, Tsachas told Raymond he needed to be "proactive."

"So what's the definition of 'proactive'?" Raymond asked.

"You know what 'proactive' is," Tsachas said.

About halfway through the meeting, Tsachas began losing patience. "I'm here for, like, half an hour, and you're playing with words." Raymond kept pressing him. Finally, Tsachas said something more pointed. "I'm not saying lock up anybody," Tsachas said. "If you come in with some stuff — let's say, female, Asian, 42, no ID, locked up for T.O.S." — theft of service — "that's not gonna fly."

As Raymond interpreted it, Tsachas was suggesting that he focus on arresting blacks and Latinos, as opposed to Asians or whites. "The 14th Amendment says we have to be impartial," he said.

Tsachas began trying to clarify his statement. "It didn't come out the way it's supposed to," he said. He went on to talk about "no IDs" and low-level arrests. According to Raymond, Smith, who is black, screwed up his face in disgust.

The room fell quiet. "I have to say I forgive you guys," Raymond said. "This is bigger than even you guys. This is coming from up there."

"I'M NOT GONNA lie, man," Raymond told me one fall afternoon in his apartment shortly after that meeting. "I know I'm doing what's right, and what's right and what's smart have always been the same to me, but when I got that 2.5 I was no longer sure that what I'm doing is smart. I was months away from being promoted. Once you're promoted, you will never be asked to meet a quota again." He paused for a moment, then said: "They expect you to pass on that pressure instead."

Raymond lives in a one-bedroom apartment in a new building in East Flatbush, near where he grew up. On the walls were paintings and photographs of Malcolm X and Haile Selassie; on the shelves were books by Marcus Garvey and Ta-Nehisi Coates. On a side table sat a carved wooden sculpture of a warrior blowing into a conch shell:

During Haiti's war for independence, slaves used conch shells to warn one another of danger and for calls to battle.

Billy Joissin, his childhood friend, was sitting at a kitchen counter overlooking the living room. "We grew from not having nothing," he said to Raymond, clearly worried about him. "Don't slide back into poverty."

Raymond said he didn't see what he was doing as a choice. His insistence on always doing what he believed to be right had allowed him to survive a precarious childhood. "If I'd done what was popular in those surroundings, I would have never been a police officer," he told me. "I was surrounded by guns and drugs — and I was surrounded by guns and drugs while I didn't eat for two days."

Despite everything, Raymond still wanted to believe he might somehow have a future in the force. He found it hard to imagine that the department's leaders would reject him just because of his lower numbers. "Everything I do points to a job well done," he said. Any week now, he expected the administration to begin promoting officers from his class.

Through October and November, he waited for the call. Finally, in early December, the promotions were announced. Among those promoted was Kenneth Boss, one of the four officers who fired 41 shots at Amadou Diallo, an unarmed Guinean immigrant, in 1999, hitting him 19 times and killing him. But Raymond's name wasn't on the list. Instead, he was summoned to the hearing with the executives to explain his situation. He brought along a sheaf of documents, including a form letter from Bratton from July 28, 2015, thanking him for his participation in the brainstorming sessions and eight letters of recommendation from people inside and outside the department. Avram Bornstein, co-director of the Police Leadership Program at John Jay, where Raymond had taken courses, called him an "outstanding example of leadership," noting his "strong moral character and his intellectual acumen." Oliver Pu-Folkes, the captain who asked him to join Bratton's brainstorming sessions, compared him to Galileo, "who was sent to the Inquisition for affirming that the earth was a sphere."

Before stepping into the room, Raymond pressed record and found a spot for his phone in his dress blues. The officials sat at the other end of the table: James Secreto, chief of housing; Thomas Galati, chief of intelligence; and Michael Julian, deputy commissioner of personnel. Julian, the first to speak, began in a way Raymond didn't quite expect. "I want to hire a thousand of you," he said. He hadn't conjured that exact number out of thin air. Julian, who is white, had recently been assigned the task of coordinating the recruitment of 1,000 black officers. That summer, the 57 black men and 25 black women who graduated from the academy represented less than 10 percent of the graduating class — the lowest percentage of black graduates in 20 years. In an interview with The Guardian, Bratton blamed the scarcity of black recruits on the prevalence of criminal records in black neighborhoods. Too many of the city's black men had "spent time in jail and, as such, we can't hire them," The Guardian quoted him as saying. (Bratton later said the newspaper took the quote out of context.)

Along with the other executives at the hearing, Julian had already reviewed Raymond's documents. He noted that Raymond had called in sick only once in seven years. "You don't get sick," he said, his voice rising with enthusiasm. "There's a lot of good about you."

Then the conversation shifted. Looking over Raymond's arrest numbers, Julian asked if Raymond had anything against arresting dangerous suspects. Raymond assured him he didn't. "Coming from a very tough community, high crime, being born and raised in the crack era, I unfortunately witnessed horrible acts," he said. "These people need to be locked up, and we need to use whatever resources we have to do so."

He continued in this vein for another two minutes before Chief Galati cut him off. "Can we back up for one second?" Galati asked. "Tell me why your evaluations are continually poor."

Raymond mentioned his direct supervisor, Sergeant Campbell. "He wasn't comfortable with those evaluations," Raymond said.

Galati: "Is it a personal thing between you and him?"

Raymond: "I have a great relationship with Sergeant Campbell."

Secreto: "So it's his boss?"

Julian: "You don't have the numbers?"

Raymond: "The numbers?"

Julian: "You don't have the numbers?"

After years in the department, Julian could most likely imagine what a commander might say to a lower-ranking supervisor who wasn't getting high-enough numbers from one of his officers. "The commander says, 'You gotta do it like this,'" he mused. "'You gotta put him down for low initiative, low drive, passive.'" He acknowledged that Raymond didn't fit that description. "You don't seem like a passive person," he said. "You look like a guy I'd want walking through the train when I'm on the train."

Raymond thanked him. "I'm at service to the public at all times," he said. "We are oathbound to serve them, and this is what I do every day." Raymond saluted, left the building and drove to Queens to meet a friend. "I didn't want to be alone," he told me. At some point that day, the executives would decide whether his service was good enough to warrant a promotion. Bratton himself would review their recommendation and sign off by the end of the week.

ON DEC. 10, a sergeant from the employee-management division called Raymond: He hadn't been promoted. According to the sergeant, the executives would revisit the decision in six months. In the meantime, he would be transferred out of the subway system to the 77th Precinct in Crown Heights, Brooklyn. He didn't look forward to this change of scenery. He knew two other officers in the 77th. They were fellow plaintiffs.

When Raymond called me with the news, he was furious. He spoke of being disappointed in Bratton, who had talked so compellingly about changing the department. "I was foolish enough to believe him," he said. He also mentioned Sergeant Campbell, who he said had refused to provide him with a letter of recommendation to show the executives.

When I reached Campbell at home, he said he had in fact written a letter of recommendation for Raymond but decided not to send it. "I have to protect myself and my job and my family," he said. Campbell described Raymond as a "good person" and added that he thought he could be a "valuable" member of the department. But he disagreed with his methods of trying to bring about reform. "There's a lot of guys in the department, even I and supervisors and other guys, who would like to see things change," he said. "But it doesn't change like that. It doesn't change overnight."

Last month, Bratton wrote in a Daily News op-ed that the police department has managed to keep crime down even as it has "cut back hugely on enforcement encounters with citizens." This would seem to suggest that the approach to policing long practiced by Raymond is both effective and, in Bratton's eyes, admirable.

In January, the city's legal department filed a motion asking a judge to dismiss the plaintiffs' charge that the department is violating the quota ban, along with several other claims. A judge is expected to rule on this in the next two months. If the case, Raymond v. City of New York, proceeds, his recordings will most likely be entered into evidence. The whole proceeding could take years. But Raymond says that he will not stop pressing, even if it means trying to take the case all the way to the Supreme Court. He claims he will never settle unless the department changes its practices. "There's no amount they could pay me to make me stop fighting," he said.

On the day he received the bad news about his promotion, we met at a health-food place in Crown Heights. Over a tempeh B.L.T., he talked about his hopes for the lawsuit; it was clear he had lost faith in his ability to change things from inside the department. After a while, his thoughts turned to his neighbors in East Flatbush — how they had protected him as a child, how he had tried to protect and serve them in turn. He looked away and gave a short, exasperated laugh. "An officer who hides in a room, peeking through a hole in a vent, is more supervisor material than me." He shook his head. "This is the system," he said, "and it needs to change."

SAKI KNAFO is a reporting fellow with the Investigative Fund at the Nation Institute. He has written for New York Magazine, GQ and Travel and Leisure.

Glossary

bigoted Showing stubbornness in one's own opinions and prejudice or intolerance toward others.

body camera A video camera worn by law enforcement officers to record their activity.

community policing The assigning of police officers to work regularly in a specific area so they form a rapport with the local community.

deadly force Physical actions that may result in death. In most cases, deadly force is legally justified only as a last resort in extreme circumstances.

dragnet In policing, a system of organized strategies to find and apprehend criminals.

facial recognition Software used to identify a person by mapping their facial features via photo or video and cross-referencing them with a database of known faces.

mollify To appease or placate.

moratorium A suspension.

police brutality Acts of violence perpetrated against civilians.

racial profiling Suspecting someone of illegal activity because of their race or ethnicity.

stop-and-frisk A policy in which police officers stop people in public spaces to search them for illegal items such as drugs or weapons.

wellness check A procedure in which someone requests that police officers be dispatched to check on someone's well-being.

Media Literacy Terms

"Media literacy" refers to the ability to access, understand, critically assess and create media. The following terms are important components of media literacy, and they will help you critically engage with the articles in this title.

angle The aspect of a news story that a journalist focuses on and develops.

attribution The method by which a source is identified or by which facts and information are assigned to the person who provided them.

balance Principle of journalism that both perspectives of an argument should be presented in a fair way.

bias A disposition of prejudice in favor of a certain idea, person or perspective.

credibility The quality of being trustworthy and believable, said of a journalistic source.

feature story Article designed to entertain as well as to inform.

impartiality Principle of journalism that a story should not reflect a journalist's bias and should contain balance.

intention The motive or reason behind something, such as the publication of a news story.

motive The reason behind something, such as the publication of a news story or a source's perspective on an issue.

reliability The quality of being dependable and accurate, said of a journalistic source.

Media Literacy Questions

1. Does "In New York, Testing Grounds for Community Policing" (on page 19) use multiple sources? What are the strengths of using multiple sources in a journalistic piece? What are the weaknesses of relying heavily on only one or a few sources?

2. What is the intention of the article "A Struggle for Common Ground, Amid Fears of a National Fracture" (on page 56)? How effectively does it achieve its intended purpose?

3. "Obama Puts Focus on Police Success in Struggling City in New Jersey" (on page 83) features photographs. What do the photographs add to the article?

4. "I'm a Police Chief. We Need to Change How Officers View Their Guns." (on page 119) is an op-ed by a chief of police. What particular point of view does Brandon del Pozo provide, and how does a policing background support it?

5. Identify each of the sources in "Police Use Surveillance Tool to Scan Social Media, A.C.L.U. Says" (on page 122) as a primary source or a secondary source. Evaluate the reliability and credibility of each source. How does your evaluation of each source change your perspective on this article?

6. Analyze the authors' reporting in "Cleveland Police Officer Contacted 2,300 Women Using Work Computer, Authorities Say" (on page 129) and "Philadelphia Police Inspector Charged in Sexual Assaults of Officers" (on page 187). Do you think one journalist is more balanced in her reporting than the other? If so, why do you think so?

7. Does Jacey Fortin demonstrate the journalistic principle of impartiality in her article "Police Body-Cam Video Appears to Show Willie McCoy Sleeping Before He Was Fatally Shot" (on page 131)? If so, how did she do so? If not, what could Fortin have included to make her article more impartial?

8. "Police Data and the Citizen App: Partners in Crime Coverage" (on page 143) is an example of an interview. What are the benefits of providing readers with direct quotes of an interviewed subject's speech? Is the subject of an interview always a reliable source?

9. Identify the various sources cited in the article "Activists Say Police Abuse of Transgender People Persists Despite Reforms" (on page 167). How does Noah Remnick attribute information to each of these sources in his article? How effective are Remnick's attributions in helping the reader identify his sources?

10. What type of story is "The Lawyers Protecting the N.Y.P.D. Play Hardball. Judges Are Calling Them Out." (on page 177)? Can you identify another article in this collection that is the same type of story? What elements helped you come to your conclusion?

11. In "Police Officer Charged With Murder in Killing of Handcuffed Suspect in Maryland" (on page 190), the journalists quote several sources. What are the strengths of the use of a direct quote as opposed to a paraphrase? What are the weaknesses?

12. "A Black Police Officer's Fight Against the N.Y.P.D." (on page 193) follows the story of Lt. Edwin Raymond's efforts to enact change from within the N.Y.P.D. What is the purpose of a long-form article such as this? Do you feel this article achieved that purpose?

Citations

All citations in this list are formatted according to the Modern Language Association's (MLA) style guide.

BOOK CITATION

THE NEW YORK TIMES EDITORIAL STAFF. *Police in America: Inspecting the Power of the Badge.* New York Times Educational Publishing, 2021.

ONLINE ARTICLE CITATIONS

BAKER, AL. "Police Leaders Unveil Principles Intended to Shift Policing Practices Nationwide." *The New York Times*, 29 Jan. 2016, https://www.nytimes.com/2016/01/30/nyregion/police-leaders-unveil-principles-intended-to-shift-policing-practices-nationwide.html.

BENNER, KATIE. "Barr Says Communities That Protest the Police Risk Losing Protection." *The New York Times*, 4 Dec. 2019, https://www.nytimes.com/2019/12/04/us/politics/barr-police.html.

BROMWICH, JONAH ENGEL, ET AL. "Police Use Surveillance Tool to Scan Social Media, A.C.L.U. Says." *The New York Times*, 11 Oct. 2016, https://www.nytimes.com/2016/10/12/technology/aclu-facebook-twitter-instagram-geofeedia.html.

BUCKLEY, CARA. "Police Training and Gun Use to Get Independent Review." *The New York Times*, 5 Jan. 2007, https://www.nytimes.com/2007/01/05/nyregion/05police.html.

DANCE, GABRIEL J.X., AND JENNIFER VALENTINO-DEVRIES. "Have a Search Warrant for Data? Google Wants You to Pay." *The New York Times*, 24 Jan. 2020, https://www.nytimes.com/2020/01/24/technology/google-search-warrants-legal-fees.html.

DAVIS, JULIE HIRSCHFELD, AND MICHAEL D. SHEAR. "Obama Puts Focus on Police Success in Struggling City in New Jersey." *The New York Times*, 18 May 2015, https://www.nytimes.com/2015/05/19/us/politics/obama-to-limit-military-style-equipment-for-police-forces.html.

DEL POZO, BRANDON. "I'm a Police Chief. We Need to Change How Officers View Their Guns." *The New York Times*, 13 Nov. 2019, https://www.nytimes.com/2019/11/13/opinion/police-shootings-guns.html.

DEWAN, SHAILA. "When Police Officers Vent on Facebook." *The New York Times*, 3 June 2019, https://www.nytimes.com/2019/06/03/us/politics/police-officers-facebook.html.

FEUER, ALAN. "The Lawyers Protecting the N.Y.P.D. Play Hardball. Judges Are Calling Them Out." *The New York Times*, 12 Sept. 2018, https://www.nytimes.com/2018/09/12/nyregion/nypd-lawyers.html.

FITZSIMMONS, EMMA G., AND JOSEPH GOLDSTEIN. " 'I Was Wrong,' Bloomberg Says. But This Policy Still Haunts Him." *The New York Times*, 21 Jan. 2020, https://www.nytimes.com/2020/01/21/nyregion/2020-bloomberg-stop-frisk-nyc.html.

FORTIN, JACEY. "Cleveland Police Officer Contacted 2,300 Women Using Work Computer, Authorities Say." *The New York Times*, 19 Mar. 2019, https://www.nytimes.com/2019/03/19/us/cleveland-police-message-women.html.

FORTIN, JACEY. "Police Body-Cam Video Appears to Show Willie McCoy Sleeping Before He Was Fatally Shot." *The New York Times*, 31 Mar. 2019, https://www.nytimes.com/2019/03/31/us/willie-mccoy-shooting-video.html.

GOLDSTEIN, JOSEPH. "Changes in Policing Take Hold in One of the Nation's Most Dangerous Cities." *The New York Times*, 2 Apr. 2017, https://www.nytimes.com/2017/04/02/nyregion/camden-nj-police-shootings.html.

GOLDSTEIN, JOSEPH. "What Racial Profiling? Police Testify Complaint Is Rarely Made." *The New York Times*, 12 May 2013, https://www.nytimes.com/2013/05/13/nyregion/what-racial-profiling-police-testify-complaint-is-rarely-made.html.

GOODMAN, J. DAVID. "In New York, Testing Grounds for Community Policing." *The New York Times*, 23 Aug. 2015, https://www.nytimes.com/2015/08/24/nyregion/for-new-york-police-a-radical-change-for-queens-residents-a-step.html.

HEALY, JACK, AND NIKOLE HANNAH-JONES. "A Struggle for Common Ground, Amid Fears of a National Fracture." *The New York Times*, 9 July 2016, https://www.nytimes.com/2016/07/10/us/a-struggle-for-common-ground-amid-fears-of-a-national-fracture.html.

HILL, KASHMIR. "New Jersey Bars Police From Using Clearview Facial Recognition App." *The New York Times*, 24 Jan. 2020, https://www.nytimes.com/2020/01/24/technology/clearview-ai-new-jersey.html.

KNAFO, SAKI. "A Black Police Officer's Fight Against the N.Y.P.D." *The New York Times*, 18 Feb. 2016, https://www.nytimes.com/2016/02/21/magazine/a-black-police-officers-fight-against-the-nypd.html.

LANDLER, MARK, AND NICHOLAS FANDOS. "President Obama Urges Mutual Respect From Protesters and Police." *The New York Times*, 10 July 2016, https://www.nytimes.com/2016/07/11/us/politics/president-obama-urges-serious-and-respectful-tone-in-protests.html.

LIPTAK, ADAM. "Supreme Court Considers a Thorny Question of Free Speech and Police Power." *The New York Times*, 26 Nov. 2018, https://www.nytimes.com/2018/11/26/us/politics/supreme-court-free-speech-police-power.html.

MARTINEZ, MARINA TRAHAN, ET AL. "Fort Worth Officer Charged With Murder for Shooting Woman in Her Home." *The New York Times*, 14 Oct. 2019, https://www.nytimes.com/2019/10/14/us/fort-worth-police-officer-charged-murder.html.

MUELLER, BENJAMIN, AND JEFFREY E. SINGER. "New York Police to Use Social Media to Connect With Residents." *The New York Times*, 25 Mar. 2015, https://www.nytimes.com/2015/03/26/nyregion/nypd-to-use-social-media-platform-to-address-quality-of-life-issues.html.

THE NEW YORK TIMES. "Training Police in Social and Communication Skills." *The New York Times*, 3 July 2015, https://www.nytimes.com/2015/07/04/opinion/training-police-in-social-and-communication-skills.html.

OPPEL, RICHARD A., JR. "Activists Wield Search Data to Challenge and Change Police Policy." *The New York Times*, 20 Nov. 2014, https://www.nytimes.com/2014/11/21/us/activists-wield-search-data-to-challenge-and-change-police-policy.html.

ORTIZ, AIMEE. "Philadelphia Police Inspector Charged in Sexual Assaults of Officers." *The New York Times*, 27 Oct. 2019, https://www.nytimes.com/2019/10/27/us/carl-holmes-philadelphia-police.html.

PINTO, NICK. "The Point of Order." *The New York Times*, 13 Jan. 2015, https://www.nytimes.com/2015/01/18/magazine/the-point-of-order.html.

POWELL, MICHAEL. "In Police Training, a Dark Film on U.S. Muslims." *The New York Times*, 23 Jan. 2012, https://www.nytimes.com/2012/01/24/nyregion/in-police-training-a-dark-film-on-us-muslims.html.

REMNICK, NOAH. "Activists Say Police Abuse of Transgender People Persists Despite Reforms." *The New York Times*, 6 Sept. 2015, https://www.nytimes

.com/2015/09/07/nyregion/activists-say-police-abuse-of-transgender-people-persists-despite-reforms.html.

ROSENBERG, TINA. "Barriers to Reforming Police Practices." *The New York Times*, 2 Aug. 2016, https://www.nytimes.com/2016/08/02/opinion/barriers-to-reforming-police-practices.html.

ROSENBERG, TINA. "A Strategy to Build Police-Citizen Trust." *The New York Times*, 26 July 2016, https://www.nytimes.com/2016/07/26/opinion/a-strategy-to-build-police-citizen-trust.html.

SMITH, MITCH. "Police and Protesters Clash in Minnesota Capital." *The New York Times*, 10 July 2016, https://www.nytimes.com/2016/07/11/us/police-and-protesters-clash-in-minnesota-capital.html.

SOUTHALL, ASHLEY. "4 Years After Eric Garner's Death, Secrecy Law on Police Discipline Remains Unchanged." *The New York Times*, 3 June 2018, https://www.nytimes.com/2018/06/03/nyregion/police-discipline-records-garner.html.

SOUTHALL, ASHLEY, AND ALI WINSTON. "New York Police Say They Will Deploy 14 Drones." *The New York Times*, 4 Dec. 2018, https://www.nytimes.com/2018/12/04/nyregion/nypd-drones.html.

STEWART, AMY. "Female Police Officers Save Lives." *The New York Times*, 26 July 2016, https://www.nytimes.com/2016/07/26/opinion/female-police-officers-save-lives.html.

STEWART, NIKITA. "New York Police Illegally Profiling Homeless People, Complaint Says." *The New York Times*, 26 May 2016, https://www.nytimes.com/2016/05/27/nyregion/new-york-police-illegally-profiling-homeless-people-complaint-says.html.

STEWART, NIKITA, AND JOSEPH GOLDSTEIN. "New York Police Will Retrain Security Staff at Homeless Shelters." *The New York Times*, 15 Mar. 2016, https://www.nytimes.com/2016/03/16/nyregion/new-york-police-will-retrain-security-staff-at-homeless-shelters.html.

TUGEND, ALINA. "Defining the Role of the Police in the Community." *The New York Times*, 20 July 2016, https://www.nytimes.com/2016/07/21/us/defining-the-role-of-the-police-in-the-community.html.

VALENTINO-DEVRIES, JENNIFER. "How the Police Use Facial Recognition, and Where It Falls Short." *The New York Times*, 12 Jan. 2020, https://www.nytimes.com/2020/01/12/technology/facial-recognition-police.html.

VALENTINO-DEVRIES, JENNIFER. "Tracking Phones, Google Is a Dragnet for the Police." *The New York Times*, 13 Apr. 2019, https://www.nytimes.com/interactive/2019/04/13/us/google-location-tracking-police.html.

VIGDOR, NEIL, ET AL. "Police Officer Charged With Murder in Killing of Handcuffed Suspect in Maryland." *The New York Times*, 28 Jan. 2020, https://www.nytimes.com/2020/01/28/us/prince-georges-maryland-police-shooting.html.

WATKINS, ALI. "Police Data and the Citizen App: Partners in Crime Coverage." *The New York Times*, 2 Oct. 2019, https://www.nytimes.com/2019/10/02/technology/personaltech/police-data-and-the-citizen-app-partners-in-crime-coverage.html.

WEISER, BENJAMIN. "Class-Action Lawsuit, Blaming Police Quotas, Takes on Criminal Summonses." *The New York Times*, 17 May 2015, https://www.nytimes.com/2015/05/18/nyregion/class-action-lawsuit-blaming-police-quotas-takes-on-criminal-summonses.html.

WILLIAMS, TIMOTHY. "Long Taught to Use Force, Police Warily Learn to De-escalate." *The New York Times*, 27 June 2015, https://www.nytimes.com/2015/06/28/us/long-taught-to-use-force-police-warily-learn-to-de-escalate.html.

WINES, MICHAEL. "Are Police Bigoted?" *The New York Times*, 30 Aug. 2014, https://www.nytimes.com/2014/08/31/sunday-review/race-and-police-shootings-are-blacks-targeted-more.html.

Index

A
Alito, Samuel A., Jr., 36, 37
Alpert, Geoffrey P., 48

B
Baker, Al, 95–98
Baker-White, Emily, 65–68
Barr, William P., 39–41
Bartlett, Russell P., 37
Batts, Anthony, 107, 108, 109, 111
Benner, Katie, 39–41
Bloomberg, Michael R., 53, 69–75, 111, 180, 202
Bogel-Burroughs, Nicholas, 182–186
Bratton, William J., 13, 20, 22, 25, 63, 99, 169, 194, 201, 204, 207, 209, 210, 211, 212
Breyer, Stephen G., 38
"broken windows" style of policing, 13, 14, 15, 71, 88–89, 201
Bromwich, Jonah Engel, 122–124
Brosnahan, Mary, 29
Brown, Allwyn, 96, 98
Brown, Karen, 178–179, 181
Brown, Michael, 47, 50, 51, 61, 115, 117, 204
Brown, Paul J., 78, 80, 82
Bruley, Mark, 139, 161
Buckley, Cara, 76–78

C
Canterbury, Chuck, 82–83, 87
Castile, Philando, 58, 60–61
Cities for Tomorrow conference (New York), 30–32
communication skills, training police in, 93–94
community policing, 7, 19–26, 31, 93
CompStat, 71, 143–144, 201–203, 204
Conforti, Thomas, 16–17, 18
Cotner, Jeff, 97
Cuomo, Andrew, 173

D
Dance, Gabriel J. X., 158–161
Davis, Julie Hirschfeld, 83–87
Dean, Aaron Y., 182–186
de Blasio, Bill, 14, 27, 53, 73, 128, 172, 173, 174, 180, 181, 204
de-escalation tactics, 27, 76, 88–92, 115, 120
Del Pozo, Brandon, 119–121
Dewan, Shaila, 65–68
Diamond, Shagasyia, 167, 171
drones, 8, 122, 125–128
Duffy, Tim, 169, 171

E
Ernsdorff, Gary, 135–136, 139, 160–161
Esposito, Joseph J., 42, 44

F
facial recognition software, 8, 122, 145, 147–154, 155–157
Fandos, Nicholas, 62–64
female police officers, 33–35, 187–189
Feuer, Alan, 177–181
firearms training, 76–78, 119–121
Fitzsimmons, Emma G., 69–75
Floyd v. City of New York, 195
Fortin, Jacey, 129–130, 131–133

G
Gangi, Robert, 22
Garcia, Sandra E., 190–192
Garner, Eric, 14, 96, 115, 172, 174, 176, 196, 204
Garvie, Clare, 148
Geofeedia, 122–124
Gidari, Al, 159, 160
Giuliani, Rudolph, 13, 71, 180
Goldstein, Joseph, 27–29, 42–46, 69–75, 114–118
Goodman, J. David, 19–26
Google, and users' infor-

mation, 134-142, 158-161
Graham v. Connor, 97
Granick, Jennifer, 141
Gray, Freddie, 96, 107, 108, 112, 123
Green, William H., 190-192
Grewal, Gurbir S., 155-157
Gualtieri, Bob, 148, 152
Gupta, Vanita, 39, 97

H

Haas, Robert, 90-91
Hadley, Jeff, 164
Hannah-Jones, Nikole, 56-59
Hartman v. Moore, 37-38
Hayes, Andrew, 21, 26
Healy, Jack, 56-59
Hedden, Harvey, 91
Hill, Kashmir, 155-157
Holmes, Carl, 187-189

I

Isaac, Mike, 122-124

J

Jarrett, Valerie, 85
Jefferson, Atatiana, 182-186
Jeffries, Hakeem, 30-31, 32
Johnson, Brian, 97, 98
Johnson, Jeh, 63, 64
Jones, Eric, 101-102, 103

K

Kagan, Elena, 36
Kalven, Jamie, 113
Kang, Joo-Hyun, 127, 174
Kelly, Raymond W., 71, 72, 73, 77, 78, 79, 80, 202
Kennedy, David M., 102, 103, 109
Kleiman, Mark A. R., 30, 31, 32
Klinger, David A., 49, 50, 51

Klugiewicz, Gary T., 90
Knafo, Saki, 193-212
Krasner, Larry, 188
Kraus, Ed, 182, 185

L

Lancman, Rory I., 175, 176
Landler, Mark, 62-64
Lenz, Justin, 22, 25
Liptak, Adam, 36-38
Lomangino, Gregory, 20, 21, 26
Lopez, Jose L., 166

M

Main, Jim, 154
Malik, Mina, 170, 171
Mance, Ian A., 165
Martinez, Marina Trahan, 182-186
Mayne, Richard, 12, 13
McCoy, Willie, 131-133
McDonald, Laquan, 96, 108, 112, 113
Merritt, S. Lee, 183
Mervosh, Sarah, 182-186
Metropolitan Police Force (London), 10-13
Middleton, Mark-Anthony, 166
Miller, Patricia, 178, 179, 180
Modell, Daniel, 196
Molina, Jorge, 134, 137, 141-142
Monahan, Terence A., 125
Mueller, Benjamin, 15-18
Mullins, Ed, 174

N

New York City Police Department
  and community policing, 19-26

  and maintaining order at homeless shelters, 27-29
  police quotas class-action lawsuit, 52-55
  and profiling homeless people, 99-100
  and racial profiling, 42-46
  and the Special Federal Litigation Division, 177-181
  and use of drones, 125-128
  and use of social media, 15-18
Nieves v. Bartlett, 36-38
nine principles of policing, 11-12, 13

O

Obama, Barack/Obama administration, 20, 57, 62-64, 83-87
O'Neill, James P., 27, 150, 175, 176, 194-195
Oppel, Richard A., Jr., 162-166
Ortiz, Aimee, 187-189
O'Toole, Kathleen, 89
Owen, Michael, 190-192

P

Padilla, Mariel, 190-192
Paolucci, Nicholas, 54, 177-178
Parker, Kevin S., 173
Patterson, Sean, 97-98
Peel, Sir Robert, 11, 12, 13, 14
Pinto, Nick, 10-14
police brutality, 32, 33, 39, 41, 42, 58, 65, 66, 106, 107, 108

INDEX **223**

police shootings, 9, 47–51, 56, 58, 59, 61, 62, 63, 76–78, 89, 95–98, 101, 109–110, 112, 113, 114–115, 119, 131–133, 162, 163, 182–186, 190–192
Powell, Michael, 79–82
Price, Richard, 31–32
procedural justice, 102–106, 107–113

R

racial profiling, 42–46, 84
Ramsey, Charles H., 89–90
Raymond, Edwin, 193–212
Remnick, Noah, 167–171
Ritchie, Andrea, 171
Roberts, John G., 37
Robinson, Georgia Ann, 33, 34
Rosenberg, Tina, 7, 101–106, 107–113
Rosenfeld, Richard, 49, 50
Rowan, Charles, 12, 13
Ruberto, Jake, 152
Rudin, Joel B., 181
Ruoff, Matthew, 19–20, 21
Rybarczyk, Michael, 129–130

S

Shear, Michael D., 83–87
Sheridan, Crystal, 170
Silverman, Eli, 201–202
Singer, Jeffrey E., 15–18
Smith, Mitch, 60–61
social media
  police officers and, 15–18, 65–68
  surveillance and, 122–124
Southall, Ashley, 125–128, 172–176
Spillar, Katherine, 33–34
Sprague, John J., 96
Stapel, Sharon, 168
Stewart, Amy, 33–35
Stewart, Nikita, 27–29, 99–100
Stinson, Sharif L., 52, 54–55
stop-and-frisk policy, 14, 42, 45, 69–75, 99, 109, 111, 112, 181, 195–196, 197, 204
Stroehlein, Andrew, 39

T

Taylor, Milan R., 23, 26
"Third Jihad, The," 79–82
Thomson, J. Scott, 114, 116, 117, 118
Torres, Ritchie, 169
traffic stop data, 162–166

transgender people, police treatment of, 162, 167–171
Trump, Donald/Trump administration, 39, 41, 116, 126
Tugend, Alina, 30–32
Tumin, Zachary, 15, 16, 17, 18
Turner, Catherine, 136

U

U.S. Supreme Court, 36–38, 95, 97, 140, 212

V

Valentino-Devries, Jennifer, 134–142, 147–154, 158–161
Victor, Daniel, 122–124
Vigdor, Neil, 190–192

W

Wasserman, Robert, 22
Watkins, Ali, 143–146
Weiser, Benjamin, 52–55
Wexler, Chuck, 20, 25, 95, 96, 97, 98, 119, 121
Williams, Timothy, 88–92
Wilson, Thomas J., 95
Wines, Michael, 47–51
Winston, Ali, 125–128
Wyant, Aimee, 150